Our Endless Needs

LM Foster

This is a work of fiction. Names, characters, places and incidents are products of the author's imagination. Any resemblance to actual events, locales, organizations, or persons, either living or dead, is entirely coincidental.

ISBN-13: 978-0999768105
(9th Street Press)

ISBN-10: 0999768107

Cover design by
Ravenna Young
www.ravennayoung.blogspot.ca

9th Street Press
www.9thstreetpress.com

Who will provide the grand design, what is yours and what is mine?
'Cause there is no more new frontier, we have got to make it here
We satisfy our endless needs and justify our bloody deeds
In the name of destiny and in the name of God.
                                        - *The Last Resort,* Eagles

JANET

"What've we got?" I asked my partner.

"We've got a mystery, Scooby."

Not for the first time, I felt like I'd awakened to find myself not an actual cop – what I'd been since I was barely twenty-one, some fifteen years now. No – all the struggles and investigated crimes, the shocks, the sadnesses, the actual trials and figurative tribulations – none of that had ever occurred.

I wasn't a cop at all, just an actress, *playing* a cop. I was become the straight man in some television show, and this guy, Sergeant Eric Parker, just transferred to Riverside from somewhere in Orange County – he was the funny cop. The cool cop. The one who said clever stuff like *We've got a mystery, Scooby.* The one who looked like he'd been sent over from central casting to play the perfect partner: intuitive, intelligent, even respectful. Oh, yeah – let's not forget good-looking and single, and eight or ten years younger than me.

Sergeant Wonderful glanced at the bleeding body on the floor. "The deceased is David Walker, age fifty-seven. Cause of death –"

"You're not the coroner, Parker."

He smiled, showing all his perfect teeth. The thought crossed my mind that his dentist must be proud. He stepped out of the way to give the police photographer some space.

"Cause of death," he repeated, "is a slug from this." He handed me a snub-nosed .38 in an evidence bag.

"Who shot him?" I asked, and thought, *The first commercial break'll be coming up soon, right after we get these expositionary details out of the way.* Maybe I'd just been on the job too long. Maybe that was why it had all started to seem scripted to me.

"His ex-wife. Mrs. Virginia Walker. She claims she thought he was a burglar."

"How long had they been divorced?"

Parker consulted his notes. "For quite a while. Mrs. Walker said about twenty-five years."

"Forced entry?" I asked.

"He had a key." Parker handed me another evidence bag. In it was a single key and a wallet.

When I didn't have any *Criminal Minds*-style leaps of intuition to apply to this, Parker smiled once more. "I'm gonna cut right to the chase here, Jan."

There it was again. I was convinced that no one said *I'm gonna cut right to the chase,* outside of television and action movies. And no one called me Jan, except my maternal grandfather, and he'd been dead for ten years. Nobody but Grampy and *this guy.*

"I said we had a mystery, and here it is. Mrs. Walker was sure her ex-husband was a burglar because, according to her, David Walker's been dead for seven years."

I glanced up from the body. "Is it him or not?"

"She says it's him. The wallet's empty except for a photograph and some cash."

"Maybe she's mistaken, then."

That sounded ridiculous to Parker. He said, "I'm sure we can scare up a picture of him. Barring that, fingerprints'll tell, but I'm assuming that a woman knows her ex-husband. She told me that David was reported missing and presumed dead – she said, as a matter of fact, that he was just declared legally dead a couple of months ago. It was a boating accident; his rented powerboat was found adrift off of Newport Beach. She said there was a Coast Guard search and the whole nine yards, but no bodies were ever found."

"Bodies? Someone was with him?"

"His son, Adam. Mrs. Walker said he was eighteen at the time."

I frowned. "Obviously, the Coast Guard got it wrong. He wasn't dead."

I even sound like TV to myself. And now Parker's gonna say –

"He's surely dead now."

"If Dad didn't die at the beach, then –"

"Maybe the son isn't dead either."

It seemed like nothing was ever easy anymore. Nothing was ever open and shut nowadays. "I hate the beach, Parker."

The good sergeant saw it as open and shut, however. He shrugged. "Haven't you ever wanted to just disappear? This guy got away with it for seven years. Now he's dead for real. I don't see as how we need to go to the beach."

2

"His eighteen-year-old son disappeared, too. Maybe Dad murdered him —"

"Then disappeared to cover it up? Maybe they just decided to disappear together."

"Maybe it was an insurance scam."

Parker shook his head. "Mrs. Walker says there wasn't a dime, and Christ, Jan, Newport Beach is out of our *juris-my-diction.*"

First Scooby Doo and now *The Matrix.* What next? Roger Daltrey's scream from the intro to *CSI?* The kid was a walking cliché. And regardless of his applied knowledge of popular culture, there'd have to be an investigation into dead-alive-dead Mr. Walker. We'd have to at least talk to Newport Beach PD, if nothing else.

A patrolman appeared in the doorway. "Someone here to see you, Detective Dunn." He handed me a business card. It said, *John T. Stevens, Attorney at Law.*

"The lawyer's here already? No one's even been charged!"

Parker rubbed his fingers together, the universal sign for *money.*

I asked the patrolman where our shooter was. He said she was downstairs in the dining room. I told him thanks, and said to Parker, "I want to talk to her again."

Fade to that Diet Pepsi commercial.

3

SARAH

My mother shot my father last night. Killed him, deader than disco, with one bullet from the snub-nose .38 she keeps within easy reach in the drawer beside her bed. She lives in that big house all alone nowadays, and she's always told me that having the pistol close made her feel safe.

She's apparently put it to the use for which it had been intended.

"I've just killed someone, Sarah." Her voice was shocked and quavery on the phone, but she wasn't crying.

Blurry from sleep, I asked her what she was talking about.

"I woke up . . . There was someone in my room. I couldn't see him so much as I could . . . *sense* him. Just standing there in the dark. I thought maybe I was dreaming . . . Then he moved. I just reacted. I yanked the drawer open and got the gun; I pointed it. I was so scared! He took another step forward, just a black shadow. I screamed – he stepped even closer. I pulled the trigger – I thought I heard his voice then, saying your name, all mixed up with sound of the gun . . ."

Was I dreaming this? No, the phone in my hand was solid and real. "He said *my* name? It's someone I know?"

She'd sobbed then, but it was just a small one. "It's . . . it's David, Sarah."

Still not quite processing her words, still not all the way awake, *David* meant nothing to me. I didn't know anyone by that name. "David who, Mom?"

A whisper, barely audible: "I've shot your father, Sarah!"

"That's impossible, Mom. Dad's – There must be some mistake!"

"There's no mistake. I got up and turned on the lights. It's him." Then she whimpered, "Where's Adam, Sarah?"

It was all too much, an avalanche of insanity dumped on me – half of my mind was still behind the wall of sleep. All I could say was, "Mom . . ."

"I've called the police." Her voice regained most of its usual authority. Someone had to take control of the situation, and as usual, it would be Virginia Walker. It certainly wasn't going to be me. "They're on their way."

"I'll be there as soon as I can, Mom."

****

I'd expected a single, silent, forbidding police sentry, standing at attention, barring my way into my childhood home with the power and awful gravitas of the state, but when I got to the house, there were two cops in front of the door. Neither silent nor grave, one was looking at his phone while the other talked to him. The phone-cop looked up at his buddy and grinned. Nonchalance wasn't really what I'd expected at a murder scene, but I was just as certain that they'd become all business if I tried to get past them.

My Uncle John was standing on the walk between me and the cops. He was pacing the short distance and speaking quietly and rapidly into his phone.

"Thanks, Jesse. You could find Waldo at a striped shirt convention."

He disconnected the call and shoved his phone into the breast pocket of his immaculate suit. Eleven o'clock at night, and John T. Stevens was still on, still looking like he'd stepped out of a *GQ* spread on the sartorial style of powerful attorneys. It had been that way all my life. He was still working, too. I knew that Jesse was one of his investigators.

He turned and I noticed that he was drawn, pale. Just like me (and Mom, too), he'd already suffered the shock of Dad's death once. He'd been devastated the first time: he'd lost weight, drank too much; he'd become a shadow of his former self. But just like me, he'd gotten over it, because whatever tragedies life serves to you, it still goes on, and you have to go on, too.

Despite the inexplicable insanity of this new situation, John smiled. "Christ, Sarah!" He embraced me, and I smelled his expensive cologne. It brought back a thousand pleasant childhood memories. "I'm so sorry." A bitter laugh. "How many times do you have to live through someone telling you that your father's –"

"Did you know, John?" I stepped back from his hug and studied his clear, gray eyes. "Did you know that Dad wasn't dead?"

Because if anyone had known this secret, it would've been him. He wasn't my uncle, not actually, not by blood. He was my father's

5

best friend, since high school; his business partner. The firm was still called Stevens and Walker.

My question was met with neither a tremor nor a blink nor a gasp; no denial or shock or resentment. John Stevens was again troubled by his friend's death, but he wasn't one of the best trial lawyers in the state because he *reacted.*

"I did not," he replied.

I hadn't actually expected any other answer, but I still had to ask.

"Have they arrested Mom? Is that why you're here?"

"It's not likely that she'll be charged for this, Sarah. I'm surprised you'd even think so."

"I'm just a secretary, John." I looked down in the unwilling shame I always felt when I had to remind him of that fact.

"You're a *legal* secretary." Familiar rebuke peeped out to answer my shame, like it always did when my career choice was on the stand. He'd never gotten over the fact that his best friend's daughter hadn't chosen a life before the bar. "I figured you'd know the most basic penal codes . . ."

"I type *correspondence.* I don't know anything about –"

"It's called the Castle Doctrine," he said with a superior sniff. "If you feel that your life's in danger, you're permitted to use deadly force in your own home to protect yourself. From what your mom told me . . . How could she possibly have known it was David? We all believed he's been dead for the last seven years. I doubt if they'll even take her in. It's just a . . . *another* tragic accident. Death by misadventure. I'm here because your mother wants me to –"

"Mr. Stevens?"

Both of us turned. Another cop was standing in the open doorway. "Detective Dunn will speak to you now."

"This is Mrs. Walker's daughter." He took me by the hand, like I was still a child. He didn't ask the cop if it was okay for me to also come in. Like my mother, Uncle John knew how to take control of a situation.

****

Mom looked elegant, like an old-timey movie star, in her black dressing gown, the one with the fur at the cuffs and the hem. She arose and embraced Uncle John, then me, then sat back down at the dining room table. Before they had a chance to speak, she introduced the detective and the sergeant to us.

Hand-shaking concluded, we all seated ourselves. The detective said, "It's not necessary for you to have your attorney present, Mrs. Walker. You haven't been charged –"

"I'm not concerned with that, Detective." Mom was shaken, but even the quaver was now absent from her voice. "I was married to a lawyer for ten years. While this is all sad and unfortunate, I know it's not a crime. I shot an intruder who was threatening me."

Uncle John smiled at the police.

My mother said, "David has deceived us – whatever his reasons were, we may never know now. He always had a flair for the theatrical – it's been his undoing this time. He should've chosen a more mundane way of returning from the dead than appearing at my bedside in the middle of the night like an apparition."

The detective exchanged a look with her partner: she found *my mother* to be a little theatrical.

"I've already told Mr. Parker what happened: I awakened to find a man in my room; terrified, I shot him. Even if David hadn't been dead for seven years, it can be called nothing other than a terrible accident.

"I've called John here to talk to you with me, and my daughter, also –" she patted my hand, "– because we have a more pressing problem than a legally dead man who is now most assuredly dead. I want you people to find my son."

In the ensuing heartbeat of silence, Virginia Walker smiled. Because her charm was instinctual, flawless, limitless, it almost didn't seem like a name-dropping threat when she next said, "While you all were on your way over here, Detective, I spoke to Paddy . . . I mean, Chief O'Connor. He's a family friend." An almost girlish giggle. "I apologized for waking him up, but considering the circumstances . . . He's already assured me that I won't be charged, and he promised that I'd be able to count on your help with this far more pressing concern. He agrees that if David was alive, then Adam must be, too."

As if on cue, Detective Dunn's phone buzzed. Her eyes narrowed, and I noticed that it seemed to cost her some effort to ignore the electronic summons. But ignore it she did, saying, "We'll do whatever we can, Mrs. Walker."

The detective's phone buzzed again and she excused herself to take the call.

JANET

The chief let it slide that I'd ignored his first call. I told him I hadn't recognized the number, as I'd never actually spoken to him before – there's a few layers of management between me and the top dog. He *had* sent me a congratulatory letter when I'd made detective, however, *signed in his own rubber stamp,* as the old song says.

The conversation was short. He introduced himself, in that kind of self-deprecating manner than men of command affect, and said it was a damn shame that David Walker was truly dead. He'd been a great lawyer, although criminal cases hadn't been his line. Paddy said not to worry about the details of the actual shooting; Ginny Walker had just been dealt a nasty shock . . .

Then the top cop said that he was confident that my team and I would give the other matter our customary diligence, coordinate with NBPD and the Orange County Sheriff and the Coast Guard and whoever else might need to be consulted to reopen the investigation into the disappearance of Adam and David Walker. We were to devote all our efforts to finding the missing boy. I told him we'd get right on it, and after requesting frequent updates, he said goodbye.

My partner walked up. "Iglesias?" Iglesias was our boss.

I shook my head. "It was Paddy himself."

Parker said unnecessarily, "I guess were going to the beach after all, then."

I nodded, and if my life really was just a police drama, Parker would've suggested that we go somewhere for a drink, to comment on the people Mrs. Walker knew in high places, to discuss the facts of the case that we already knew, to speculate on those we didn't.

I could picture it all so clearly. We would've wound up back at his immaculate, minimalist and trendy bachelor pad, and – the case forgotten for the moment – we would've fallen into bed before the next commercial break. It was about time for such adventures, if my life was a cop show: Parker and I had been working together for about three months.

Aside from feeling lately like all the questions and answers were scripted, my life didn't follow the television police procedural formula when I wanted it to, however, and I really didn't want to get involved with Parker. Did I?

No. It was nuts. I didn't know him at all. The only other major crime we'd investigated had been a jewelry store burglary. That one *had* been open and shut, an inside job. It'd all been captured on the security camera, and the disgruntled employee/suspect had even been conveniently at home when we went to arrest him. He came along quietly, as they say. No muss, no fuss.

No, I didn't know Parker, not as a person, as a man. He seemed to be a good cop, thorough and intuitive, like I say, but that didn't mean I should be wanting to get to know him better. Not just yet. On the other hand, he was damned attractive, and those cinematic ideas kept eddying through my mind, of white sheets cut up by bars of moonlight, and Parker taking off his gun and his shirt and his –

"I asked them all to come downtown tomorrow, to launch this thing," he was saying. "Ten o'clock." When I nodded, he told me good night and walked over to his car with nary a hopeful smile nor even a backward glance.

SARAH

With surprising quickness, the crime scene was photographed, forensics gathered, the body removed. No grizzled old coroner arrived at the scene to determine the cause of death, as they always do on television. Just a couple of guys with a gurney. The cause was obvious enough, I guess. Mom had already identified the body, and Uncle John had concurred. I couldn't bear to look. If they said it was Dad . . . Then it must be him.

There was no police tape in front of the house, or even inside; no press arrived. After a very short time, all was quiet again. Nothing to see here, folks . . .

JANET

Rita Iglesias was a hard-bitten woman of forty-three or so. Another TV cliché: she'd worked her way up through the ranks, and it had made her tough as those oft-mentioned nails. She still had some ambitions of perhaps making chief herself someday, so she was succinct: "Don't fuck this up, Dunn. The Walkers are personal friends of ol' Paddy, and while he didn't seem to take too much of an interest when this lawyer and his kid were reported missing and presumed dead . . ." She thumbed through a folder. "He seems to be taking an interest now. There'll be a quickie hearing about the shooting . . . You won't have to appear. Don't worry about it. Go see those idiots at the beach, and . . . You know what to do. Find this kid."

That was twice now that I'd been told not to worry about definitely-dead-now David Walker; twice I'd been told by the brass to find his son. It warmed the very cockles of my heart that Iglesias had so much confidence in my skills. Not to mention the fact that if I didn't turn up this seven years' missing person – dead or alive – it would be my ass on the line and not hers. The chief had called me personally – he knew my name. If Parker and I failed, my boss would show the proper embarrassment, put someone else on it, and we'd wind up investigating car stereo thefts from Walmart parking lots.

****

For an uncomfortable moment, there was some confusion as to whether or not Mr. Stevens was there in the capacity as Mrs. Walker's counsel. I told him that she didn't need one at this time, and he finally agreed to be tell us what he knew about Adam and David Walker later. He said he'd take the daughter and go get a coffee, and Parker and I sat down to talk to the shooter – er, the chief's friend, the lady who wanted us to find her son.

She wrote out her statement about the shooting – it was brief – signed it without reading it over and handed it to Parker. She didn't inquire as to what would be the next steps regarding the circumstances of her ex-husband's death. She knew that it would all be handled – and discreetly.

Parker had jokingly predicted the headline: *Headshot Returns Zombie Lawyer to the Grave.* But I knew better. Mrs. Walker's buddy Paddy had already kept it out of the papers. Her ex-husband's mysterious resurrection and immediate return to the spirit realm would never see a by-line. Not unless we found Adam. And maybe not even then.

But I wasn't as through with David Walker as my boss and the chief and his ex-wife were.

"So the seven years just ran out recently?" I asked.

"About three months ago," she said.

"You were beneficiary to your –"

"David was my *ex*-husband, Detective. I wasn't beneficiary to anything. We divorced ages ago. All property and assets were divided up then. When he was finally declared legally dead, I got nothing more. Sarah received nothing more. There wasn't even any life insurance."

Parker asked, "And you had no idea that he wasn't really dead?"

Mrs. Walker shook her head. "I surely wouldn't have shot him, if I'd I known it was him. Not before I made him tell me where Adam is."

"Could you tell us about the . . ." Parker looked at the file.

"The boating accident?" I supplied.

She sighed. "Maybe I should start at the beginning. I'm sure that you people have the whole history of my family there in that folder, numbers and dates and the like, but there's a great deal that isn't there in black and white. It would be quicker if I told you about *those* events, instead of this back and forth – *tell us about the accident,* and so on. If I tell you everything that came before David and Adam wound up at the beach that day, maybe it'll give you the insights you need to find him."

She glanced around the room. "You're not recording this are you?" She pointed at the black half-globe of the camera in the ceiling. "That thing's not on, is it?"

I shook my head. "You've made a written statement about the incident, so there was no need to tape you. Now we're just trying to understand all we can about why your ex-husband would've wanted to fake his own death."

"And take Adam with him." Mrs. Walker shook her head. "I cannot even begin to understand either of these things, Detective, but perhaps you'll be able to get some clue to his motivations if I tell you the entire story."

She gazed at Parker now. "Everything I've done in my life – the things that I must tell you now – they haven't always been the most honorable. I have some little social standing –"

You're friends with the chief . . .

"– and that's why I asked if I'm being taped. What I'm going to tell you – maybe it'll be useful to you in finding Adam. But some of the details . . . They don't need to leave this room."

Parker stared right back at her. "We'll maintain confidentiality as much as possible, Mrs. Walker."

She smiled, but it didn't quite reach her eyes. "I'm sure you will, Sergeant. It's not necessary for the Walker dirty laundry to reach the outside world, but I'm afraid I must air it for you. Like I say, maybe you'll find something in it that'll lead us to my son. Why David would do this . . ."

She shook her head again, then took a deep breath, let it out. "I met David while I was visiting friends in San Francisco. He was going to SFSU."

Parker consulted the file. "You're quite a bit older than your husband." He was all business. He wanted to let Mrs. Walker know that whatever closets she was going to throw open, whatever skeletons she was going to reveal, he wasn't going to be fazed by them. He was a professional.

"I'm ten years older." She gave me a look that said she didn't consider ten years to be *quite a bit,* like she assumed I'd agree. She gauged that I was about ten years older than Parker, and surely I considered him as up to his tasks as he obviously did, right?

"I was twenty-nine when we met, and he was nineteen. It was love at first sight." She smiled smugly. "His parents weren't too happy, but once they discovered that I wasn't out for the family fortune, they accepted us." When Parker looked blankly at her, she clarified. "I have my own fortune, Sergeant."

I'd skimmed the file, and knew that Virginia Walker wasn't kidding. She came from old money. Some great grandfather had been there with North and Gage and the rest, at the founding of Riverside. It only followed that she'd be friends with the chief of police.

"We married; Sarah was born. We returned to Riverside. David transferred to UCLA, and John came with him. After they passed the bar, they hung up their shingle here in town –"

"Right out of law school?" Parker asked in surprise. When Mrs. Walker just smiled, he remembered those family fortunes, now blended.

Virginia Walker smiled again, more genuinely this time. "Everything was beautiful. We were happy – David and I and our little girl and our friend John." She sighed. "Then, when Sarah was about ten, Billy Munro came to stay the summer with us."

My mom does that, I thought absently, while Parker scribbled the name down. He was the note-taker of our team, *befitting his youth and vanity,* and also because he and I preferred it that way. It allowed me to study the witness, when I wasn't thinking about non sequitur bullshit, like the idea that my mother always did what Virginia Walker had just done. Whenever she was telling a story, reckoning when it had occurred on the timeline of her life, I was Mom's yardstick. *When such and such occurred, Janet had to've been about six . . .* It was a mother thing, I guess. I'm not a mother, thank all that's holy.

"Billy was one of David's roommates from college," Mrs. Walker continued. "I'd never met him before, though he'd shared the house in Frisco with David and John and Max."

Cue Parker. "Max?"

"Max Haycroft," Mrs. Walker dutifully replied, and Parker dutifully wrote it down. She frowned. "You'll definitely want to talk to him, Sergeant. I didn't suspect him at the time, but now that I know that David faked his death . . . Max had to've been in on it. I'm positive."

"Do you know where we can find Mr. Haycroft?" Parker asked.

Virginia Walker waved her hand dismissively. "Start with a Google search, Sergeant."

She smiled at me like we were pals, and got back to her story.

"I couldn't get enough of David Walker from the moment I'd seen him, shooting darts in that crowded college bar. How I'd allowed my friends to drag me to a college bar in the first place . . . It would later seem to me that there'd been some guiding hand, the inevitability of fate. I'd gone all the way to San Francisco, only to meet a man that was from my home town. Surely the most attractive man I'd ever seen.

"He was surprised when I approached him, although his slick, gray-eyed buddy John wasn't surprised. I would later learn that he'd been David's wingman since high school. That hadn't been that long ago at the time, and if I was the first grown woman to approach his

14

good-looking friend – like I say, David was surprised, but John was not.

"That expression – love at first sight – it was really so much more than that. I was pushing thirty – the friends I was visiting were a married couple from my own college days. They had a four-year-old son. I'd begun to think that all of that – marriage and children – had passed me by. I'd always been a loner, a poor little rich girl. Men had been just playthings to me, diversions, never in any way *equals.* Just ways to pass the time.

"But from the moment I saw David, I knew he was *the one.* Brilliant, ambitious, thrifty, forthright and true, this diamond-in-the-rough Boy Scout – he wasn't even old enough to be in that bar. Yet I knew that he'd be my husband, the father of my children.

"And since my biological clock was fast-ticking, since thirty loomed on the horizon, I set immediately to the task of bringing it all about.

"In the three months or so before David and I wed and moved back to Riverside, I'd never met Billy Munro. I'd met John, the first night. The embodiment of rich college boy privilege, John's attitude broadcast that if David was too dumb to take what was being offered, he'd surely step up. And I met Max, but I never got to know him very well. I never had a conversation with Max where he wasn't illuminated by a computer screen.

"I'd certainly heard enough about Billy, though, and I'd surely seen enough pictures of him. In that short three months, David and John and Max had each showed me pictures – *that's me and Billy* – and then they'd tell some outrageous story about him. Apparently, he was bon vivant, ladykiller, scoff law, truant. Man about town. All three of them admired Billy, to the point, it seemed to me, almost of boyish worship. I wouldn't meet him for ten years."

I caught Parker glance at the clock, but I was intrigued. Virginia Walker had said she wanted to tell us about her husband, and she had, but the sad, wistful quality to her voice – that was there, I thought, not because the marriage to the love of her life had eventually ended. It was there because of this Billy Munro.

She continued. "I was out on the veranda with Sarah. Suddenly, we heard a burst of masculine laughter. There were three voices, and three men coming up the walkway: John and David, and arm in arm with them, another.

"'This is our friend, Billy,' David said. 'He just breezed into town this morning.'

15

"Billy was . . . surprising. He and David looked so much alike – they could've been brothers. The same black hair, the same blue eyes. But while David had always been rather . . . earnest . . . Hardworking, studious, devoted . . . Billy was something else entirely.

"Yes, David and his college buddy looked alike, but a dark enticement danced and sparkled in Billy Munro's blue eyes, and for the second time in my life, it was like love at first sight." Mrs. Walker paused and looked significantly at me. "But not exactly love."

Parker tried to make eye contact, but I ignored him. I sensed that what was to follow was the dirty laundry. It was gonna be a confession, and it's always good to be looking at the subject when they confess.

She sighed. "I was fascinated with Billy, Detective. It wasn't only me; David and John hung on his every word; even ten-year-old Sarah was enthralled. He'd been out of town or out of the state or out of the country – it never occurred to any of us to find out which, precisely – because the important thing was that he was back now, at odds and ends for the summer, until he returned to San Francisco in September. He had a job waiting for him there. David immediately volunteered to put him up until then; he insisted in fact."

Now Virginia Walker again addressed Parker. She was hale and vibrant, coiffed and made-up as befitted an old-money grand dame. She might be holding court at some art auction or charity function, or whatever it is that rich women do with their time – looking at her, you'd never guess that she was spilling family secrets in a dingy police interrogation room. According to the file, she was sixty-seven – a little old lady. Yet she was unlike any senior citizen that Parker had ever interviewed: her light blue eyes glowed and sparkled as she related what came next, and it amused me to see him look away from the intensity of her gaze.

"Billy brought Camelot to Riverside that summer, Sergeant." Parker blinked when she briefly burst into song. *"The rain may never fall till after sundown; by eight, the morning fog must disappear. In short, there's simply not, a more congenial spot, for happily-ever-aftering than he-e-e-re . . .*

She grinned briefly at me and I grinned back. Then she sobered and again spoke to Parker. "I lived Guinevere's life, almost from the first day he arrived. I loved David, surely, but Billy . . . the passion in his eyes was undeniable." She sighed, resigned at her inability to

16

resist temptation. Parker held her gaze for another moment, then looked down at the file in front of him.

Mrs. Walker said to me, "We carried on behind David's back. We felt guilty – I was David's wife, and he was David's best friend from college. Unspoken between us was the idea that perhaps these feelings, these *urges* that we had for each other, would pass when he left in September. It lent a kind of . . . I don't know . . . a kind of *finality,* I guess, to our moments together. We knew it couldn't go on forever, but for the present . . .

"I was sure that David didn't know. On the other hand, I was just as sure that John *did* know. It was there in his eyes, whenever he'd look at me: accusation, condemnation, betrayal – as if it was him and not David that I was betraying.

"David and I always hosted a big party on Labor Day. I . . . *spoke* briefly to Billy that afternoon. He was scheduled to leave in a few days, to go back up north. But we didn't talk about that, as it was something to which we both looked forward and dreaded in equal measure. Our . . . our *affair* had to end. But we didn't talk about it. He told me he had some business to conduct, but he'd be back for the party. He kissed me goodbye . . ."

Mrs. Walker covered her face with her hand and fell silent. Parker glanced over at me, and he suddenly seemed very young. He couldn't relate – Parker had never indulged in a forbidden passion. The idea that was it possible to love two people at the same time was foreign to him. He perceived the old lady only as an adulteress; his concept of loyalty was starkly black and white.

She cleared her throat and spoke again. "David went into the office that day; he returned with John just as our guests began arriving. He was distant and sullen, and he began drinking almost immediately, something he rarely did. John wouldn't look at me, wouldn't speak to me.

"I didn't have time to reflect on David's odd mood, or the fact that John didn't stay for much of the party. I had a houseful of people to entertain, and of course, Sarah to look after. It was a good gathering – happy and light; great conversation.

"I didn't even notice that Billy hadn't returned until a little before ten, when I reminded Sarah that it was her bedtime. Our guests had become loud and drunk, and she was only ten years old, and I'd already allowed her to stay up an hour longer than usual.

"She stamped her foot, and said she didn't want to go to bed. 'Uncle Billy said he was gonna bring me some sparklers,' she told

17

me. 'He said they we're illegal here, but he was going to bring me some, anyway. He said they always had fireworks on Labor Day when he was my age! I don't want to go to bed till I get my sparklers!'

"I told her that she'd just have to wait until tomorrow to get her contraband fireworks, as Uncle Billy wasn't back yet, and it was past her bedtime. She wanted to throw a tantrum, but knew I wouldn't be having that – not with a houseful of people. And she was confident that if Billy'd said he'd bring her sparklers, he'd keep his promise. Like I say, she was devoted to him. Because she was ten, tomorrow was a million years away – but she went up to bed without further argument.

"As she stomped out of the kitchen, I called after her – 'It'll all be all right, Sarah. You'll see your Uncle Billy tomorrow.'

"David walked into the kitchen; he looked fondly after his daughter, then turned to me. His smile vanished and he said, 'She won't, you know.'

"I was tidying up, and didn't really notice that he was staring at me. I said, 'She won't what, David?'

"'Sarah won't be seeing Billy tomorrow. And neither will you.' He took a step forward and grabbed my wrist so I'd look at him. 'I know what's been going on, Ginny.'

"I'd never seen David drunk unless it was in celebration, and then he was always playful and happy. He was neither now. Bitterness and fury enveloped me along with the smell of whiskey on his breath.

He said, 'I might've expected it from him . . . *Never underestimate the desperation of a poor boy,* John always says . . . But you! The haughty debutante! To think that you'd wallow with a nobody like Billy Munro!'

"'I'm forty, David,' I said. 'I'm hardly a debutante.' I told him he was drunk and he was imagining things.

"'Yeah, I'm drunk, but I'm not imagining anything.' He cackled, but it ended in a kind of sob. 'You're found out, Ginny. But there's not going to be any happily-ever-after. No starting from scratch up north with Billy. Your penniless lover's gone. And he's not coming back.'

"'He was always leaving, David,' I said, trying to sound neutral.

"I mentioned Billy's job in San Francisco, and David said, 'The job fell through. Some time ago, actually. Billy thought he'd just stay on here indefinitely, *fucking my wife . . .* '

18

"David fought his anger down, allowed his bitterness full rein. He said, 'My best friend. *Your* friend. But there's another friend Billy likes better than either of us, Ginny. *Money.* I bought his loyalty this time. All I had to do was fork over the cash. He's never coming back. He chose money over you.'

"'He was always leaving, David,' I repeated. 'Now that he's gone, we can get back to how it used to be.'

"He uttered that cackling sob again, shook his head. He said, "No. Virginia Nicole Leeds is not gonna have her cake and eat it too, this time. I want a divorce. I'm gonna stay at John's. I'll have the papers drawn up in the morning.""

Virginia Walker again covered her face with her hand; another sigh escaped her.

"David never considered reconciliation. Not for one second. I'd betrayed him with his best friend, and there was no going back from that. We never really had another conversation. Anything that needed to be said was said through our attorneys.

"The divorce settlement was equitable; I kept the house. Sarah's child support was generous. I'm sure you're aware that there are only two grounds for divorce in California: irreconcilable differences and incurable insanity. Insanity must be proven, but it's not necessary to go into a great deal of detail about differences in open court."

Especially when you're wealthy, I thought.

"Still, David could've dragged my name through the mud. He could've tried to take Sarah away from me. But being a lawyer himself, I don't think he wanted to pay one of his brethren any more than he had to. He just wanted out. I was dead to him. And Billy . . ."

Now Parker looked up and again met Virginia Walker's eyes. He wanted to know if there'd been a happy ending to this sordid, not uncommon story, after all.

She smiled humorlessly. "Billy stayed bought, Sergeant. I never heard from him again. Not a single word."

"Did you try to contact him?" Parker blurted out. He *so* wanted that happy ending.

Mrs. Walker shook her head. "I figured that he hadn't fled to darkest Africa or to Mars, even if the Frisco thing had fallen through. Even if he surely didn't talk to David anymore or even John, all of them undoubtedly still talked to Max. There was no way that Billy didn't know that David had left me, that we'd divorced.

"It'd always been destined to end. Billy *took the money and ran,* as they say. It was undoubtedly for the best." Mrs. Walker sighed.

19

"Six months after that Labor Day, almost to the day, my divorce was final. About three months after that, my son was born."

Silence dropped so completely that I could hear the tick of the clock on the wall. I almost grinned at the look of dumbfounded surprise on Parker's face. He'd been so caught up in Mrs. Walker's story of passion and infidelity and divorce, he'd forgotten all about her son.

I hadn't forgotten him. He was the reason we were all here.

Parker recovered immediately, and asked the most relevant question. "Was he . . . Is he . . . Is your son . . . Is David his father?"

I said he asked the question. I didn't say he asked it well.

Mrs. Walker stared unblinking at him. "David's listed as Adam's father on the birth certificate, and he voluntarily expanded the child support order to include him. Yet he never met his son, never once visited him, all the years he was growing up."

"Is David Adam's father?" Parker asked again.

"My son grew up without a father, Sergeant," she replied with a bit of an edge. "Since neither of the possible suspects was around, I never saw the need for any kind of scientific testing. *Legally*, Adam is David's son. *Actually,* he is *mine*. And I want him back."

"If David never participated in Adam's life, then how did they come to be on that boat together?" I asked.

"David was fond of theatrics, as I've told you. As far as I knew, he'd never spoken a word to Adam, had no interest in him whatsoever, past the monetary considerations of child support. Before our divorce was even final, long before Adam was born, he and John had moved their office to LA. John moved it back here to Riverside, after the accident. He's been a comfort to me for the last seven years."

Parker wanted me to look at him at this admission, but I kept my eyes on Mrs. Walker.

"Then one day, out of a clear blue sky, David showed up on the doorstep. He said that he was there to see his son. Adam would be eighteen in a few weeks, and David said he wanted to ask him about his plans for college, to see if Adam was planning to follow in his footsteps and become a lawyer.

"I was completely gobsmacked. I hadn't spoken to this man in more than eighteen years, and there he was, smiling. He didn't come into the house, however. He just stood on the veranda and waited while I fetched his son.

20

"Adam was as surprised as I was. He looked over his shoulder at me in confusion as David took him by arm and led him to his car. He didn't return until the next day. He called, telling me that he was having a great time . . . *bonding* with his dad."

"What did he say when he came home?" I asked.

Mrs. Walker shrugged. "Not a whole lot. He said he found his father . . . *intriguing*. He admitted that he'd often wondered what he was like. It was the first time he'd ever said that to me."

"So Adam didn't know the circumstances of your divorce?" Parker asked. "He didn't know why his father had never been around?"

"Irreconcilable differences, Sergeant. It had all happened before he was born. I was all the parent he needed, so he'd never expressed an interest in his absent father."

"What about Sarah? Did she know why David had suddenly —"

"Sarah was only ten years old at the time. *Sometimes mommies and daddies decide they'd be better off living separately* was enough for her.

"It wasn't as if David abandoned *her*. He sent a car for her every other weekend; she spent birthdays and holidays with him. When she was old enough to drive herself, he bought her a car. I think Sarah enjoyed the arrangement better than she would've had we stayed together. She never had to listen to her parents fight. She never knew a father who was tired or distracted . . . David was no doubt always been glad to see her, always ready to devote his full attention to her."

"So when he showed up at your door — didn't you think it was odd, after all that time?"

"Hell yes, I thought it was odd, Sergeant!" A blue flame of annoyance flared briefly in Mrs. Walker's eyes. "But what was I supposed to do about it? My son was intrigued — he was almost of age, and it wasn't as if David was some complete stranger he was suddenly keeping company with —"

"But he was a stranger," I said. "From what you've said, Adam didn't know his father at all."

"But David *was* his father, nonetheless. So there really wasn't anything I could say. David never came back to the house again, nor did he ever speak to me. But he and his son hit it off. Adam went to visit him in LA; Sarah went along a few times. Two weeks later, David took Adam to Vegas to celebrate his eighteenth birthday.

"Then, about five or six months after my ex-husband arrived back into our lives again, two very solemn and serious policemen showed up at my door. There'd been an accident . . . They'd found the boat . . . David was gone again, this time permanently. From my life, from Sarah's life. And this time he'd taken Adam with him."

Mrs. Walker paused, then said, "It's not easy for me to tell you people all this. What happened with Billy all those years ago . . . It was little more than selfishness on my part. The poor little rich girl once again indulging her whims." She sighed. "I can't say as I was ever proud of what I'd done, but on the other hand, I didn't feel particularly guilty, either."

When Parker blinked at this, she smiled. "Life is for the living, Sergeant. Perhaps you'll recognize that before you get too much older. *All you touch and all you see is all your life will ever be.* Billy was the most fascinating creature, and for that one idyllic summer, he was everything to me."

"Everything? But you lost *everything!*" Parker exclaimed, a trifle unprofessionally, I thought. "Your marriage –"

"Perhaps my marriage had run its course, Sergeant. The only thing I lost was David, and like I say, maybe it was time for him to move on . . . He'd been so young when we'd married. He, and John, too, became much more successful in LA than they ever would've here. Two thirty-somethings, ambitious . . . And I had Sarah, and a late in life surprise. I was forty-one when Adam arrived.

"So my life was full. I didn't have time to think about what Billy might be doing. I didn't have time to consider if David was bitter, or if he hated me. The idea that I might have to someday pay the piper for the selfish tune I'd called that long ago summer – that idea never crossed my mind.

"But after the solemn policemen left, it began to dawn on me. When I held my inconsolable daughter while she sobbed – she'd dearly loved her father *and* her brother – when John choked out on the phone that he'd find out what'd happened, if it took everything he had . . . It occurred to me that the other shoe had dropped.

"The joys of my life had come in seasons: first David, then Sarah, then Billy. And Adam – a gift in approaching old age, to replace the loneliness I would've otherwise felt because my marriage had ended. It occurred to me that whatever betrayal and heartbreak and fury David might've felt . . . I hadn't had to deal with it at all. He'd simply left.

"I'd forgotten about David, for all intents and purposes. But he hadn't forgotten about me, had he? Neither me, nor the thing I treasured the most. He waited for eighteen years . . . then he breezed back into town and took my son from me."

Again the silence was so complete that I heard the second hand on the clock. Mrs. Walker again spoke. "I've had seven years to go through the stages of grief. Denial was the briefest." She laughed harshly and Parker jumped. "I've never been one to delude myself. My son was gone and he wasn't coming back. And why was that? That's when the anger came, and to some degree, it's stayed with me all along. Anger and blame. *David did this. He* took Adam from me."

She smiled with a touch of embarrassment. "The bargaining stage of grief was fruitless, as it always is, and it was expensive. When the Coast Guard called off the search for their bodies, I was hysterical, so John hired private searchers. They looked, they billed . . . but they never turned up anything.

"I never experienced the depression that they say is an inevitable part of grieving. It's not my nature – I've always felt that, for good or bad, what's done is done. Feeling sorry for myself wasn't going to bring Adam back. And I had my anger to sustain me. *David did this!*" She slammed her open palm onto the table, then covered her eyes. Parker didn't look at me.

Mrs. Walker took another deep breath. "But acceptance finally came. My son was dead, and I had to figure out how to live the rest of my life without him. As I say, John's been an enormous comfort, and Sarah . . . I think we've comforted each other.

"And now . . . Words cannot express my surprise . . . The fear, the adrenaline . . . I'd just shot an intruder . . ."

A lesser woman might've had a heart attack, I thought.

"When I turned on the light and saw . . . All the anger rushed back. I shrieked in rage when I saw that it was David. I might've even kicked him. He hadn't been dead at all, even though he was dead now – so that meant . . . He'd made me suffer for seven years! Where was my son?"

I thought that there might've been a tear there in her eye, along with a brief expression of pleading. "So I've told you all that I did, because maybe it will somehow help you to find Adam."

SARAH

The interrogation room was a cheap-office shade of gray, and too much air conditioning made it cold. Mom squeezed my hand and then left. Detective Dunn was concerned and businesslike, and her partner was warm and friendly.

"Tell us about your brother," he said.

I shrugged. "There's not a lot to tell, Sergeant. We were ten years apart. He was always just the cute little kid that lived at my house. Mama's baby.

"I moved out the first time when he was about ten or so. We talked and texted while he was growing up. I went to his birthday parties, met his little friends. He was eighteen when he . . . died. I'd just moved back home again about six or eight months before. He was just starting to get a little interesting – then he was gone."

"How was his relationship with your dad?" Detective Dunn asked.

I didn't really know what to tell them. "There was no relationship, not until the end. Like I say, Adam was Mom's pride and joy, especially when he was a baby. He was everything to her, and she delighted in keeping him entertained, so I'm sure he didn't miss me when I went to see Dad on the weekends. He never asked about where I'd been or what I'd been doing. Mom didn't ask, either.

"By the time I was old enough to drive down to LA, Adam was only six. He had his own little kid life. He was never overly curious about his big sister's. I don't know what he asked Mom, but he never asked me anything about Dad."

"It must've been hard on you when your parents divorced," the sergeant said. His eyes were large and brown and filled with sympathy. He was young, though – maybe only twenty- three or four. Too young for me to be noticing his big brown eyes.

"I didn't grasp what'd happened for a little while. To tell you the truth, at first, I was more upset that my Uncle Billy had taken off without even saying goodbye."

"Who?" Detective Dunn asked.

I laughed. "My Uncle Billy. He wasn't really related to me, although he and Dad looked like they could've been brothers. John and Billy – I called them both *uncle*. They'd all been roommates in college.

"He came to stay with us one summer . . . The summer before Mom and Dad got divorced, actually. Billy was so nice and fun. It seemed like I'd known him my whole life, even though he'd only stayed with us for three or four months. When he took off without saying goodbye – I was upset about that for *years*. Being a little kid, I thought that he'd left so abruptly because of something I'd done. It took me a long time to get over it. Neither Mom nor Dad ever offered any kind of real explanation, just something about a job up north somewhere."

The detective and her partner were both studying me, as if they were gonna get some kind of deep psychological meaning out of the idea that I was upset that we'd never heard from Uncle Billy again, so I tried to deflect their analysis. "It was just rude, that's all."

My mother had commanded me to be straightforward with these people. She seemed to think that they were the modern equivalent of Sherlock Holmes and Watson; she was convinced that if we were all brave and honest in answering their questions, it would enable them to find Adam.

Mom was usually the most cynically realistic of thinkers, but her emotions had taken her over with the idea that my brother was still alive. I thought she was kidding herself. These were just regular cops, not any more or less bent on solving this mystery than they were on solving any other. Besides, I believed that if Adam *was* still alive – that in itself was a big if – then he apparently didn't want to be found.

"And then your dad left you, too," the young sergeant said, like he was some kind of therapist. "Right after your Uncle Billy." If he next said, *How did that make you feel?* I thought I might laugh in his face. It'd all been a lifetime ago.

"Dad didn't leave right away," I told him. "I mean, he did move out of the house, but he came back. He and Uncle John built me a folly in the woods. He said that whenever I went out there, I could remember that he'd built it for me, and then maybe I wouldn't miss him not living with us anymore. But I didn't really have time to miss him. I saw him every other weekend."

They looked at each other in confusion, then Detective Dunn finally spoke. "I'm sorry, Miss Walker – what did you say? Your dad built you a . . . a *polly?*"

"A *folly*."

When they still looked blankly at me, I unwillingly remembered something my mother used to say to me when I was little, thinking herself the height of hilarity: *poor people are dumb.* I pushed that elitist claptrap from my mind. Perhaps they'd just never heard the term before.

"That's what Mom always called it. It was a playhouse. It was really just a big room, but Dad and John put in a skylight and dormer windows and a window seat, and wooden curlicues on the eaves. They painted it pink and white."

The sergeant – what was his name again? He was looking at his phone. He murmured, *"In architecture, a folly is a building constructed primarily for decoration . . . or of such extravagant appearance that it transcends the range of garden ornaments usually associated with the class of buildings to which it belongs."* He looked up at me and smiled. He had a beautiful smile. "Is it extravagant?"

I couldn't help but smile back. "Not really. It's like one of those fancy sheds you see on the cover of gardening magazines. When I was a kid, I spent a lot of time out there –"

"Where is it, exactly?" the detective asked.

Apparently their canvass of the crime scene hadn't extended outside of my old bedroom. Mom had chosen it to be hers, giving up the one she'd once shared with Dad, when I'd finally left home for good, about three years ago. I was thirty-two years old then, too old to be still living at home, even if it was a giant house. And Anthony had said we were going to live happily ever after. That hadn't happened, but I liked the apartment we'd shared. I still lived there; I hadn't run home to Mama again, when Anthony and I had ended it.

I told Detective Dunn that the folly was in the woods. "Between the house and the golf course."

The room was suddenly quiet, and I realized that they were waiting for me to continue talking, and I wasn't, because I was staring at Sergeant Whatshisname – he reminded me of Anthony a little bit – and he was staring back at me.

He was very cute, but he had to be at least ten years younger than me. About the same age as Adam, if Adam was still alive. I shouldn't be staring at him. This was supposed to be a . . . *a professional* interview. Something I might say might help them to find my brother.

The detective seemed a little annoyed at my silence, so I tore my eyes from the sergeant's and started talking again.

26

"So, yeah. The folly. The playhouse. Dad and Uncle John built it for me, right after Uncle Billy took off. I helped as much as a little kid could, holding boards and stuff, and between trips to Home Depot, Dad explained that he wouldn't be living at the house with us anymore.

"It took a couple of weeks to build the thing. We had to wait for the concrete to dry, and . . . Dad or Uncle John picked me up from school every day and I helped with it. I couldn't remember ever having spent so much time with Dad, and by the time it was completed . . . I dunno. I just accepted how things were gonna be. He say everything that you're supposed to say to make a kid feel okay about divorce: that even though Mommy and Daddy weren't going to be living together anymore, they both still loved me. Stuff like that."

The cops were now both staring at me as if I was imparting some great psychological parenting sleight of hand or something. It was a little unnerving. I concluded, "Anyway, it worked. I had the best childhood ever, even if I did come from a *broken home.*"

"As you got older, did you ever wonder why –"

"Sure, I wondered, Detective. But one doesn't interrogate Virginia Walker. I imagine you may've already discovered that. Over the years, I asked her a few times what went wrong with her and Dad. She'd just say, *Some things don't work out.* If I'd press, she'd get annoyed and say that things that happened when I was only ten years old really weren't any of my business."

Detective Dunn's expression was neutral, unreadable. "What I was going to say was, did you ever wonder why your dad never visited your brother?"

The sergeant looked embarrassed that I'd not only interrupted his partner, I'd also taken the discussion off in a direction that they didn't care about. My parents' divorce and what I'd thought about it were not the issue here.

"I asked Dad about it a few times. He's another one that doesn't really stand still for interrogation. When Adam was a baby, he'd say he didn't know what to do with a baby; when he was a little older, he'd say that Adam would miss Mom. By the time he was ten or so, Dad would say, *Ah, I don't know him and he doesn't know me, Sarah. There's no point.*

"And since, other than me bringing it up, he never asked about Adam, and Adam never asked about him . . . I just accepted that, too. It was just how things were. I had Dad, and Adam had Mom. But then . . . ." It amused me to watch them lean forward, hanging on my words. "I can tell you the exact day when Dad finally discovered his son.

"I hadn't seen him for a couple of months. I was about twenty-eight at the time – the standard weekend visits had pretty much stopped about the time I'd started college. I had my own life. But I still got down there to see him every now and then, even if it was just for lunch. And we talked and texted daily.

"I'd just . . . ended a relationship, had just moved back home with Mom. I was at odds and ends for the weekend."

Detective Dunn glanced at her partner, but the sergeant wouldn't look at her. He didn't want to acknowledge that *poor little rich girl from a broken home wasn't married at twenty-eight, was in fact living with her mother again* look on her face. I was sure he'd noticed that I still didn't have a ring on my finger, just as I'd noticed that he didn't have one on his. The detective didn't have one either – I pegged her as a divorcee. She was about the same age as me and she had the look of someone who'd once taken the marriage plunge, someone who'd loved and lost. She was married to the job these days, no doubt.

"Dad said that he was sorry that things hadn't worked out with Steve. He said he was painting his living room, Uncle John was bringing the beer, and I was welcome to come on down and spend the weekend, like in the old days. He said manning a roller would help me forget my romantic troubles.

"So I went. At one point, I was up on the ladder, painting, and my phone beeped. It was sitting on the coffee table, and . . . I both hoped and dreaded that it was Steve sending me a text."

Detective Dunn nodded in understanding. She was familiar with that uncomfortable, queasy feeling of hope and dread, your constant companion every time the phone rings when you've just broken up with someone.

"I said, 'See who that is, will ya, Dad?' because he was sitting right there. He picked up my phone and told me that Sprint was kindly reminding me that my bill was due on the 17th. Maybe I looked sad or maybe I looked relieved. I dunno. I couldn't tell you exactly how I felt at that moment.

"Dad asked, 'Is this the villain in this love play?'

I looked over my shoulder. He was holding up my phone, nodding at the wallpaper pic. I told him, 'That's your son, Dad.'

Uncle John's eyebrows went up and he crossed the room to look at Adam's picture. It was from Halloween, the week before. I'd was handing out candy with Mom – what else did I have to do? Adam was going to some party, and I took a picture of him before he left. He was in a cowboy getup, all in black. The hat and the little kerchief; a black jacket, and striped pants. He was leaning back against the railing with his hand on his gun, giving his best *What the fuck do you want?* bad boy sneer to the camera. It was a great shot. It was the next pic in the gallery after I'd deleted all of Steve, so I'd just slapped it up there for wallpaper, temporarily."

"Do you have a copy of –"

"I took all of Adam's pictures off my phone when he died. Dad's, too. Every time I'd look at them, I'd cry. So I put them in a folder and buried it on my computer. But I thought you might like to see any pictures I had of Adam . . . I'm sure Mom didn't have the same ones as me." I showed them the old shot of my seventeen-year-old brother, dressed up for Halloween, and a few more, that I'd put back on my phone for them. "I can email them to you, if you want."

Detective Dunn handed me her card, and while I send the pictures, I continued with the story.

"'Of course that's Adam, David!' Uncle John said. 'He looks just like you!'

"I'd never seen that much of a resemblance myself, past the fact that they both had black hair and blue eyes. Dad's hair was gone to salt and pepper, so that made the resemblance even fainter to me.

"Dad and Uncle John studied Adam's picture in silence. The thought crossed my mind that maybe neither of them had ever even *seen* Adam before. I told them to scroll through, there were plenty of him on there, and I went back to painting the wall."

I paused for effect, then told the cops, "At the end of May, Dad showed up at the house, wanting to meet his son. Right before Adam turned eighteen."

"Your mother said that you all hung out together after that. You and your brother and your Dad." When her phone beeped with my email, Detective Dunn handed it to her partner.

I shrugged. "Once or twice. Mostly Adam went down to LA by himself."

The sergeant looked up from perusing the pictures I'd sent. "How did they get along?" he repeated.

29

"They got along really well. If I was an outsider, I would've thought that they'd known each other all their lives. They laughed and joked . . . Just like a regular family."

"Nothing seemed odd at all to you?" the detective asked.

"The only thing odd about it was how often Adam immediately started going out of town to see Dad, once they'd met. Adam had been talking to someone online for months. He told me that he was really into this girl. He said neither of them had worked up the courage to actually meet in person yet, but it was gonna be soon. He said that she was totally intriguing, that he was interested, like he'd never been in anyone before. He told me that he'd been spending most nights home, in his room, sharing secrets and talking online till the wee hours. He said he hardly saw his friends anymore. He was really excited. But when Dad showed up, he seemed to forget all about it."

"Did you ask him why he stopped talking to her?" the cute sergeant asked. I imagined that he might have a few online friends himself.

"Once. He said he hadn't forgotten about her, that they still chatted sometimes. Then he said he didn't want to get caught in the traffic, and gave me a hug goodbye."

"So you never got a name?" Detective Dunn asked.

"No. I never brought it up again. Adam was looking forward to going to Vegas with Dad for his birthday, and we talked about that."

"What about your Uncle John?" the sergeant asked. "What did he think of David and Adam's reunion?

"The last time I saw Uncle John was that afternoon we painted at Dad's. I talked to him on the phone a few times afterward – I thanked him for the gift cards he sent at Christmas and stuff like that. He never mentioned Adam. I didn't see him again until right after the accident. He'd been out of the country. He flew back when he heard . . . about what happened."

They gave me a silent moment to reflect on the demise of my brother and father, then Detective Dunn said, "And nothing's ever occurred to make you think that your father or brother weren't really dead?"

I shook my head. "Nothing."

"Is there anything else you think we should know?" the sergeant asked.

"When I shook my head once again, he rose and clasped my hand in both of his, thanked me for my time. He gave me his card and told me that they'd be in touch if they learned anything.

Detective Dunn echoed these platitudes and rather abruptly showed me to the door.

****

Uncle John was standing outside the police station, on his phone, as always. He ended the call when he saw me coming down the steps, and said, "Will you wait for me until this thing with the cops is done, Sarah? There's something we need to discuss."

I nodded. If John Stevens wanted to discuss something with me, his always-commanding persona broadcast that it would, without a doubt, be in my best interest to attend.

"You don't have to wait here . . ."

"I'm going back to the house. I'm sure Mom'll want to hear about my interview."

"Great. I'll text you when I'm finished." He gave me a paternal hug and went up the steps into the station.

JANET

It wasn't necessary for me to ask Parker his thoughts, although I didn't think he'd tell me all of them, anyway. He didn't stare contemplatively off into space, or gaze fixedly at the table in front of him, but I could tell that whatever he was thinking about Sarah Walker, it didn't entirely revolve around solving the mystery of why her father had come back from the dead, only to be immediately dispatched again, or where her brother was.

I won't say that sparks had flown between them, as it's a worn-out expression, another television cliché. He was a professional, and she was my age, a little old for him; and she was not really in the state of mind to be considering romance. But there'd definitely been *something* there in the couple of long stares they'd shared.

I wasn't too sure how I felt about that.

He looked up abruptly from his notes and said, "Maybe there was some kind of revenge angle, like Mrs. Walker said. David hated his wife because she'd cheated on him, so first, he befriends her son —"

"But why wait all those years?" I countered. "If David wanted to turn Adam against his mother, why not visit? Why not be a part of his life, be a father to him?"

"David's not his father, Jan."

Parker didn't wait for me to say, *What do you mean?* He was too convinced that he knew what he was talking about for that. He said, "The only thing the deceased had on him was a key to the house, and a wallet, right? The wallet had three hundred bucks in cash in it — it's one of those old-fashioned ones, with the little cellophane sleeves. There was no driver's license or credit cards or anything, but there was one picture, remember?"

"It was of his ex-wife." I hadn't done much besides glance at it, in its sleeve, through the evidence bag. Old pictures of the known players weren't of much use. We needed some ID.

"They made us a copy for the file," Parker said. "Come to find out, the picture was folded over. There were two people in it. It wouldn't fit in the sleeve, so he folded it."

The copy of the picture was in the file. There was Virginia Walker, young. Younger, anyway: she looked a trim and exceptionally well-preserved forty or so. There was a rude crease in the photo, and beside that, there stood a strikingly attractive, dark-haired man, much younger than Virginia.

"Who do you reckon that is?" Parker asked. He picked up my phone, scrolled, then set it down again. The resemblance between Adam Walker and the young man in the photo was undeniable. The same wavy black hair, the same arrogant blue eyes.

"Maybe that's David," I said.

Parker was ready for this supposition. He pulled another picture from the file and set it beside the other two. *"This* is David. From Newport Beach's missing person's file. Provided by the distraught daughter at the time of the accident."

My mind's eye darkened up the hair, and thinned the face out a little bit, erasing the years from David Walker. He was good-looking, and I could see how he might've looked like this other guy when he was younger – *They could've been brothers,* Mrs. Walker had said, and Sarah had said the same thing.

But the young man standing beside her in the creased picture was not her husband; and her husband was not Adam's father.

"I'm gonna guess that this is Billy Munro," Parker said. "He's Adam's dad."

"Mrs. Walker said she didn't know who Adam's father was."

Parker smiled. "She lied. If she loved him as much as she said she did –" here he rolled his eyes – "how could she forget what he looked like? And I'm sure she's got a few pictures of him squirreled away somewhere. Maybe even another copy of this one. Adam looks just like him. There's no way she didn't know. And once David saw pictures of Adam, there's no way he didn't know, either."

"He knew all along," I said. "That's why he never went to see him."

"The revenge angle's looking better all the time, Jan. Maybe David killed Adam, and staged it to look like they both died."

I didn't like it. It was too . . . perfect. Just like Parker himself – my perfect partner solves the perfect crime simply by checking out a few photographs. This wasn't TV. We weren't going to get all the answers before the last commercial break. There were still too many questions.

"If David wanted to punish Virginia by killing her son, why did he wait till he was almost eighteen? That's a *long time* to wait."

"Maybe he didn't think to do it until he saw the pictures. Here was the kid he'd supported all his life – mama's baby. Maybe he'd thought for all those years that Adam *was* his kid. But once he saw his picture, he knew. Maybe all the hatred and betrayal came back at once. Maybe he decided he'd hurt her the way she hurt him."

I still wasn't buying it. "Then why did he come back again now? After seven years?"

Parker had an answer for that one, too. "To tell her what he'd done. To gloat. *Oft have I digg'd up dead men from their graves, and set them upright at their dear friends' doors, even when their sorrows almost were forgot; and on their skins, as on the bark of trees, have with my knife carved, 'Let not your sorrow die, though I am dead.'*

"In fact, maybe David *did* tell her. Maybe that's why she shot him. She doesn't want to confess to murder – that's the reason for this whole *find my son* plea. Maybe she just wants us to find his body."

The kid never failed to amaze me. He really was too much. Not only good-looking, but with just the right kind of a perceptive, analytical . . . *poetic* mind. But I couldn't think about that now.

I gave him back a quote of my own. *"I'll have grounds more relative than this,* Parker. Let's see what the lawyer has to say."

****

A uniform showed John Stevens into the interrogation room, and in he strode, smiling expansively, featuring us both with that firm, two-handed handshake of which Parker himself was so fond. *I'm here to be of any help I can,* said that smile and handshake.

He was impeccably on point and the question crossed my mind – are all rich people good-looking? Of course they're not. But this one certainly was. If Parker was a youthful ideal made flesh, then John Stevens was the definition of a silver fox.

I could tell that my partner was impressed with the lawyer's expensive suit, but to me, clothes don't always make the man, and I noticed that, not unlike Mrs. Walker, his smile didn't reach his watchful gray eyes. We sat, and I asked, "What kind of law do you practice, Mr. Stevens?"

"The kind that makes money, Detective." He grinned.

"So not criminal, then," I returned with my own little smile.

34

His smile widened, and my grandmother's voice said in my head, *A gentleman is simply a patient wolf.* "Oh, we've had our share of debutante drunk drivers and heroin-possessing heirs. But mostly we handle estate matters and the occasional divorce case."

"We?" I said.

"It used to be just David and myself. But after he . . . disappeared, I took on two other attorneys."

"Were you involved in the Walkers' divorce?" Parker asked.

Stevens laughed. "You mean, in a legal capacity? No, Sergeant. That would've been a conflict of interest. Todd Bellman from Sharp and Singleton handled David's divorce."

"Would you say that it was acrimonious?"

Stevens appeared to be as impressed as I was with this big word from Parker. "All divorces are acrimonious. There's always disillusionment, heartbreak, bitterness. I don't think anyone gets married with the idea that it's going to end someday."

"Some people do," Parker disagreed. "That's why there are pre-nups."

"You've got me there, Sergeant," the attorney replied with a careless shrug. "But there wasn't any of that kind of premeditated preparation in David and Ginny's case. They were so in love –"

"Despite the age difference?"

It occurred to me that Parker was very much stuck on this point. It made me reconsider his interest in Sarah Walker. She (and I) were both older than him. On the other hand, maybe he kept bringing it up because the concept *intrigued* him.

"Ginny was unlike any of the girls David had previously known. There's not one shade of the neurotic to her. She's comfortable in her own skin, so to speak. She knows what she likes, what she wants. And what she wanted was David.

"He immediately discovered that he didn't have to jump through hoops to please her. She didn't run hot one day and cold the next. She had no hidden agendas. She just wanted to be in his company. She loved him. That kind of simplicity is a rarity in this world, and if she was a couple of years older than him – that didn't bother David at all."

Stevens glanced at me. "They were deliriously happy together. I know that sounds like a cliché, but it fits. They loved each other, they loved Sarah. They loved their life together."

I returned his steady gaze. "But it didn't last."

35

"No." Stevens looked down at his immaculate hands, clasped together loosely on the table in front of him. "It didn't." He looked up at me again. "There's a saying about people, that when they have one tiny flaw . . . *Their virtues else be they as pure as grace,* this one defect corrupts them. That's how it was with Ginny. The things that David loved about her – that she always seized what she wanted, that she denied herself nothing – he came to hate those qualities about her, eventually."

Parker opened the file and slid the picture of Virginia Walker and the young, dark-haired man across the table.

"Wherever did you get this?" Stevens asked in surprise. "Surely, Ginny didn't –"

"It was in David's wallet," Parker supplied. "The only thing in there, actually. This picture and some cash."

The attorney considered the photo in silence for some seconds, then he looked up at us blankly. At that moment, I had no doubt that he was a very good lawyer. He wasn't going to reveal anything. He was going to let us tell him what we already knew, before he told us anything more.

"Are you surprised that David still kept a picture of his ex-wife, after all these years?" I asked.

Stevens positively *giggled*. "If that was what this was, yes, Detective, I'd be very surprised."

Parker opened his mouth to speak, but I held up my hand. "It's a picture of David and his wife. If it wasn't Mrs. Walker that he wanted to remember – why would he want to keep an old picture of himself?"

Stevens smirked to let me know that I wasn't as smart as I thought I was, and I certainly wasn't as smart as him, but he'd give me points for trying. "That's not David, Detective, and I think you know it. They did look a lot alike, but that's . . . That's a friend of ours from college. His name is Billy Munro."

"Why would David keep a picture of this guy in his wallet?"

Stevens grinned. "Why, indeed, Detective. That's a very interesting question."

He took a deep breath, as Mrs. Walker had done; I sensed that perhaps another sort of confession might be coming. But whatever he was going to say – I was sure that it wouldn't in any way reflect badly on Stevens himself. If we needed to get him to admit to anything . . . *personally dubious,* we'd have to be alert and ask the right questions.

"David and I met in junior high, and we instantly became friends. By sophomore year, I had dreams of being a rock star – I thought I could play the guitar. My father was horrified, of course, and David agreed with him. He said I wasn't that good, and the only way to be successful in life was through hard work.

"We didn't have to work that hard, of course." Stevens winked at me, alluding to those family fortunes. Apparently he came from money, too. "My dad was a doctor, but medicine was entirely too grubby an enterprise for me, so David suggested that the law could be our ticket, as it'd been for his father.

"Just like that, we decided that we'd go to law school. All parents were of course thrilled. Now that a goal had been set, we studied hard, got good grades, all that bullshit. We learned all those important life lessons that one learns in high school. All the awakenings of adolescence, so to speak."

Parker narrowed his eyes thoughtfully. I thought I could actually hear the gears turning in his head. But all he said was, "About girls and the like?"

Stevens nodded. "Whatever life had to offer, David and I were in it together. He was my best friend." The attorney frowned; this show a grief – his best friend was dead, twice – suddenly made him look old.

Parker took no notice. He nodded at the picture. "Mrs. Walker said Billy Munro was David's best friend."

The lawyer's frown deepened; he winced, blinked rapidly – all quicker than it takes to describe it. Past that little bit of grief, it was the only emotion I'd seen from him. A ghost of iciness remained in his eyes when he said, "Ah, yes. Our boy Billy."

Stevens leaned forward in his chair, readjusted himself a bit. When he spoke again, his manner was once again . . . I guess I'd have to call it *jovial.*

"We met Billy the first week we were at SFSU. He was in the lobby to our dorm and just started talking to us, and by the end of the conversation, we were on our way to the run-down painted lady he shared with a guy named Max Haycroft. Dorm life just wouldn't suit two guys of our obviously discerning tastes, Billy told us.

"There was a party going on when we got there, and there was Max at the door, collecting five bucks' cover. We would later learn that Max rented the place from a relative – a great-aunt, or a cousin twice removed, or something like that, so he didn't pay anything near a San Francisco kind of rent. But he still had to keep the lights on and pay for his necessities. It wasn't like he was gonna get a job or anything, so he ran the big house like a business.

"He insisted that all the parties be bring your own – no keggers at Max's. That way he could recycle the empties for cash. There was also the gate charge for entrance to the party, and he skimmed the poker games and the guys shooting dice, and even the dart games in the basement. Billy said Max'd been considering renting out the spare bedrooms to a couple of their more enterprising co-ed friends and taking a cut of that action, but that might've just been a joke.

"Into this all-day, all-night, merry-go-round of Bay Area collegiate decadence now strolled Davey and Johnny from the bucolic backwater burg of Riverside. At Max's, we discovered all the vice our little hearts could imagine: gambling, drugs, sex, alcohol. Anything we wanted, Max could procure it. All pay as you go. All in the name of keeping the lights on.

"David fell head-first into all of it the very first weekend. I turned my back for a second on Friday night, and he and Billy had disappeared. Max told me they'd decided to squire two girls to a more secluded venue. They showed up alone at Sunday noon, all conspiratorial smiles and boozy giggles. Housemother Haycroft was pleased.

"But David hadn't come to San Francisco to party, at least not 24/7. He liked Max and he *loved* Billy . . ." The photo of Billy and Virginia Walker was still on the table in front of Stevens, and he spun it around and pushed it back toward Parker. He winked. "Who wouldn't love Billy?"

Parker asked, "Are you saying that David and Billy were . . . more than friends?"

Stevens laughed. "It was college, Sergeant. You went to college, didn't you?"

If Stevens thought he would rattle very-young Sergeant Eric Parker with a reference to – no – with an *inference of* homosexuality, he was dead wrong. Parker returned the silver fox's sly grin with one of his own, and said, "I did indeed, Counselor."

How proud of him was I? I didn't have time to wonder if he was agreeing from clever professionalism or from actual personal experience.

Stevens continued. "So, there we were, with every imaginable means to get *riggety-riggety-wrecked, son*, at our fingertips." The old lawyer winked at Parker again. "But like I say, David wasn't there just to have a good time. He had ambitions. By the end of the week, he had a deal worked out with Max. The four of us would give the place a good scrubbing and a paint job – inside at least – on David's dime. And then David and I would move in and pay Max enough rent so that he wouldn't have to run card games and sell drugs and charge five dollars at the door for parties anymore. Parties would be, thereafter, limited to once a week.

"Max was more than down. He was an IT geek, and all those people around, *all the time,* was cutting into his coding time. And his equipment had an affinity for sprouting legs and walking off, no matter how many deadbolts he put on his door.

"Max was happy, and I was happy. David and Billy were *very happy.*"

"You're telling us that David and Billy Munro had a relationship in college?" I said.

"You're leading the witness, Detective," Stevens said with a chuckle. "I'm saying nothing of the sort." He *chortled.* "Like I say, it was college. Boys and girls away from home for the very first time. David and Billy. Billy and Max. Billy and me and the entire winsome house of A Pi –"

"A Pi?"

"Alpha Omicron Pi, Detective. It's a sorority." He glanced at Parker, who raised his eyebrows in embarrassment at my ignorance.

"Billy had *relations* with all of them, but you couldn't call any of them *relationships."* He grinned at Parker, amused at his own wit, and Parker grinned back.

"It was actually in the middle of that Greek escapade when David met Ginny. Billy was MIA – he actually spent very little time at home, once he didn't have to be manning the door and collecting the take.

"Our rent payments to Max allowed Billy a little bit more freedom to be out amongst 'em in the big, bad world. It wouldn't occur to me till years later that maybe poor boy Max had sent good-looking, equally as poor Billy over to the rich boys' dorm to scout him some pigeons, for exactly the roles we wound up filling. Perhaps David and I were played on that score. I dunno."

Stevens shrugged. "Anyway, Billy'd been gone for a couple days, so I took a break from my sorority friends, and David and I went to some dive over on Taraval somewhere. We mostly did our drinking at home, seeing as how we weren't *quite* twenty-one at the time, but the bouncer was a friend of Max's and the bartender was a *good* friend of Max's, and our IDs *said* we were twenty-one, so we went over to the place to have a few beers and shoot some darts.

"You mentioned that Ginny's older than us, Sergeant? It wasn't something either of us even noticed." Stevens shook his head in admiration. "She looked like a million bucks, tax-free, all curves and hollows and shiny brown hair and flashing blue eyes. She just came up and started talking to us. I thought David's jaw was gonna hit the sticky floor, so I tried my best lines, but after a very short time, it was obvious that this sharp, self-assured gal wasn't interested in me.

"It wasn't that David was shy – no one could live at Max Haycroft's house for very long and remain shy – but David had never been shy. You got any pictures of young David Walker in that file, Sergeant? He was no Billy Munro, but he was the same type – the black-haired, blue-eyed, all-American white boy. David had no trouble attracting the ladies.

"No, he wasn't shy, but he was amazed with Ginny, nonetheless. Like I say, she was different from the crafty young things he was used to. She didn't ask what kind of car he drove or what his major was. She didn't attempt to giggle seductively and ask what he liked to do for fun. She asked him about his hopes and ambitions. What he dreamed of being when he grew up." Stevens sighed and readjusted himself in the chair again. "Three months later, they had to get married."

"Had to get married?" I blurted out in surprise.

Now Stevens grinned broadly at me. "Ginny didn't tell you that? You should have all the relevant dates in your file. Do the math. It shakes out that darling Sarah was born not *quite* nine months after their romantically rebellious quickie elopement. Big debutante weddings take time to plan and all."

When I continued to gawp at him, Stevens said, "Do you think David would've just dropped all the dark pleasures of Max Haycroft's house – not to mention a prestigious SFSU School of Law degree, to get married in his freshman year? To come back to *Riverside?"*

"A UCLA School of Law degree isn't exactly ITT Tech, Mr. Stevens," Parker said dryly.

"Again, you have me, Sergeant. *Go Bruins,* and all. But David and I – we didn't get the same kind of *enjoyment* out of going to UCLA that we'd been having at SFSU, now did we? No more Max, *no more Billy* – just a little cramped apartment in LA during the week."

Stevens chuckled again. "Don't let me lead you to believe that we suffered in any way. David's dad floated him a loan for that house by the golf course – old Mr. Walker was glad to see that his son had his whole life already mapped out for him, before he was even old enough to buy a drink.

"During the week we were students in LA, but on the weekends, David played house with his beautiful wife and lovely daughter, as if he was already the successful attorney he would eventually become. And I went along for the ride."

He reached for the picture in front of Parker and again studied it thoughtfully. "What did the former Mrs. Walker tell you about Billy, if anything?"

Parker said immediately, "She told us that you knew about the affair."

The attorney pursed his lips and nodded with a trace of – was it sadness?

"That I did, Sergeant."

No. It wasn't sadness. Was it resignation? Spite, maybe?

"It was me that told David. He hadn't a clue. He was so glad to see Billy again. To David, it was just like old times. But ol' pal Billy and his beloved bride were making a fool of him, so I –"

"Why would you tell him?" Parker demanded. "Mrs. Walker said that it was gonna end –"

"She told you that, did she?"

Stevens looked at me for confirmation, and I nodded. "She said he was supposed to go back to Frisco at the end of the summer."

Stevens laughed bitterly. "Billy wasn't going anywhere. His thing with Ginny wasn't ever going to end. He was just gonna stay on there, living off of David –"

"Fucking his wife," Parker said.

Stevens raised an eyebrow at the vulgarity, then said, "David asked Billy to meet him at our office. He told him that he knew what was going on –"

"You were there?"

"Yes, Detective. David was my best friend. I'd been the one to tell him the bad news . . . Of course I was there. David told Billy he knew about the affair. He offered him some money to break it off."

"How much?" Parker asked.

Stevens closed one eye, trying to recall. "I think it was twenty grand."

Parker tried mightily not to show his amazement at this figure, and he almost succeeded. Stevens caught his astonishment and grinned. "Billy said, 'I have to go back and pack . . .' and David told him that we'd packed for him. He pointed to the suitcase, standing next to the door. David held out a thick manila envelope. Without any hesitation whatsoever, Billy took it. He counted the money, then picked up his suitcase and left, without another word."

Before Parker could speak, before silence could drop, I asked Stevens again, "So why would David have Billy's picture in his wallet?"

Stevens ran his finger over the thick white line that had been the crease in the original photograph. "Maybe it *was* Ginny he wanted to remember."

"Now you're changing your story, Counsellor," I said.

"How can anyone be sure of the motivations of another?" he asked innocently.

"You seemed sure," Parker said.

Stevens shrugged. "Billy and David were once very good friends, Sergeant. The hardest thing about the decision to marry Ginny and move back here, to transfer to UCLA and leave the Bay Area behind – it was that David would also have to leave Billy behind.

"Neither of us had heard from him in ten years, then he just showed up, down on his luck, needing a place to stay for the summer. David was touched – he'd be able to . . . to *provide* for Billy again, just like in college.

"Then his good friend betrayed him. And so did the woman he loved so much. I think he kept this to remember Billy because . . . I dunno. Billy was what he was – he was like Satan himself. Give him an inch and he'd become your ruler." Stevens pushed the picture away and looked up at us. "I think David expected his wife to . . . *resist* all that."

"So you're saying that David kept Billy's picture because he forgave him?" Parker asked.

Stevens shook his head. "No. David didn't forgive him. Nor did he forgive Ginny."

"Then why did he keep –"

I held up my hand and Parker shut up. We were getting nowhere with this discussion of David Walker's motivations for keeping an old snapshot.

I was sure that David Walker hadn't been carrying around a wallet with only cash and a memento in it. There had to be ID somewhere. He had to have a car stashed, maybe a hotel room. He hadn't just materialized out of thin air in Virginia Walker's bedroom. Regardless, this analysis of an old picture was getting us nowhere.

I picked up my phone from the table and called up Adam's photo, set it in front of the attorney. "What can you tell us about Adam?"

Stevens glanced at the picture. "He was a good-looking kid, wasn't he?" Then he met my eyes. "Billy's son."

"Are you sure that he's –" Parker began, but again I held up my hand. I wasn't concerned with more pointless analysis of the missing kid's obvious paternity.

"Did you ever meet Adam Walker, Mr. Stevens?"

"Only once or twice, Detective. All the time he was growing up, David and I had never spoken of him. Not for his entire existence. Then, somehow, he came up in conversation one weekend when Sarah was visiting. She showed us his picture. Before ya know it, he came down for a visit. They discovered that they had very much in common – Adam was a chip off the ol' block, as the saying goes."

Stevens paused and scrolled through the pictures of her brother that Sarah Walker had sent to my phone. "I heard that they eventually made plans to go to Las Vegas for . . . something."

"Adam's eighteenth birthday," Parker supplied.

"Ah, yes. That was it. Unfortunately, I didn't get to attend that bacchanal. I was busy with a case, then I was called out of the country."

"For?"

Stevens grinned at Parker. "The client invited me to accompany her to Europe. A little celebratory tour after all the work I'd done on her contentious divorce. David had declared himself on vacation – he was going to Vegas and all – so after the gavel dropped, I also went on an extended sabbatical.

"I exchanged a few texts with him while I was overseas, but we didn't talk. The former Mrs. Anderson kept me quite entertained, and on the return trip, I didn't have time to wonder why I hadn't heard from David for a few days. I'd just landed at LAX when I got the call from Ginny about the accident."

I asked Stevens the same question I'd asked Sarah. "And nothing's ever occurred to make you think that they weren't really dead?"

He replied the same way she did: "Nothing. Although . . . I'm sure you read the report? About the boat?"

I nodded. Parker had a copy of it in the file in front of him. He didn't remove it to refresh the attorney's memory, however.

Stevens said, "The boat was a rental. A fairly big powerboat, if I recall. That in and of itself was odd. If you'd told me that David had died in a skiing accident – snow skiing – that would've made more sense. He was an avid skier. But he'd never been on a boat in his life."

"Maybe it was Adam's idea," Parker suggested.

"Maybe it was. But he didn't prove to be much of a sailor, either, did he? I guess there was some minor damage to the front end of the boat, like maybe they'd hit something. But whatever it was – it wasn't enough to sink it. It didn't even take on water. And both lifejackets were onboard."

"The Coast Guard's theory was that they hit some submerged object, and maybe one of them got knocked overboard." Parker still didn't bring out the report. "The other one killed the engine, then tried to save the guy in the water. He fell in, too, and they both drowned."

Stevens nodded. "A tragic accident. But why didn't they find the bodies? Don't drowning victims eventually surface?"

"The Coast Guard conducted the routine search –"

"Oh, it was more than routine, Sergeant. Virginia Walker's precious son was missing. On her behalf, I called all of her not-uninfluential friends – they persuaded the Coast Guard to search for several days longer than is customary. Then, when they couldn't make any more excuses for wasting the taxpayers' money looking for bodies that apparently weren't going to turn up, I hired private searchers. They didn't find anything either."

"So you thought it was suspicious?" I asked. "At the time of the accident? A fake drowning *is* the most common method people use when they want to disappear."

"Is it? I guess I've never given it any thought."

"Or a fake suicide," Parker added. "Leave a note, say you're going to jump off a bridge, or walk out into some body of water until your hat floats, or take off on foot across the Mohave. Anything that would result in a missing body."

Stevens shook his head resolutely. "I never suspected that David and Adam weren't really dead. I figured it was just incompetence on the part of the authorities that they were never found. Or, I thought maybe the sharks got 'em. But now we know they didn't die, don't we?"

"We know *David* didn't die," I said.

Again Stevens shook his head. "It was a scam, Detective. I know that now. They were in it together. If it'd been just an accident with only one casualty, David wouldn't have made himself disappear over it. He was a lawyer. Accidents happen every day. Hell, he would've sued the boat rental company for allowing the two of the out without proper training."

"Maybe he killed Adam," Parker said slowly, "and disappeared to cover it up."

Stevens laughed. He guffawed; he slapped the table. "What possible motive would David have to kill Adam, Sergeant?"

A shadow of indignation crossed Parker's face. I hadn't precisely laughed at his pet theory, but now John T. Stevens, Attorney at Law – whom he'd immediately liked – was doing just that.

"Because he wanted to get even with his ex-wife. For cheating on him. For making him pay a lifetime of child support for a kid that clearly wasn't his . . ."

Stevens laughed some more. He was utterly undone with levity. He even wiped away a tear. Yet when he finally got a hold of himself, he did so completely. He stopped laughing abruptly, and his derision was like acid. "You watch too much TV, Sergeant. You think that David waited for nearly twenty years to get even with Ginny for fucking the local party boy? And he chose to get even with her by committing premeditated, cold-blooded murder? Because surely, this whole thing had to be premeditated. One doesn't just take a three-hour cruise and fall off the world. Life doesn't imitate *Gilligan's Island*.

"Time heals all wounds. Trust me when I tell you that it took very little time – David was over the wound Ginny and Billy had dealt to him before that Labor Day weekend had passed. He didn't stew and plot for twenty years – Christ, how melodramatic can you be? He put the whole thing from his mind – Ginny, his marriage. They were only together for ten years –"

"You went on and on about how much in love they were, Mr. Stevens," Parker countered. "I'd think that such a love isn't forgotten overnight."

Another grim burst upon Stevens' face, but once again, I noted that his eyes remained cold. "What are you, Sergeant? Twenty-two? Twenty-five?"

"I don't see what difference –"

"Maybe you know a lot about love, being twenty-five." Stevens glanced briefly at me. "But I'm willing to bet that you don't. It lives. It dies. It's forgotten. Other loves are remembered. New loves come along. Maybe some people carry a torch, maybe they plot revenge against those that *done 'em wrong* for . . . for *twenty years.*" The old attorney giggled again. "Or maybe that's just a plot from *CSI* or *Murder, She Wrote* or whichever one is your favorite.

"The only thing that David ever thought about in connection with his marriage was his daughter. He had a life – a thriving law practice – Ginny and her indiscretions and their by-product didn't even cross his mind. No words about them ever passed his lips. I was his friend, his business partner. I know what I'm talking about."

"Then why did he suddenly decide to befriend his – *Billy's* son?" I asked.

Stevens raised his hands and dropped them back onto the table. "Why not? Who knows? But it certainly wasn't so he could take him out on a boat and murder him and then fall off the world. If this is your line of investigation . . . I'm telling you, you're barking up the wrong tree. David and Adam disappeared *together.*"

"And why do you think they did that, Mr. Stevens?" Parker asked.

Again, that shark's grin. "If I was a policeman, I'd have time to watch TV, Sergeant. Get all my ideas for what motivates people to commit murder, to rob banks, to fake their own deaths, from prime time." He winked at me. "I have not a clue why they did it."

Parker didn't want to look at Stevens' patronizing smile, so he again consulted the file. "Mrs. Walker says she thinks your old buddy Max Haycroft might've had something to do with it. Why do you suppose she'd think that?"

"It's as good a place to start as any, I guess," Stevens replied blandly. "Max undoubtedly would know what to do to create new identities. He made a mean fake ID in college." Stevens smiled. "Seriously. He could do it. He used to teach IT at Cal Poly."

"Used to?"

"I suggest a Google search, Sergeant. Max was always all over the internet. And for a brief period, it was all over him. Magnus Julian Haycroft. Quite a name for a poor boy, isn't it?"

Stevens turned to me. "Is there anything else you want to ask me, Detective? I have a rather pressing afternoon meeting."

Parker remained silent, still stinging from Stevens' ridicule. I didn't have anything else, either, so I thanked the attorney for speaking to us.

"If you think of anything else you want to ask me, just call." He laid a business card on the table, wished us luck in the investigation, gave Parker a *no hard feelings, kid* slap on the back and let himself out of the interrogation room.

Parker picked up the card and murmured, "Oh, we'll definitely be calling you, Counsellor."

I smiled. "Aren't we supposed to give him *our* card? Isn't he supposed to call *us* if he thinks of anything else?"

Wasn't that how it always went on *CSI?*

SARAH

Uncle John didn't come into the house. He'd texted that he was in a hurry, and asked me to meet him outside.

I hadn't been inside his immaculate, primrose yellow Jaguar XKE since I was a teenager, but the old leather smelled the same. The car was built in 1968 – Dad had always called it a dinosaur. He'd never had any use for antiques; he'd always leased his cars, alternating between BMWs and Benzes every two years. Uncle John had driven just this one for as long as I could remember – he called it his baby, and said it was cheaper than a wife. It was, of course, the very definition of sporty, but it wasn't a convertible. John Stevens would never have owned a car that would've mussed his hair.

He smiled and said, "Are you free for the rest of the afternoon, Sarah? I'm afraid we have to take a little ride."

He knew that I was. My job . . . Like I say, the apple hadn't fallen too far from the tree, but I'd never had the ambition to become a lawyer, to Uncle John's eternal chagrin. And yeah, it was true that I didn't have to work at all, but I couldn't bear an idle life. The life my mother had.

I'd called in sick, and what were they going to do if I didn't come in for a few days? Fire me? It wasn't likely. I was the late, great David Walker's daughter. Mom and her friends at RPD had seen to it that no one knew how recently late he actually was. I'd just told them at work that I had the flu. I had plenty of sick leave.

John told the GPS to take us to the T-Mobile Store in Barstow and I laughed. "I have Sprint. Why are we going to Barstow?"

He shifted and shot the low, fast car through a hole in traffic before telling me, "We're going to pay your Uncle Max a little unannounced visit."

"My Uncle – who?"

"You don't remember your Uncle Max? He visited a few Christmases when you were little."

The name meant nothing to me, and I said so. "Why are we going to visit him?"

"Your Uncle Max used to be a Professor of Computer Information Systems at Cal Poly Pomona, though he's fallen on hard times. Now he's assistant manager at the T-Mobile Store in Barstow, or so Jesse tells me."

"Why are we going to visit him?" I repeated, and, "How is he related to me?" Both of my parents were only children.

"He's not actually related to you, any more than I am. Your dad and I roomed with him for a little while in college. I can't believe you don't remember him. Max is rather hard to forget."

"The only one of you and Dad's college roommates I remember is Uncle Billy," I said.

"And I imagine you don't remember him very well. It's been what – twenty-five years?"

I frowned, feeling all the old resentment again. "Whatever happened to him, anyway? He just took off. He didn't even say goodbye. It was so rude."

John shook his head. "That's how he was, honey. Here today, gone tomorrow. We lost touch after he went back up north."

"I've looked for him on Facebook a couple of times, but never found anything."

"People our age are a little too old for Facebook, don't you think?"

"You're on Facebook."

He grinned. "Yeah, but I'm cool."

I loved Uncle John, but sometimes he talked to me like I was five instead of thirty-five. And it irked me that sometimes I just went along with it. "Uncle Billy was cool."

"Uncle Billy was the coolest. Way too cool for Facebook." He grinned again. "Now your Uncle Max –"

"Quit calling him that, John. I don't even know the guy."

"– he was cool."

"What's his last name? We'll see what cool Max's Facebook looks like."

"Oh, I doubt he has much of an online presence anymore. At least not under his real name. I dunno. Maybe. It's been awhile. Surely the villagers have put down their pitchforks by now."

I stared at him, but he just looked ahead at the road. Suspiciously, I asked, "What did he do?"

"What he always did. Just with the wrong people."

"The suspense is killing me, John." I held my phone up.

"Magnus Haycroft," he told Ok Google.

Google seemed to hesitate – long enough for me to wonder if my father's old college roommate had gone berserk and murdered a classroom full of – and then, there it was: *University Professor Accused of Sexual Harassment by 26 Students.*

I glanced over at Uncle John and he looked back at me with amused embarrassment. The article was dated from three years ago. I read it aloud.

"POMONA, CA — A federal complaint has been filed against a Cal Poly professor, claiming that he used illegal drugs with students and pressured them into having sexual relationships with him. Magnus Haycroft, 55, has been employed by the university for nearly two decades.

"Since the allegations surfaced publicly last month, the number of alleged victims has risen to 26, stretching back years, according to James Alexander of Straub and White, the complainants' legal team."

"Yikes," John said. "Jimmy Alexander. He's a real bulldog. Champion of the downtrodden, and all that. As long as they can pay."

"'Professor Haycroft abused his powerful position,' one of the victims told The Times, *on the condition of anonymity. 'He was teacher, leader, advisor – he held all our futures in his hands. If we didn't go along with what he said – he threatened us with poor grades. He said he wouldn't give us references. References are vital for advancement.'*

"How could anyone do that?" I said.

"Oh, I doubt there was actually any coercion involved," John said. "Max never needed to force anybody."

I frowned. "That's not what I meant. Who would trade sex for a grade? Coerced or voluntary? It's just a grade."

"Some people are more ambitious than you, Sarah. Some people *need* that grade, because they're gonna *need* that job."

"I *need* my self-esteem," I told him and read aloud again. *"Another student, who is not part of the suit, told us, 'I'd heard that Mr. Haycroft was known for sleeping with his students, but I never would've imagined that so many would come forward. On the first day of class, he did seem a little odd. He used foul language, told dirty jokes. I figured he was just trying to be cool, put us at ease. But it was a little much for the first day.'"*

"I told you Uncle Max was cool."

"'Haycroft propositioned and/or seduced so many students at Cal Poly and other schools, that the type he preferred –

characterized as "statuesque blondes and brunettes" was common knowledge all over town,' according to the complaint."

I waited for another comment, but my chauffeur just shrugged.

"He was promoted to full professor a decade ago, despite a handful of complaints already lodged against him.

"'Professor Haycroft's depredations are by no means a new phenomenon,' Alexander said. 'A recent poll of students and grad students across the nation has revealed that they've come to expect sexual harassment by staff as par for the course of life on campus.'"

"Did anyone ever harass you at school, Sarah?" John asked with a curious grin.

"Not even once," I told him. *"'Professor Haycroft has out-Heroded Herod in his exploitation of the students enrolled in his lectures,' states the 175-page federal complaint. 'Students were encouraged to dress provocatively for after-hours' study-groups held at Haycroft's residence, and alcohol and drugs were frequently present.'*

"After several phone calls went unanswered, Haycroft finally sent the following email to The Times. *'I will continue to support all my students, even if they choose to transfer out of my classes. The pressures of higher learning are crippling enough without the whispers and finger-pointing that will ensue for them now that these allegations have made the press and are being tried in the court of public opinion. None of them deserve that added stress.'"*

"How diplomatic of him," John said.

"After the complaint was made public, Haycroft was forced to step down from teaching and take administrative leave. The investigation is ongoing. What happened to him? Did he go to jail?"

"I'm sure they drummed him out of the AV Club –"

"The what?"

"If he had tenure, I'm sure it was revoked. He would've been sacked, fired, let go, Sarah. And the ladies – only women were mentioned as complainants in that article, right?"

I skimmed it again and nodded.

"If no criminal charges were filed, I'd imagine that the ladies sued him in civil court. Pain and suffering and loss of future income, don't you know. They sued him back to the Stone Age, no doubt."

I was amazed. "You don't know? I thought you said you were friends?"

"I lost touch with Max a long time ago, Sarah. Way before he was taught this unfortunate lesson in women's rights. But he's working at a T-Mobile Store, so I'm betting he didn't come out of it very well. I wonder if he got to keep his balls."

"Why are we going to see him again?"

"Your mother's sicced Sergeant Dudley Do-Right and her partner on him. Max, being in the IT field – Ginny figures he must've helped David and Adam to disappear. She's probably right.

"I want to get to him before the cops do. Max never did care for cops too much, and if he did provide your father and brother with new identities, there just might be some charges the cops can make stick against him this time. Max might tell us where Adam is, because he surely isn't gonna tell them."

****

John parked the Jag in a deserted corner of the shopping center's parking lot – had to guard against those door dings – and we hiked across to the Barstow T-Mobile Store.

There were one or two customers inside, each being helped by young, eager employees. There was a slightly unkempt older party behind the counter, and as we approached, he said, "Welcome to T-Mobile. How can I be of – well, I'll be a son of a bitch."

"Don't be, Max," John said, extending his hand. "At least not on my account."

The old guy ignored the hand. "What the fuck do you want?"

Out of the corner of my eye, I saw a teenage girl and her mother look over at the profanity.

"David's dead," John said, still smiling.

"David's been dead." He glanced at me, then said, "This is not news, Johnny. So I ask you again, what the fuck do you want?"

John lowered his voice. "Ginny shot David last night, Max. He is, as we speak, lying on a slab in the morgue in Riverside."

Utter surprise crossed Max's face. I was sure it was genuine.

John spoke in a conversational tone again. "Do you get a break from enslaving the masses?" Smiling, he glanced around the store. "Is there somewhere we can talk?"

"I don't have anything to say to you."

John's sunny smile evaporated. "Here's what I have to say to *you*, Max. David didn't fall off that boat and drown. He's been alive, lo, these many years, and you knew it. He showed up at her house in the middle of the night like a prowler, and like a prowler, Ginny shot him. She's convinced her boy's still alive, too, and who could she think of, that might've helped him and David disappear without a trace? No one but you. She's sicced the cops on you, Max. I imagine that they'll be out to this garden spot to see you, probably tomorrow."

Max was not fazed. "I'm not afraid of the cops. There's not a thing left that I've got to hide. I'm a pure as the driven snow, these days. I don't know anything whatsoever about David not being dead." He glanced at me once again. "And even if I did, I wouldn't help you. Where were you when I needed a fucking lawyer? You wouldn't even take my phone calls."

"You got caught, Max. Thirty women spoke up. You were indefensible. Why would I take on a case I knew I couldn't win?"

"Because we were friends, that's why."

When Max glanced at me a third time, John said, "This is David's daughter, Sarah."

A ghost of charm sparked in Max's tired eyes. "I thought you looked familiar. I met you a couple of times when you were a little girl." He offered his hand and I shook it, then he glared at John.

"You're gonna need a lawyer again, Max," John said. "I'm here to offer my –"

"I wouldn't have you represent me if you were the last mouthpiece on the planet, Johnny. That ship has sailed. I don't need a lawyer, anyway. I don't know what you're talking about."

"I'm talking about fraud, with a capital F, friend." John smiled afresh at the alliteration. "You had to supply them with new social security numbers, drivers' licenses. Funds transferred offshore, then transferred back, into new accounts . . ."

Max laughed. "Bank accounts are the least of my worries right now."

"Still paying restitution, are we, to all those poor, mistreated girls?"

"You need to leave now, Johnny, before I come over this counter and beat your smug ass to death. Then those cops from Riverside won't have wasted their trip."

John held up his hands. "Whatever you want. I was just giving you a heads up, offering my help –"

"Fuck you, John. When I needed your help, you were in a meeting." Max Haycroft said to me, "Sorry about your dad, Sarah."

I nodded and left the store. John was already in the parking lot.

"Fuck him," was all he would say about it, but I could tell he was pissed. "Let the cops get it out of him."

53

JANET

Parker said, "We need to look at David's bank accounts, Jan. See if he was making any transfers of money . . ."

"We know he did it, Parker. The question is *why*. There's no reason to be slogging through bank statements."

"If we follow the money, we might be able to find where *it* went, then maybe we might find out *where* they went. The *why* . . . If we find Adam, he can tell us the *why.*"

I sighed, not looking forward to a transaction by transaction examination of a rich man's seven-year-old financial records, looking for evidence of a crime – it wasn't actually even a crime. There's no law against falling off the earth. I'm sure the boat rental people got to keep the damage waiver on the boat, and until we turned up some fake identification, there wasn't even any proof of fraud. There hadn't been any life insurance.

So we'd actually be combing through David Walker's bank statements looking for evidence of preparation for a not-really illegal *action* that we already knew had occurred. *Look! He hit the ATM for the $300 limit, twice that week!* The never-ending joys of police work.

My phone beeped and the front office informed me that there was a guy on the line that said he had some info on the David Walker case.

I snapped my fingers at Parker, told the operator to patch the guy through, and put my phone on speaker. "This is Detective Dunn."

"Hello, Detective. My name's Max Haycroft. I understand you want to talk to me."

"Who told you that, Mr. Haycroft?"

"John Stevens."

"Son of a bitch!" Parker whispered.

"Yes, Mr. Haycroft, we were wondering if you might have any information about –"

"I know what you're wondering, Detective. I've been wondering a few things myself, for quite some time now. Maybe we can help each other. Say tomorrow, about noon?"

"That would be great, sir."

"I'll see you then."

****

Parker and I discovered that Magnus Julian Haycroft seemed to have lived a charmed life, despite John Stevens' rather dark description of his activities whilst a student at SFSU. He had no criminal record – not even a parking ticket, as the old saw goes. Parker bored me to tears with the list of his *cum laudes,* his academic achievements and awards.

He'd seemed to've been a veritable pillar of the information technology education community, right up until all of it came crashing down, in a big, ugly, smoking heap, when some twenty-six current and former students came forward with accusations of illegal drug use and serial sexual harassment.

"Out-Heroded Herod," Parker snickered, skimming the federal complaint.

No criminal proceedings were ever undertaken – no one said Haycroft had ever *raped* her, nor were any of them underage when the alleged malfeasance occurred – but he lost everything, nonetheless. He was forced to step down from his position. Credentials, reputation: all gone. He was nowadays a fifty-eight-year-old nobody peddling cellphones is Barstow.

He indeed looked like someone who'd gone through the ringer – he was only a year older than John Stevens but looked at least five. He hadn't bothered to dress up for the interview, wearing shorts and flip flops and a ratty t-shirt advertising some act I'd never heard of called *The Pat Travers Band.*

At first glance, the ex-professor looked like he might've just come in from pushing a shopping cart full of aluminum cans – Stevens had said he'd been a big recycler, hee, hee. This image was wiped immediately from my mind by the fierce intelligence that crackled in his eye, and the air of educated snobbishness that stubbornly managed to cling to him. He wasn't drunk, and he wasn't crazy; he was just *worn.*

Parker and I introduced ourselves, and I asked, "Will Mr. Stevens be acting as your legal counsel, Mr. Haycroft?"

He scowled, and opened his mouth as if he would hold forth at length; then, seeming to think better of it, he simply said, "He will not. Do I need legal counsel, Detective? With what am I being charged?"

"Nothing yet, Mr. Haycroft," Parker said without any inflection whatsoever. "Some people just feel more comfortable with their attorney present when they talk to the police."

"Mr. Stevens is not my attorney. Not in this lifetime."

I saw Parker's surprise, but he didn't show it to Haycroft. "No? But you gentlemen are friends, right? He let you know that we'd be looking for you."

"Perhaps you'd better tell me what it is you want to know, Sergeant. I'm sure we'll get around to the depth of my friendship with Johnny before too long."

Parker obviously didn't care for Haycroft, but I was warming up to the fractious old coot. I said, "I'm sure Mr. Stevens told you of David Walker's recent death."

"He told me that Ginny shot him. Funny how that didn't make the news. It was all over the news the first time he died."

Parker said coldly: "What can you tell us about that, sir?"

Yeah, my partner really didn't like Max Haycroft. I felt like I was caught in the oldest cliché of them all: good cop/bad cop.

The disgraced professor shrugged. "Something about a boat. They drowned. In Long Beach or somewhere, right?"

"When was the last time you saw David Walker, Mr. Haycroft?" I asked.

"He showed up at a New Year's Eve party I was throwing. Out of the blue. I hadn't seen him or talked to him since college."

"When was this, exactly?" Parker asked.

"The New Year's before he died. He just crashed my party, saying he wanted to catch up on old times. I have no idea how he found me."

"A Google search, perhaps."

The ex-professor scowled at Parker. "Perhaps. I was still teaching at Cal Poly at the time." He shrugged. "I was a little drunk, so I let them in and we went out to the back patio to talk, where it was quieter."

"Them?"

"Yeah, he had that kid with him." Haycroft made quotation marks with his fingers. "His *son.*"

My partner's eyebrows went up. Here was a witness placing David and Adam together on New Year's Eve, nearly six months before they supposedly met for the first time. He asked, "What happened next?"

"We went outside and talked about a whole lot of nothing for about ten minutes. David did all the talking, asking how I liked it at Cal Poly, and hadn't we been having nice weather, and had I gotten everything I wanted for Christmas. Pure inane bullshit. Then the kid got up to get a beer, and I asked David what the fuck he was doing showing up at my house with Billy Munro's son."

Parker blinked guilelessly. "Who?"

"Billy Munro. He was my best friend in college. During your investigation – you haven't heard anything about Billy?"

Parker shook his head.

"It doesn't surprise me," Haycroft said.

Parker asked, "How do you spell that?"

Haycroft spelled it for him, and Parker dutifully pretended to write it down. "Why do you say you're surprised we haven't heard of him? Who is he?"

"I'll get to my lack of surprise that you haven't heard about Billy momentarily, Sergeant. It's actually my main motivation for coming in here to see you, instead of waiting around for you to come up to Barstow and see me.

"What I'm going to tell you *first* about Billy – it all happened about twenty-five or six years ago. He and I were still living in Frisco. I was . . ."

Haycroft shook his head, waved his hand. "It doesn't matter what I was doing. The important thing is – Billy was unemployed. That Liberal Arts degree hadn't translated into any kind of a real-world job. When summer arrived, since he didn't have anything else to do, he told me he was gonna go down to Riverside and visit David and Johnny.

"I didn't hear much from him all summer, and when Labor Day came and went and he still hadn't come back home, I got to missing him. So I called down to Stevens and Walker, looking for him. David wasn't in, but I talked to Johnny.

"He always was a gossipy schoolgirl. He was absolutely *giggly* when he told me the dirt. Billy and Ginny had been carrying on all summer, and David had found out about it. Johnny said that the affair had broken up David's marriage, that divorce proceedings were underway, as we spoke.

"'Where's Billy now?' I asked. Johnny said that David had paid him to break off his thing with Ginny and get the hell out of Dodge."

Haycroft paused. He looked at Parker and then at me and then back at Parker. My partner assumed a believable expression of surprise and said, "Wow."

Haycroft nodded. "Yeah. I'll get back to all that in a minute. You wanted to hear about the last time I saw David. It's damn near twenty years after the sordid events of that summer. David and I are sitting on the back patio, and the walking, talking embodiment of his wife's cuckoldry has just gotten up to get himself a beer. I asked David what he was doing there with Billy's son, and he said, 'He thinks he's my son, Max.'

"I didn't have any comment for that. I read a study once – there was some tribe in Africa that didn't have any concrete customs regarding monogamy. To the researchers, it seemed that their practices might lead to some confusion about paternity, yet when DNA tests were done, everybody was correct about who everybody's daddy was. They did the same kind of tests in some little town in Europe – England or Scotland or something – and it shook out that *mama's baby, daddy maybe* was actually an extremely accurate appraisal there. DNA tests don't lie – quite a lot of adultery had been taking place in this Christian, supposedly monogamous community." Haycroft grinned. "So I didn't ask for any explanation. It didn't shock me that David had been raising Billy's bastard. That kind of thing happens every day. It wasn't any of my business, so I didn't say anything about it. Instead, I asked him, 'What the fuck do you want, David?'"

I blinked. "Why were you so . . . abrupt with him? I thought you guys were all friends in college? You and John and David . . ."

"And Billy." Haycroft smiled grimly. "Patience, Detective. I'll lay it all out for you, by and by. I asked David what he wanted, and that's when he started to talk about the thing that *you* want to talk about. He said the kid was in some kind of trouble –"

"What kind of trouble?" Parker asked in surprise.

Haycroft waved his hand. "He didn't specify. He asked if I could help him to make the kid disappear –"

"Like, kill him?" Parker thought his original theory might be making a comeback.

"No, Sergeant. Not kill him. Why is it that you guys want to talk to me? It's because you think that I provided the ever-important, new and improved paper trail for David and the kid to set out upon, once they mysteriously disappeared from Long Beach. Am I right?"

"It was Newport Beach," I said.

58

Our Endless Needs

"Long Beach, Newport Beach, whatever. They're all the same to me. I hate the beach."

"So David told you that he was planning to –"

"David didn't tell me that *he* was planning, anything, Sergeant. He asked me if I could come up with a new identity for the kid. He said he'd pay me, any amount I wanted. I told him, 'Yeah, I can do it.' It's really a very simple thing. But then I told him that I wouldn't do it for *him*, not for all the money in the world."

"Why not?" Parker and I asked in unison.

Haycroft smiled humorlessly again, shook his head. "I'm about to drop the dime here, as they supposedly said in the old gangster flicks, and you want to know my motivations for refusing to commit fraud?"

We nodded.

"Ah, I see my reputation has proceeded me. Gotta love gossipy Johnny. While I was certainly capable of doing what David asked, if the price was right, and while I had no moral compunctions against doing such a thing – you're just going to have to wait a few more minutes to find out why I wouldn't do it for *him*.

"I looked through the sliding glass door, and there's the kid – what was his name?"

"Adam."

"There's Adam, beer in hand, chatting up a few of my grad students. One of them was Charlie Wang. Write this down, Sergeant. *Charles Xavier Wang.* Like from the X-Men. I guess his dad was a big fan.

"He was a smart kid; more ambitious than he was talented, but ambition will take you a long way in this world. But he was talented enough. He had a rather regrettable penchant for twinks . . . Ah, Christ, how Charlie must've laughed when I got hung out to dry by those humorless bitches!" Haycroft shook his head at the ironies of his life.

"Anyway, I look through the door, and there's Adam, deep in conversation with Charlie. I said to David, 'There's the man for this job. I'm sure Charlie can come up with what you need.'

"He asked me why I wouldn't do it for him personally, and I said, 'Seen Billy lately, have you, David?

"He said, 'I have not.'

"'Nor have I,' I said. 'Not once. Not in nearly twenty years. Not since you found out that he was fucking your wife.' I nodded through the glass door. 'But, on the other hand, you probably don't miss him.

59

You've got his son. It must be like looking at Billy every day, am I right?'

"David stood. He said, 'Thanks for nothing, Max.'

"'I'm sure Charlie'll help your boy out,' I told him, then added, 'Did the cops talk to you?'

"He said, 'What?' and I told him that when Billy hadn't come back by the end of that September, I'd reported him missing. The cops said that they couldn't do much. I told David, 'They said that Billy was free and way over twenty-one, and from what I'd told them, he'd been more or less missing since June. But I'd talked to him a few times over the summer – then, after Labor Day, nothing.'

"'I paid him twenty thousand bucks, Max,' David sneered, like he was talking about pocket change. Then he said, 'Just like I told Ginny – money was always Billy's best friend. If enough money's involved – he'll fuck anybody for it. Everybody, eventually. The fact that he never came back home – it was just your turn to get fucked.'

"'Yeah,' I said. 'But did the cops ever talk to you?'

"'You're drunk, Max,' he told me. 'I never talked to any cops.'

"He went into the house; soon he *and* the kid were talking to Charlie. I made myself another drink, and didn't think too much more about it.

"Charlie never mentioned making any deals with David. On the other hand, I never asked him. He graduated that June. I think he might've gone to work for Texas Instruments. I'm not sure. But how many Charles Xavier Wangs can there possibly be?

"I feel bad about narcing him off – maybe you guys can tell him it was skilled police work and not his old prof that led you to him. I'm sure if you cut him some kind of deal – it is only fraud after all – he'll cooperate and give you whatever names he gave to David and the kid."

Haycroft again looked from Parker to me then back to Parker again. Apparently he didn't like what he saw there; he addressed me. "I've given you want you wanted, Detective. Once you light Charlie up a little bit – I'm sure you'll be able to find Ginny's son straight away. Once that case is closed . . . I've got another one for you. One of a far more serious nature than a little harmless fraud."

Haycroft sighed. "As you may have gathered, I've lived a very interesting, very *busy* life. Once upon a time, Billy Munro was my best friend. He'd always claimed to be an orphan. He was always the life of the party, so he never had a steady squeeze. The world was always his oyster, but once the slurping was over – nobody ever cared enough about Billy to wonder what happened to him next. Nobody but me.

"I missed him when he disappeared; I missed him enough to file a report. I was angry when it went nowhere, but . . . Like I say, I was busy. I rationalized. Maybe Billy took David's money and took off to Australia like he'd always wanted to. But it just wasn't like him to not say goodbye.

"Life goes on. I'd think about Billy every time I saw a good-looking, dark-haired white boy. Then I'd think of other things until I wasn't thinking about Billy anymore.

"But when David showed up with *Billy's son,* all grown-up, I felt all that anger again. That's why I wouldn't've helped him for the entire joint assets of Stevens and Walker. After they left my house, I thought about going to the cops again. I wasn't so far away then, in San Francisco, as I'd been when Billy'd disappeared – I was right over there in Pomona. I could easily go speak to the Riverside cops. But this came up, and I put it off, and that came up, and the months went by. And then David was dead."

"Did you believe he was really dead?" Parker asked.

Haycroft shook his head. "If it just would've been him, I would've wished it was true. But when I read that it was him *and* the kid, I knew that Charlie'd worked a little digital prestidigitation for them. My anger faded again. David was as gone as Billy was, so what good would it do to bring it all up again? Who would care?

"Then before you can say *consenting adults,* I had troubles of my own, and really didn't give a whole lot of thought to David *or* Billy."

Haycroft's voice hardened. "Now Johnny Stevens shows up in his expensive suit and that shitbox old jag, smiling down his nose at me and warning me that, *Oh no, the cops are coming for you, Max,* because *he's* convinced that I helped David disappear. He's so sure he's right – this smug, entitled bastard – he *knows* I did it. I helped David fake his own death – what's it been, five years ago now?"

"Seven," Parker said.

Haycroft winced. "Time certainly does fly. Johnny was *so sure* I'd helped his buddy out, simply because David had *asked* me to. Because that's how it works for rich boys. David and Johnny – they'd never had to do anything more than *ask* for anything. Ever. Request, sign the check, and voila, problem solved.

"Johnny figured that David came to me and I jumped at the cash, even though I wasn't exactly hurting for money at the time.

You can take the boy out of the ghetto, but you can't take the ghetto out of the boy, am I right?

"He was standing there yesterday, grinning at me across the counter – he *knew* I'd done it. And he was so sure I'd tell him where the kid was, so he could be the hero and deliver him back to Ginny and bask in her appreciation and gratitude. I know he was going to offer me some money, but I didn't give him the chance. I told him to get fucked.

"Seeing Johnny after all these years infuriated me. He was so sure that I'd provided David with whatever he needed to disappear, all the while simply overlooking the undeniable fact that David had murdered my best friend. He was sure that *seven* years ago, almost twenty after Billy'd disappeared – I must've forgotten about all that by then, am I right? Even if I did remember – I still would've helped my ol' college buddy David out. *For money.*

"And since I could surely use some money now, I'd just as surely overlook the fact that slick Johnny had to've been in on Billy's murder, too. I'd tell him everything he wanted to know, if he just slipped me a few bucks. He was mistaken.

"So here's my request, Detective. After you find Billy's son and bring him home to his adoring mother, I want you to put a few of those taxpayer dollars to work for . . . for *justice*, for a change. First, see if you can find a single trace of Billy Munro, subsequent to the summer he spent here in Riverside. And when you find not a single driver's license renewal or passport application, not one bank transaction or credit card receipt, I want you to put a little pressure on Johnny Stevens for me. Tell him you know David killed Billy; ask him where they hid the body.

"Johnny's not gonna cop to shit, I'm sure – time and the law and *corpus delicti* are all on his side – but you can give me a call, Sergeant, and tell me about the look on his face when you bring him in and accuse him of it. When you tell him that I sicced you on him. That'll be enough for me. I think that would even be enough for Billy."

The clock clicked off ten noisy seconds before Parker stammered, "We'll do what we can, Mr. Haycroft."

****

The former professor took a business card from each of us and scrawled his cellphone number on the back of a grubby one from the Barstow T-Mobile and tossed it on the table. He silently shook our hands and left.

Now Parker stared contemplatively at the table in front of him. But I knew he wasn't thinking about Sarah Walker.

Finally he said, "This is big, Jan."

I shook my head. *"Let me cut right to the chase, here, Eric.* On this side, we've got a missing adulterer; the orphaned party boy. His buddy – the sex-crazed schoolteacher – is apparently the only one who's ever missed him. We've got a dead lawyer. We've got a live lawyer. On the other side, we've got a very influential rich woman who doesn't care about any of them. All she cares about is –"

"We're talking about murder in the first degree here, Jan," Parker said, and all I could think of was that redheaded guy and his shades. *Murder in the first degree.* Seriously. Who says that?

"I think it's more important than a missing person," Parker added.

"Allow me to reiterate. Missing nobody. Accused misogynist that sells cellphones. Dead lawyer. Live lawyer. No evidence. No body."

"What if we find the body?"

"Did I ever tell you I'd invented a new word, Parker? It's a verb. To *back-burner.* Today I back-burner; yesterday I back-burnered; often I have back-burnered. That's what you're gonna do with your ideas for a *murder in the first degree* investigation right now. You're gonna put them on the back burner – you're not even gonna turn on the gas. If Billy Munro's dead, he isn't gonna get any more or any less dead while we look for Adam Walker.

"That's the case that Iglesias and the fucking chief of police have assigned to us, partner. Just like the good professor said: once we return Adam Walker to his loving mother, then we can look into all this love-triangle/murder shit. The chief'll be all over it then."

Parker frowned sullenly for some seconds, lamenting the reality of how the whims of live, influential people often take precedence over justice for ones that had been missing (but unmissed) for twenty-five years. At last he smiled. Then perfect Parker asked the perfect question: "What do *you* think?"

"I think ol' Billy's under the *polly.* And I think you do, too. And once we get a court order, we'll just go right ahead and dig him up. And since it would be wasting the taxpayers' money to pin it on the dead lawyer, maybe we'll just pin it on the live one. As an accessory, if nothing else."

"That's my girl!" Parker slapped the table in front of him, jumped up and hugged me.

If my life was a cop show, what followed next would've been a moment of awkwardness, while we both regretted his delightful physical display. But that's not what happened.

Parker smiled. "I don't care what anybody says about you, Jan. You're all right." He winked at me and left the room.

It was still a cliché, but it was a good one. It demonstrated . . . *potential.* I picked up Haycroft's card and the file, and picturing that trendy bachelor pad again, I followed Parker down the hall.

He stopped abruptly and asked, "Do you think she was lying?"

"Who?"

"Sarah. I'm sure Mrs. Walker didn't know, but . . . Sometimes brothers and sisters share things with each other that they keep from their parents. But Sarah said the same thing, that Adam didn't meet David until May. Max Haycroft said they showed up together on New Year's Eve." Parker frowned. "Do you think she was lying? Do you think that she knew David and Adam had met six months before her mother thought they did?"

I shook my head. "I don't think she was lying, Parker. Like she said – I don't think that she and Adam were all that close."

"Why wouldn't Adam tell her? Or his mom? Why would he keep it a secret?"

I shrugged. "Miss Walker said Adam was a mama's boy. Maybe he thought his mama wouldn't be too happy about him hanging out with this guy who'd never given him a moment of his time all his life. Maybe David *told* him that Mrs. Walker wouldn't be too happy about it. I don't know."

"Why do you suppose that Adam –" Parker snapped his fingers. He grinned. "Adam got in contact with David because he was in some kind of trouble, Jan! That's what Haycroft said!"

I nodded. "But he said David didn't specify –"

"I bet it had something to do with the girl!"

"What girl?"

"Didn't you listen to what Sarah – Miss Walker – said?"

She didn't say much, Parker, and nothing of any use to our case, and I was mostly watching her watch you.

"I'll play the tape for you."

Oh, yeah, about that. We record everything that occurs in interrogation rooms, whether the shooter, er, the police chief's buddy, wants us to or not. It's procedure, and I'm sure Paddy wouldn't have it any other way. Parker was offering to replay Sarah Walker's interview for me, since I'd apparently missed something he'd found relevant.

"Just tell me what she said."

"She said that Adam had been talking to some girl online, *for months*, that he said he was really into her."

Right. I remembered now. I *had* thought all that about Adam's cyber-love had been irrelevant, because, "Miss Walker said that Adam said that he never met this girl in person."

Parker was undaunted. "Maybe he lied about that, too. Maybe he'd not only met her, maybe he'd gotten her in the family way, and he got in touch with David to ask for his advice. After all, David had had to marry his mother because she was pregnant with his sister."

"Adam probably didn't even know about –"

"He could do the math, couldn't he? It's just like Stevens said. We've got all the relevant dates in our file." Parker consulted it, counted on his fingers. "Sarah was born just seven months after David and Virginia got married. So, if Adam had gotten some girl pregnant, he'd ask his dad what to do about it about it."

"And David's solution was to fake their own deaths?" I shook my head.

"Maybe she was . . . I dunno. Maybe she was underage or something. But I'm sure of it, Jan. This girl Adam was talking to online – this girl he was so interested in, according to Sarah – she had something to do with why Adam got in touch with David. Why he lied to his mother and sister about knowing him months before he showed up at the house."

"I guess anything's possible," I said, but I shook my head again. Parker really did watch too much TV.

SARAH

Being Virginia Walker's daughter, I'd never been permitted the luxury of deluding myself about what is real and what I just wish is real. Every other luxury, surely. But not that one.

Some things just don't work out. That was the sum of what she'd told me about her break-up with Dad. If I chose to treat it as one of the great mysteries of my life, that was certainly my prerogative, but the truth of it was none of my business. The details would remain unrevealed, so it was probably best for all involved if I just accepted the reality that Dad lived somewhere else, and got on with my little girl's life.

Mom never bad-mouthed Dad, so I never had to defend him. In recalling events of their marriage, she was always pleasant. Not wistful or regretful, by any means – everything had been wonderful up until that one summer's conclusion, and then the none-of-my-business had commenced, and *sometimes mommies and daddies decide they'd be better off living separately.* I could seek a better explanation from Dad or Uncle John or the man on the street – none of whom every told me anything more – or I could just let it go.

That worked for me.

Dad left, and Adam came along, and by that time, Mom had already begun to teach me the logic and rationality that was her worldview. Fantasies and wishing were fun, but did I really believe a jolly fat man came down the chimney and delivered presents, etc., etc.? Sure, it was enjoyable to picture such a magical thing – it was called *fiction* – but, seriously? What was my brain for?

When I was sixteen and came home outrageously late from one of my very first dates, Mom didn't yell or threaten punishment. What was right and wrong between men and women were fluid concepts to her, and the opinions of others regarding one's habits – well, everyone was entitled to their opinion, no matter how narrow-minded.

She said that while love was indeed grand – it was one of those times when she fondly recalled Dad – I would simply be playing Russian Roulette if I failed to take the precautions that were necessary in the adult world that I so obviously wanted to join. I could hope that the boys wouldn't think me too free with my charms; I could hope that biology wouldn't take its inevitable course. Or I could accept that things too easily achieved are not valued, and that I would grow up overnight if I got pregnant – and guide myself by these *facts*.

Later, whenever one of my relationships would end – when I'd left home in paroxysms of joy and then crawled back sadder but wiser – Mom would ask me if I hadn't known that the whole fiasco was doomed from the start. Whatever the irreconcilable differences had been this time, hadn't I really seen them all along? Surely, it'd been fun to ignore them and hope that they'd go away, but reality can only be put off for so long.

Yet when Dad and Adam died, Mom paid for the continuation of the search for them because hope wasn't just for fun anymore. It consumed her for a time – her darling boy simply couldn't be dead. But eventually she accepted the reality that Adam was gone. It was simply foolish to hope for an impossibility when you knew the true score.

But once more, impossible – dare I say, *irrational* – hope had returned to Virginia Walker. She twittered happily to me on the phone, talking about all the things we'd do and the places we'd go once Adam came home. All the catching up we'd do! The question of *why* he'd decided to disappear was not something she mentioned discussing, however.

Of course, he'd come back to live with her at the big house: she was having his room painted. It had not been kept, shrine-like, the way he'd left it. When that first uncharacteristic hope had died in her, Mom's realism had reasserted herself, and she'd disposed of the things my brother had left behind. But still the room had stood empty for seven years, and now . . . How welcoming a fresh coat of paint would be!

Mom's sudden unshakeable optimism was jarring. I wanted to scream, *Who are you, and what have you done with my mother?* I was still the same person that Virginia Walker had raised: I was still realistic. If Adam wasn't dead, then he probably didn't want *to come home*. I couldn't suddenly become delusional as my mother had done.

Her unrealistic hope made me feel unreal myself, adrift, cut off from the way I'd always known the world to work. I had to talk to someone about it. It couldn't be Mom – she was having Adam's old room remodeled, for Christ's sake. Uncle John was also optimistic.

He was fairly sure that the police would turn Adam up, whether he wanted to be found or not.

I didn't know how I felt about all that. If Adam didn't want to be found, maybe it was best that he stayed dead to us. But that seemed a traitorous thought – just look how happy Mom was at the idea that he'd be coming back. My mind was troubled. I couldn't sleep. I needed to think about something else; I needed someone to talk to.

I didn't lie to myself about my motivations for giving attractive young Sergeant Walker a ring, about three days after my interview. I gave a mental nod to the idea that I was calling him to inquire about the case on Mom's behalf, but that was only a small part of the reason. Sure, he might be the person that would eventually bring the prodigal son back home – yay, hoorah, and all that. But with the unrelenting honesty that had been ingrained in me since childhood, I knew that the real reason I called Sergeant Parker was because I was very much attracted to him, despite the fact that he was just . . . Well, he wasn't. He *wasn't* just a kid. He was a mature, responsible adult. He was a police detective.

Right. He was young for me, but so what? Spending a little quality time with him – if he was amenable – would serve a dual purpose. I might have a little fun – something that had been absent from my life for a while, even before the fresh tragedy of my father dying all over again – and it would also appear to Mom that I was as hopeful as she was about the imminent return of my brother. A win-win, anyway you looked at it.

I was appropriately apologetic – the investigation was still *in its early days,* as they say on TV, and I knew I shouldn't be bothering him already. But I really needed to talk to someone about the whole thing . . .

Now, Sergeant Parker could've thrown up a wall of professional detachment – he was a cop, not a therapist. If it wasn't some new detail that I had for him, well, he was a little busy at the moment. But he was a man, in addition to being a cop, so he was curious as to what I really wanted. He was more than happy to meet with me.

To underscore that our conversation wasn't going to be *entirely* devoted to the case, I suggested happy hour at Mickey's, a bar not far from the station. Would he be off-duty by five, and thereby permitted to have a drink?

He laughed and said that it sounded great, that he'd meet me there about five. My mood lightened exponentially. He was cute.

****

Mickey's was crowded, but my policeman friend seemed to know the waitress – he called her by name – so our drinks arrived promptly.

I again apologized for bothering him so soon, and he said that it was no bother at all, ending his sentence with *Miss Walker.* I told him to call me Sarah, and he told me to call him Eric, and once that common familiarity was established, I thought it best to ask him if they had, indeed, made any progress.

He told me that today, Detective Dunn had gone to Newport to review the case with the people who'd been directly involved. He said they also had a lead on the person who might've helped Dad and Adam disappear.

"Is it my Uncle Max?"

His smile communicated that I was correct, but he really couldn't comment. So I decided I couldn't comment either. I didn't tell him that I didn't think he was gonna get anything out of Uncle Max.

"I have to be honest with you, Sergeant – Eric. I'm not completely sure how I feel about the idea that Adam might be coming home."

His expression was neutral; he waited for me to elaborate. I said, "It's just that . . . For whatever reason, Adam obviously decided that he wanted to spend the . . . the rest of his life with Dad. He made himself dead to the rest of us. I'm just thinking . . . Maybe he should stay dead."

"What was he like, Sarah? Was he . . . I dunno – Was he *sheltered?* You gave me the impression that he was kind of a . . . a mama's boy."

I laughed. "What exactly is a mama's boy, Eric?"

"Someone who's . . . I dunno," he repeated. I got the impression that he didn't want to offend me. "Someone who thinks about what his mother's opinions might be, before he speaks or acts."

"Adam's mama isn't like others," I said, and drained my drink. "She can't abide shyness. *No one ever got anywhere in this world being shy,* she always told me. Adam knew he was the most important thing in the world to Mom, that's true . . . And that's why I can't understand why he did this to her. I guess it shows he wasn't a mama's boy at all." A darkness clouded my happy mood – Mom's pride and joy had hurt her, but she'd forgotten all about that because he might be forced to come back soon, against his will – but I shook my head, physically pushing it away.

"Adam was a regular teenage kid," I told Eric, "A little smarter than average. Surely smarter than me. He skipped the seventh grade, but he didn't become shy because he was put in with kids a little older than him at school. He didn't hide behind Mom's skirts – she would've just pushed him out in front, if he'd tried. He went to school; he went to parties, to concerts. I'm sure he had a beer, smoked a joint. He went out with his friends –"

"Do you recall any of their names?"

"I didn't know any of them by name. Like I say, it wasn't like we were all hanging out together. I only met a few of them, in passing."

"What about girlfriends? You mentioned a girl that your brother was talking to online before your dad showed up. Can you remember anything else about her?"

I couldn't see where he could possibly be going with that, but Mom had said to tell them anything they wanted to know, no matter how superfluous it might seem to me.

"He said that she was fascinating."

"Did he say how they'd met? Was it through a dating site or a chat room or something like that?"

Did anybody still use chat rooms? But I had to remember, it'd been seven years ago. Did anybody still use them then? I was sorry that I couldn't give him more information.

"You have to understand, Eric." I liked the feel of his name on my tongue. "I was pushing thirty at the time, and my brother was still a teenager. I'm ten years older than him – I really wasn't up on the ways and means of how high school kids meet and greet."

"Ten years isn't that big a difference." He smiled with a kind of shyness, but he didn't look away.

I smiled back. "I think it's more a matter of the time in your life than the years. You're what, twenty-three?"

He laughed. "That's the second time someone's misjudged my age lately. Do I really look that young? I'm almost twenty-seven."

What had Uncle John called him? *Sergeant Dudley Do-Right.* It was accurate. Cop or no, a kind of innocence wreathed him. It didn't make much difference if he was twenty-three or twenty-seven. *It's*

70

not the years, honey, it's the mileage. He was still a whole helluva lot younger than me, in a lot of ways.

I ignored this and said, "You'll agree that your twenty-seven is a lot closer to my thirty-five, life-experience-wise, than Adam's seventeen was to my twenty-eight. At the time, that ten years was a *huge* difference."

I grinned at him. "I don't remember Adam ever talking about a steady girlfriend. He was a confident individual – no son of Virginia Walker's could've been anything else – and he was smart and good-looking, as well. I doubt that he would've devoted his time to just one girl."

"Just that one he met online, huh? You said – she intrigued him. *She was different than anyone he'd ever known.* He never told you her name?"

"Her screenname was *Searching.* That's all he ever told me. Maybe he didn't know her real name."

"What was she searching for?"

"I have no idea." I smiled at him again. "Love in all the wrong places, perhaps."

I was becoming bored with all this. Although I was sure my brother had had a love life at seventeen – he was very attractive, and he was a child of a modern mother who'd always been rational and realistic about relations between men and women – I'd been neither privy to any details about the girls he'd dated, nor at all interested in it at the time it as going on, and now . . . I didn't think it had a bearing on why he'd disappeared. He'd taken off with Dad, not some online temptress.

Eric sensed my annoyance and broke off the interrogation. He signaled his waitress-pal for another drink, and we talked of other things.

He asked about my job; I catalogued it briefly. I asked him about his parents, and where he'd gone to school. He said something about UCR, but brushed off the particulars. How one spent one's college days is a big indicator of socioeconomic status; I didn't think he wanted to tell a poor little rich girl about how he was still paying off his student loans.

We skimmed all the subjects that people who are tentatively interested in each other trot out. A little environmentalism, a little politics – just enough to see that we were basically on the same page. It was somewhat tedious to me – I didn't care overly about his stand on global warming, or which crook he thought he might be supporting in the next election. Exploration of philosophies could come later, if at all.

I would've admitted it, had anyone asked – at the moment, I was only interested in discovering how fluid *his* morality was. I was looking for something to take my mind off my troubles, and despite the age difference, we were both adults, were we not?

One drink turned into three or four, as Bradley mentioned in that cautionary tale from my long ago youth, and while we did leave and get into Eric's car, we surely didn't drive to any place real far. Hee, hee.

I might've been just a *teensy* bit over the safe-to-drive limit – Officer Obie didn't *say* he was making sure, but friends, Obie was – about ten o'clock, he mentioned something about having work in the morning, and offered to give me a ride home.

It wasn't like I was falling down drunk, however. I didn't make a fool of myself. My offer of a nightcap, while transparent, was delivered in a ladylike fashion. I was Virginia Walker's daughter, after all.

He shook his head, but he smiled. "Some other time, definitely." He kissed me perfunctorily, chastely, quickly. "But I've got a ton a research to finish. I'll call you. For dinner, maybe?"

He was adorable. Young and cute, but maybe not as innocent as all that. I nodded, and gave him a little bit longer kiss goodnight.

JANET

I wound up being stuck in Newport Beach overnight.

It's always a dicey thing when you have to go to another jurisdiction and ask about a closed investigation. One that they'd deemed *solved,* for all intents and purposes. When it was clear that their conclusions had been premature, defensiveness was automatic. It took a flair for the diplomatic not to bruise any egos.

Chief O'Connor's office had already called and briefed NBPD: one of the subjects of an old missing-and-presumed-dead case had turned up as the live perpetrator of a break-in. The homeowner, exercising her second amendment rights, had sent him back to where the boys from the beach had formerly placed him, after that rented boat had turned up empty. Discussion of all this was on a strictly need-to-know basis; there was a press black-out about it. Only the two detectives that had signed the report and their supervisor were told I was coming.

The Walker case surely hadn't been the first drowning-without-a-body case they'd ever investigated, and it probably wouldn't be the last. But I got the impression that maybe it was the first one that'd ever been re-opened, and especially by some Inland Empire jurisdiction: Detectives Bailey and Rivera were solemn and wary when they shook my hand. I'd never received a colder welcome from colleagues.

I set out to thaw them out right away. "It's a long drive down here from Riverside," I said. "The traffic's murder."

"It always is," Bailey said gravely.

"Is there somewhere we could get something to eat?"

Proud of the amenities of their dominion, they took me to a place right on the beach, and with the sea breeze ruffling my hair, I ordered the lunch special. Again, I couldn't escape the feeling of being an actress instead of a real cop. I just went with it, and let the clichés fall. "I'm going to level with you, gentlemen. That's why I wanted to get away from the office. I'm sure you gave this investigation you're utmost –"

"The Coast Guard stretched out the search for *days,"* Rivera said. "Maybe you should go talk to them."

"I don't want to talk to them," I replied, and gave him my most winning smile. "They're so . . . *military.* I'm hoping that after I talk to you, I won't have to bother with them. The Walkers were friends of my chief's, so he wants me to . . ." I actually said, *"cover all bases.* I'm just here so he can tell the rich lady that he's being in-depth in his search for her son.

"I think your report speaks for itself – a couple of guys that had never been on a boat before fell off and drowned."

"That's about it," Bailey said.

"So I'm gonna ask what I was sent down here to ask: was there anything odd about it at all? Anything that didn't make it into the report?"

The detectives told me that the only thing odd about the case was the thoroughness that went into its investigation. From on high came instructions to go over the boat with a fine-tooth forensic comb – fibers, fingerprints, blood, DNA. There was no blood, and nothing else that shouldn't have been there was uncovered. Regarding that extended Coast Guard search – the detectives figured that the missing men were important to someone else who was also important. I told them that they were correct on that.

"Did anyone suspect it was a scam?"

"Not for a second," Bailey said. "We looked into it as a possible homicide, for a minute. But that didn't hold up."

They told me what I already knew. A brief check into the assets of the decedents revealed that there was no life insurance to be paid out, no property or bank accounts to be inherited.

"The kid lived with his mother," Rivera said. "The ol' man lived in a condo that belonged to his law firm. I guess the partner got that . . . But it was already a part of the joint assets, so we didn't think it was enough to kill the guy over."

Our lunch arrived. I said, "So you guys don't have anything new to tell me. That's just how I like it."

Because, really – the fact that David Walker had faked his death was just that. *A fact.* There was no need to be offending these two beach cops with the idea that I was just going to cruise down here from hot and dry Riverside and miraculously uncover something they'd missed. If I wanted to wade through financial records and look for clues there, I could do that at home. The brine-soaked revelations here, beachside – there weren't any.

Bailey and Rivera relaxed, and we enjoyed our lunch. We spent the rest of the afternoon going to the pertinent sites – here was the pier from which the Walkers had disembarked, there was the boat rental place, now under new ownership. No one employed there now was employed there at the time of the accident.

It was really just an excuse for an afternoon out of the office, for all three of us.

Newport Beach PD graciously put me up in a nice hotel for the night, and the next day, in the spirit of thoroughness and interjurisdictional cooperation, I went over the file with them. As I expected, procedure had been followed to the letter. Mrs. Walker's influential friends had seen to that. Nothing had been overlooked.

David and Adam Walker had gone boating on a sunny day in October and had not returned. While the *fact* that person or persons unknown had picked them up somewhere and spirited them off to somewhere else was now undeniable, there was not one thing in the case file that pointed to who those persons were or where those places might be.

I thanked the detectives for their time, their hospitality and their professionalism, and got back on the freeway towards home.

****

I got back to the station about 2:30. I thought Parker looked a little tired when he asked me, "How was the beach?"

"Bright and hot and breezy," I told him. "Did you miss me?"

"I certainly did," he replied with an endearingly genuine sincerity. "I pictured you taking names and kicking asses, stomping all over sandy, barefoot toes –"

"It wasn't like that, Parker."

"Like everything at the beach, I've found that police work is pretty kicked back there. That's why I transferred up here."

"I didn't know you worked at the beach."

"I worked in Orange County," he said, purposely, mysteriously not specifying which jurisdiction. If I was that interested, I could look it up. "From the way some of the crimes were investigated . . . It might just as well have been *all* the beach."

Whatever that means.

He added, "Take these Newport guys. It's obvious from the report that they didn't give this the attention that it warranted."

"Who are you, the police police?" I giggled. It was great to spar with Parker. Even though I'd only been gone overnight, I'd missed him.

"I'm jes sayin' . . . How could they not've suspected that it was a scam?"

"I'd imagine that they have a lot more body-less drownings there than we have here in the land-of-not-much-water. Their investigation was thorough, by the book, Parker. They even looked at it as a homicide for a hot second. But there was no evidence that it was anything other than what it appeared to be. A tragic accident."

"But we know better." He made a big production of sliding a folder across his desk. "I've got some good news and some bad news and some really unexpected, kinda awesome news. What do you want to hear first?"

He was kinda awesome.

"So the best part won't seem like an anticlimax, why don't you start with the good news?"

"I found Charlie Wang."

"Oh, wow, Parker, that's –"

"Wait for it . . . Here's the bad news: he's dead." He flipped open the folder. "Motorcycle accident, about two years ago, in Frisco. He never worked for Texas Instruments, like Haycroft said. He was working for Transamerica. Right there in that big, pointy building."

I asked Parker why he was smiling – the computer major's being dead put us back at the beginning, with nothing.

"Mr. Wang left behind a husband, Andrew Holly-hyphen-Wang. He works at Symatec. Another *IT geek,* as Mr. Stevens so poetically put it. Pack your bags, Jan. *The loveliness of Paris seems somehow sadly gay,"* he sang and batted his eyelashes at me. *"The glory that was Rome is of another day . . ."*

"I fail to see why you think the tenuous-at-best connection of Charlie Wang's . . . What would this guy be? His widower?"

Park shrugged, but continued to smile.

"I don't see why you think this guy warrants a trip to San Francisco."

"He's in the same field. Maybe Charlie told him about what he did for David and Adam. It deserves an interview. It's the only lead we've got. And . . . You've forgotten about the awesome news I've got for you." He winked. "Whilst I was running through the records of births and deaths and marriages . . . Neither Mr. Wang's marriage nor his death certificate took too long to find. It's just like that old pervert said. There was just the one *Charles Xavier Wang."*

"You wrong the scholar, Parker. He was never convicted –"

"Ri-i-ight. All those girls just made that shit up." He turned over papers in the file, not looking at me.

I gave him my best motherly tone. "What's a'matter, Parker? Did someone sexually harass you in college?" When he looked up, I added, "Or maybe no one offered you such an opportunity for easy grades, and you didn't appreciate all the pretty girls that seemed to pass . . . What? Effortlessly? Miraculously?"

He ignored all that. "Since I found Mr. Wang, his husband, and his unfortunate end so quickly, I looked up a couple of other names in the marriage and death records. No death certificate for Billy Munro, anywhere in these United States. So either he's alive, or . . ."

"He's under the polly."

Parker smiled brilliantly. "Maybe his wife can tell us."

The paper he handed me read *State of California Certification of Vital Record, City and County of San Francisco, License and Certificate of Marriage.* The name of the First Applicant was William Seth Munro –

"How do you know that's our Billy?"

"It's him, Jan." Parker snatched the marriage license back. "I checked with SFSU Admissions. The birthdate and the parents' names match. I called your buddy Haycroft – that's his old address."

"What did Max say about Billy's wife?"

"I didn't tell him. I figured he didn't know, or he would've told us –"

"How could he *not* know?"

Parker held up his hand. "I just asked him if this was the address he'd had in college, where he and David and Johnny and Billy had lived. He said it was, I thanked him, and hung up.

He handed the marriage license back to me. "So, William Seth Munro, aged twenty-two, married Guadalupe Maria Rodriguez, age nineteen. He would've been about a junior in college at the time, right?"

Parker nodded. "It gets better. I looked at the property tax rolls, and found an address whose owners are listed as Guadalupe and William Munro. They've owned it since right after they got married."

"So maybe he's not dead after all. Maybe he just chose to disappear into wedded bliss."

"I don't think so, Jan. The dates don't add up. Billy got married when he was twenty-two, and he was still friends with Haycroft ten years later, when he went to see David. After that, it's just like the professor said. There's never been a driver's license renewal or a passport application. No financial info. Nothing."

I had no explanation for the lack of records, so I just repeated, "Maybe Billy went back to his wife and didn't tell Max. Maybe he wanted to share that twenty grand between just the two of them."

"I don't think Max ever knew Billy married this girl, or he would've mentioned it to us. Just like Adam Walker's true parentage – maybe Billy got Lupe pregnant, married her on the down-low – and he didn't think all that was any of Max's business." Parker grinned. "Regardless, there's only one way to find out. *And on a hill, it calls to me-e-e-e . . .*"

"What did I tell you about this Billy Munro thing, Parker?"

"It's all arranged, Jan. Go home, pack a bag, get a good night's sleep. We're on the 7 am flight to SFO."

"How? You didn't mention –"

"What did you tell me about this Billy Munro thing, Jan? Since you were at the beach, I took the Charlie-Wang's-husband angle in to Iglesias, and she okayed the trip."

SARAH

On the phone, Eric stumbled over *Hi,* then said, "I'm gonna be out of town tomorrow. I just wanted to let you know, so you don't think I'm . . . I'm ignoring you."

When I didn't reply right away, he added, "It's about the case."

"Just send me a text if you're thinking about me," I said blithely. "And thanks for all the hard work."

He didn't seem to have a response to that; there was an almost awkward pause. Then he said, "I'll call you when I get back. We'll do that dinner."

"Are you sure . . . Is it okay for us to be . . . seeing each other?" If talking to Uncle John sometimes made me feel like a stupid child, talking to Eric made me feel like a naughty teenager. "I mean . . . Since I'm connected to the case?"

He laughed. "Well, you know what they say about begging forgiveness and asking permission. I'll see you in a couple days, Sarah."

JANET

Parker ignored me while we waited to board the plane; he returned emails, sent texts, and played games on his phone. It wasn't like we could discuss the case in a crowded airport terminal, nor on the plane. So once in the air, we played tic-tac-toe on the back of the in-flight magazine for the hour-long hop to San Francisco. Apparently he didn't have any two-player games on his phone.

He was really just as fun and entertaining as he could be. As much as I could ever wish for in a partner, professionally or personally. I thought that it was sincerely a goddamned shame that Iglesias hadn't sprung for an overnight stay in Frisco. But I really couldn't expect her to stop and consider my secret yen for a little off-duty, out-of-town-aloneness with Parker – like she would even suspect such a thing. And there were those budgetary concerns.

A couple of hours in the City by the Bay should be more than sufficient. The guy we were there to talk to wasn't a fugitive; he wasn't wanted for anything. It wasn't like we had to get the jump on him. Parker had already called and made an appointment for the interview.

It all could've been accomplished over the phone, in my estimation, but Parker had convinced Iglesias that a face-to-face meeting was necessary. I reckoned that she was only human, too, and was not immune to the smile and enthusiasm of a young go-getter like Parker.

His true motivation to fly up the coast was unfortunately crystal clear to me. After we were through talking to Mr. Holly-Wang, he wanted to get the jump on Mrs. Munro.

****

We grabbed a taxi at SFO and arrived at Symantec right on time for our scheduled meeting with the witness. Mr. Holly-Wang was a bespectacled man in his forties. He met us in the lobby, and like anyone who gets an unexpected call from law enforcement – law enforcement from four hundred miles away, no less – he didn't want to speak to us at his place of employ. Parker said that was fine, and we walked up the street to Starbucks.

"What is it that you want me to tell you about Charlie?" he asked, dumping a few packets of sugar into his coffee.

"First, I'd like to apologize for the intrusion," Parker said, big brown eyes solemn and serious. "We're sorry for your loss."

The guy looked at me and I nodded my condolences, but I didn't say anything. Not yet. This was Parker's show.

"We're investigating a cold case," he began. "Two missing persons."

Our witness again looked at me. "From Riverside?"

I said, "Yes, they were from Riverside, but they disappeared in Newport Beach, Mr. . . . ."

"Just Holly," he said. "I dropped Charlie's last name when he died. I didn't see as there was any point . . ." He trailed off, then glared at me. "What has Charlie to do with missing people? Are you trying to tell me that you think he killed someone?"

Mr. Holly was clearly annoyed, so I shut up again, waiting for Parker to turn on that boyish charm.

"Not at all, sir. Then it would be a homicide investigation." He smiled . . . *respectfully.* "That's not it at all. In fact, the reason that the case has been reopened – we have evidence to indicate that these gentlemen – Adam and David Walker – disappeared intentionally, and that they're not really dead at all. Did your husband ever mention those names to you?"

Holly shook his head.

"Did Charlie ever tell you that he'd provided new identities for anyone?" I asked, *cutting to the chase.*

Mr. Holly frowned. "When did this happen?"

On his phone, Parker called up a newspaper clipping from *The Press-Enterprise* that he'd scanned from the file. *Prominent Local Attorney and Son Missing after Boat Turns Up Adrift.*

Holly didn't read the article; he enlarged it only to look at the date.

"This was before I met Charlie," he told us. "It was while he was at Cal Poly. Working with Max Haycroft, God's gift to higher education."

"You know Professor Haycroft?" Parker asked.

"Only by his bad reputation. And from what Charlie told me about him, which didn't alter my low opinion of him." Holly sighed and set his coffee aside. "What you're talking about – providing new

81

identities for missing persons – is illegal. When I met Charlie, not long after he was through with school, he had an . . . *interest* in that kind of thing, true.

"He'd done a little hacking, a little clandestine *file sharing* . . ." Holly made the air quotes. "But all of us aren't *Anonymous,* Mr. Parker. I convinced Charlie that his forays into the dark side, while exciting and certainly profitable . . . I considered it his former professor's influence. I'm sure I don't have to tell you that Max Haycroft walked a tightrope above a sea of questionable behavior for years. Eventually, he fell off."

And drowned, I thought.

"If Charlie did any tinkering with social security numbers or other identification while he was at Cal Poly . . . He could surely have done it. He was brilliant to begin with, and he also learned all kinds of illicit tricks from Max, and not all of them related to the processing of information.

"But once he met me . . . I persuaded him to use his talents out in the daylight. No more jail-breaking devices for strangers he met in bars. I told him to get a job with a reputable place – with his ability, the sky was the limit. I told him that he'd make a lot more money, and he wouldn't wind up disgraced like his mentor.

"In other words, Charlie could've done what you're suggesting. But if he helped those men disappear while he was still in college, he never discussed it with me. I'm sorry I can't be of more help, especially after you've travelled all this distance."

Well, *that's the name of that tune,* as Grandpa used to say. Parker rose and shook Holly's hand, thanked him for speaking to us. As he recited the standard line about *if you think of anything else, give us a call* and handed him his card, our utterly un-helpful witness asked, "How did you get Charlie's name on this, anyway?"

I said blankly, "It came up during the course of the investigation," which, of course, is no answer at all.

Holly nodded, unsurprised at the procedural obfuscation, and said to Parker, "Maybe you should look up ex-Professor Haycroft. If you think Charlie knew these men, maybe Max did, too. Maybe he was the one who helped them to become missing persons.

"He shouldn't be too hard to locate. I hear he's a door-to-door vacuum cleaner salesman in Bakersfield. Or something equally as fitting." He offered a nasty grin, and shook our hands again.

Watching him walk briskly down the crowded sidewalk, I remarked to Parker, "Now there's something you don't see every day. A righteous man."

"I get the impression from Mr. Holly's *righteousness* that maybe Max and Charlie were better friends than Max led us to believe. Perhaps what he is, is not so much righteous as jealous." Parker grinned. *"Selling vacuum cleaners door to door.* I guess it's true what they say – they all know each other."

When I blinked stupidly at this unexpected show of stereotyping, Parker winked. "Computer geeks, Jan. They all know each other." He sighed. "The circle remains unbroken. Max says Charlie did it. Charlie's husband says Max did it. Charlie's dead. Max says he didn't do it."

"All we know for sure is that *somebody* did it."

"Fuck it," Parker said. "Finish your coffee. Let's go see Mrs. Munro."

****

We knocked on the screen door to a modest little house. The front lawn and porch were immaculately kept, with potted plants lining the steps. A woman of about Parker's age opened the inside door; by her side was a little girl of about six.

Parker introduced us, and we showed the woman our badges. "We were wondering if we might speak to Guadalupe Munro?"

The woman said that she was sorry, but we must have the wrong address. There was no one there by that name. As she went to close the door, like something out of a movie, the little girl tugged on her hand. "But Mama," she said, "Abuela's name is Guadalupe. Just like me."

Parker smiled at the child, and bent so that he was at her level. "Maybe your abuela *is* the lady were looking for." He stood up and said to her mother, "Is Abuela at home?"

The woman frowned. "Can I see your identification again?" She opened the screen door to get a closer look at our badges, then said, "Hold on. I'll see if she's here."

She took the little girl by the hand and closed the door.

"Abuela means *grandmother,"* Parker told me unnecessarily. I hadn't spent my entire life in Southern California without picking up a little Spanish.

83

The woman that returned appeared to be in her mid-fifties. That would be about the right age for Billy's bride. She said, "My daughter says you want to speak to me, officers?"

Parker was slick. "We just need a moment of your time, Mrs.?"

"Gonzales," the daughter supplied.

"We have just a few questions, Mrs. Gonzales." Parker smiled politely at the other woman. "If you could excuse us, Mrs. –?"

"Diaz." She wasn't ready to go quite yet. "What's this about? What do you want with my mom?"

"It's okay, Vera," Mrs. Gonzales said. "Go on in the house."

Vera reluctantly complied, and Mrs. Gonzales showed us to chairs on the front porch.

Parker began. "We'd like to ask you a few questions about your former husband, Mrs. Gonzales. Billy Munro."

Even if I didn't know that Parker hadn't found a record of it, the suddenly guilty look in her eyes told me that there'd never been a divorce. He was *still* her husband. I didn't know who Mr. Gonzales might be, but –

"Is Billy in some kind of . . . legal trouble?"

Parker shook his head. "Not at all. He was reported missing a while back, and we're revisiting the case."

That was twice now that Parker had trotted out the *this-is-only-a-cold-case* trope. What he'd told Holly – that we were currently looking into the disappearance of the Walkers, some seven years ago – that was basically the truth. That David's accidental murder had prompted the reopening of the investigation, that a rich and influential old woman was now demanding that we locate her son – these were details that Mr. Holly hadn't needed to know.

But as far as Billy Munro's *ancient* missing person case and our investigation of it went . . . While what Parker had told Mrs. Gonzales wasn't entirely a lie, it wasn't quite the truth, either. There *had* once been a report filed on Billy, right here in San Francisco, by his friend Max. But it had been a lot longer ago than *a while back*. And while Parker might be able to convince Iglesias to open an RPD investigation *someday,* that hadn't occurred yet. So all that actually existed was a quarter-of-a-century old report made to SFPD. From what Max had said, it hadn't even been investigated. There probably wasn't even a file anymore.

Parker was so far out of his *juris-my-diction,* in so many ways. The total impropriety of this interview made me a little uncomfortable that I was right there with him.

Mrs. Gonzales asked, "Where are you from, again?" Parker showed her his shield and she said, "Riverside. David moved to Riverside. Was it David that reported Billy missing? David . . ." She concentrated, reaching into her memory for the name. "David . . . Walker?"

Since he was already out on a limb, conducting unauthorized interviews for nonexistent investigations, Parker decided that shimmying out a little farther couldn't do anything but help our chances of gaining some useful information.

"It was Max, Mrs. Gonzales. Max Haycroft reported Billy missing."

She smiled. "Yeah, Max was Billy's friend, too. But not like David. David *loved* Billy."

"We've heard that," I said, tiptoeing right on out on that limb with Parker. "When was the last time you saw him?"

"David? Or Billy?"

"Billy."

"God. It's been . . . It's been thirty years."

Vera peeked her head out the screen door and asked if everything was all right. Mrs. Gonzales waved her hand and the worried woman went back into the house.

"You confused my daughter, asking for Guadalupe *Munro.* That was all a very long time ago, before she was born. She doesn't know about my –"

"About your sham marriage to Billy?"

Mrs. Gonzales blinked as if Parker had slapped her, and the words *police harassment* stenciled themselves across my vision for a split second.

Parker reached out and patted the stunned woman's hand. "It's okay. We're not hardly from Immigration, Mrs. – Lupe. We're just trying to find Billy. All we know about him is what Max's told us. He said Billy was his best friend, but he didn't tell us about you . . ."

"That's because he didn't know about me, Officer Parker. I mean – Max knew me. But he didn't know that Billy had married me."

"So you could stay here."

And the hits just keep on coming. How could Parker possibly know that?

"We're just trying to find out what happened to him," my partner repeated. "According to Max, he's been missing for a long time. Anything you could tell us about him –"

"And Max," I added. "And . . . and David."

"Anything you can remember might be of help in figuring out what happened to him."

When she hesitated still, I asked, "How did you first meet?"

She took a breath, hesitated for another second, then let it out slowly. "My brother Andre sometimes worked as a handyman. I met them – Max and David and the other one . . . John – when David hired Andre to paint Max's house. I wouldn't meet Billy till later.

"I was about eighteen. I'd just . . ." She trailed off, then stopped. She looked distressed, and again I wondered what the fallout would be if she decided to call down to Riverside and tell our boss that she hadn't appreciated Parker's accusations.

He smiled and patted her hand again. "Like I say, we're not from Immigration, Lupe. Anything you tell us about how you came to be in this country . . . It won't leave this porch."

Parker's charm put Mrs. Gonzales at her ease. He was *amazing*.

"My brother had recently . . . brought me here from Mexico."

It startled me that Mrs. Gonzales didn't say *Me-he-co*. She seemed to have no accent at all. Her granddaughter might call her *Abuela,* like in the old country, but to listen to her speak, she seemed as much a native Californian as Parker or myself. It was true that she'd been here for a long time, but I thought she also must've made a concerted effort to lose her accent.

"Andre and his wife and his baby daughter lived in a tiny, cramped apartment. There wasn't really enough room for me, too, but we got by. Rosa didn't speak a lot of English – she worked as a maid in a hotel. I stayed at home and watched the baby. Andre . . . Andre did handyman work and . . ." She smiled sheepishly. "Anything else he could to make a little money. That's why he knew Max.

"He came home one day to tell us that Max wanted him to paint his house. He told me that I could help if I wanted – that way he wouldn't have to hire someone else, and all the pay would stay in the family. The neighbor could watch the baby again.

"So dressed in painters' whites, wearing a little white hat, I went with my brother over to Max's big, old, run-down house."

"What did you think of him?" Parker asked.

"'Cómo te llamas, Corazón?' he asked. 'Llámame Max. Habla usted Inglés?'

"I told him that I did, and told him my name. He dropped the Spanish immediately and said, 'Welcome, Lupe. Our house is your house. Your brother and I go way back.'

"Andre asked him something about the color for the living room, and he waved his hand. 'This is all David's deal, Flaco. Whatever he wants.'

"So Andre introduced me to David, and also John. David picked a color – it was a light green, I think . . .'"

"What did you think of them?" Parker asked again. "How did they . . . treat you?"

"Do you mean, did they flirt with me?" She giggled like a schoolgirl. "My brother was with me, Officer Parker, and he was a scary sort to a couple of rich, white college boys. Max wasn't afraid of Andre – they were old friends. So Max flirted with me a little bit, but it was in a cute way. I could tell that he wasn't sincerely interested in an eighteen-year-old girl there to help paint his house.

"John and David – maybe they knew better than to flirt with me. My brother was Max's friend, his . . . connect. He might be . . . *dangerous*. David was nice and friendly and polite, and so was John, but . . . I don't know. After a while, it occurred to me that they weren't flirting with me because they were afraid of Andre. They both seemed to have other things on their minds."

Lupe paused and considered Parker for a heartbeat. "Whatever it was . . . I dunno. John seemed frequently annoyed with David, and David seemed like he was thinking about something important, and it was bothering him. He was . . . I dunno, *introspective* . . . *distracted*. I figured he had a girlfriend, she wasn't around for some reason, and he was missing her."

"You got all this while you were there painting the living room?" I asked in surprise.

Lupe smiled. "My painter's helper job didn't last for very long. Later in the afternoon, Max came out of the kitchen – John and David were also helping to paint – and Max said to me, 'Forgive me, Corazón, I don't want to appear sexist –'"

"Not Max," Parker said and grinned.

"'Nor racist,'" Lupe continued, 'but I seem to have ruined the Chili Verde. It's really bland. Can you give me some advice?'"

"Andre glared at him, thinking it might be a play to get me alone. Max held up his hand and said, 'Seriously, dude. My stew is weak.'

"'Mess with my sister, and I cut you, Gringo,' Andre replied in his best East LA growl. Everybody laughed and I went out to look at Max's *stew*.

"I added some garlic and more jalapenos – Max had been hesitant on that – and a pinch of ground cloves. I opened the fridge and looked in the cabinets to see what other ingredients they might have. Max stood there like a little kid, underfoot. So I told him I'd finish *the stew*, and he could go out and help with the painting."

Lupe smiled. "The college boys raved about my Chili Verde, saying it was the best they'd ever tasted." She giggled again. "It was John that suggested that I come and cook for them. He begged me, really. He said if I'd come by a couple times a week and cook them a meal this great, he'd pay me whatever I asked."

"That sounds like him," Parker murmured.

"You've talked to him?" Lupe asked. "What was his last name?"

"Stevens. Yeah, we've interviewed him about Billy's disappearance," Parker lied. "Unfortunately, Mr. Stevens hasn't seen him in a long time, either."

At least that was the truth.

Lupe continued. "Andre didn't like the idea. He knew the kind of stuff that went on at Max's house – he'd often been the one to supply the . . . cheer. He was concerned that maybe John was making a play for me." She smiled fondly. "Andre thought all the men in the world were out to take advantage of his little sister, so why not John, too? John was a ladies' man to Andre. He always had *hot and cold running girls,* according to my brother. But I wasn't concerned."

"Why not?" I asked.

"Andre willfully overlooked anything that didn't fit in with his views. He saw John with a lot of girls, so John was a ladies' man, maybe out to get at his sister. The fact that John might've also liked men – John, and maybe his good buddy, Max, too – Andre just didn't dwell on that. What would Mama say, if she found out her oldest boy was friends with a bunch of maricónes?" Lupe winked.

"You might say that everybody loved everybody else at Max's house," she explained with a giggle. "It was always fun to try to guess who was gonna come out of which bedroom with whom on a Sunday morning. That was different than anything I'd ever seen before, but it surely didn't offend me.

"Mostly, I think that Andre didn't want me over there because he still thought of me as a little girl. He was my big brother, a man of the world. He knew about things that went on in that world – even if he didn't participate in them – things that his innocent little sister couldn't even guess went on.

"I told him that I wasn't innocent, and definitely not a little girl anymore. Didn't I have a boyfriend in Mexico? I appealed to his sense of *economics*. These college boys were offering really good money for not much work. Andre couldn't argue with that – so I became their chef." She smiled. "That's what they always called me: *Chef Lupe*. A few meals a week turned into most meals."

Her expression sobered when she gazed at me. "I was there all the time, Officer Dunn. So I overheard some of the things that Max and John said. They were both ladies' men, just like Andre thought, but it wasn't always ladies that they discussed, when they thought I wasn't paying attention. I never did figure out why John was sometimes so irritated with David, but eventually I met the person that David had on his mind, the one that distracted him so much. The one that he loved."

Lupe paused, looked at us carefully. Then she sighed with a kind or resignation: her time at Max's house hadn't all been Mexican feasts and making guesses at who was bedding whom. Something darker was coming.

She reluctantly continued. "No, I wasn't a little girl anymore, but maybe I wasn't as grown up as I thought I was. I was used to the men I knew looking out for me – my boyfriend, Elonso, back home, and my brother, here. I hadn't yet realized that a girl has to watch out for herself, that she has to be careful about the situations she puts herself in.

"There was a party at Max's. The house boomed and shook with music and the laughter of lots of drunken people. They traipsed in and out of the kitchen – they said hi, and asked me what I was cooking. It was a huge pot of menudo . . .

"Then, the kitchen was empty for a second, so I stepped into the little bathroom, just down the hall. When I opened the door to come back out – there was a man blocking my way.

"He grinned and said hi. I said hi back, but he didn't step out of the way to let me pass. In fact, he . . . he shoved me back into the bathroom and slammed the door. He said that I was pretty, and he'd like to get to know me a little better . . ."

Lupe stared at a patch of sunlight on the floor of the porch. "He grabbed me and threw me against the wall. The whole room suddenly stunk of liquor – the smell came off of him like sweat. He started kissing my neck and tearing at my clothes. I screamed and almost got away. He grabbed me again and threw me onto the floor. I bumped my head . . . He threw himself on top of me. I screamed again, but the party was so loud. I kept trying to get away, but he was so much bigger than me, and he was grabbing my legs, reaching under my skirt . . ."

Lupe looked up at me. "Then the door flew open – it crashed against the tub, and somebody grabbed my attacker and pulled him off of me. Somebody hit him – it made a *splatting* sound. They dragged him out of there . . .

"And then another guy crouched down beside me, and gently pulled my skirt down over my knees. I sat up and he put his arms around me, and told me I was safe now. I was sobbing hysterically, and he helped me up. He had the bluest eyes I've ever seen. He took me through the kitchen, away from the people crowding around. He took me up the back staircase to his room.

"He asked me my name; he held me tightly and stroked my hair while I cried. When I had myself under control a little bit, he sat me down on the bed and told me to wait, he'd be right back. He opened the door – there was a girl standing there, and she came in and asked me if I was okay.

"I looked down at my torn blouse and started to cry again. She hugged me, and then started opening drawers in the guy's room, until she found a long t-shirt for me to wear, to replace my ruined blouse.

"By this time, the guy had come back. The girl told him I was feeling a little better, and left the room. He smiled at me – I looked silly wearing a skirt and a long t-shirt – and he asked me if I really was doing okay. I started to cry again and again he held me.

"He said, 'If it makes you feel any better, Lupe, Max and John and David have taken care of that asshole. He'll never bother you or anyone else again.'

"Then he told me what they did . . ." Lupe smiled grimly at us. "Since you guys are policemen, maybe I shouldn't tell you . . ."

My young partner was visibly shaken – the tale of the assault had been painful enough, and now Lupe was going to relate how Max and John and David had dealt with her attacker. After our brief conversations with the two still living and now old *college boys,* coupled with what he believed had become of Billy, I imagined that Parker wasn't quite prepared to hear about their undoubtedly vigilante-style justice. He thought he might have another murder investigation on his hands. He croaked, "That's not necessary, Lupe."

She crowed laughter, and we jumped. "Oh, they didn't kill him, Officer Parker! Max would say later that if they'd would've killed him, then he wouldn't't've *learned nothing*. Not to mention all the paperwork, he said.

"What they did – Max and John and David and probably a few others – they stripped the guy down to his underwear. They put a piece of duct tape over his mouth; they duct-taped his hands behind his back; they taped him to a lamp post, somewhere out of the way. They hung a sign around his neck that said, 'I tried to be a rapist.' And they left him like that.

"John told me later that the police had found him eventually, and took him in. He claimed that he hadn't raped anybody, that he was drunk and didn't remember how he came to be taped to a lamp post. John said that they kept him in jail for the seventy-two hours that they were allowed to keep him – then they had to let him go, because no one had reported any rape."

"You didn't report it?" I asked, quite unprofessionally aghast.

Parker patted Lupe's hand. "You were in this country illegally. You were afraid to come forward –"

"And I hadn't actually been raped. Just scared out of my wits. And Billy – it was Billy who took me up to his room, away from the stares – Billy comforted me. He sat with me, and put his arm around me. He talked to me, told me everything was going to be okay, like I was a child. He sent the girl to fetch me some clothes – I remember that they were very stylish and fit perfectly. She was nice, too. She told me I could keep them.

"Max got rid of all his party guests, and when I felt comfortable enough, Billy took me back downstairs. John hugged me, and told me what they'd done to the guy. I was scared for a minute – surely, he'd come back, pissed off, after he got loose . . .

"John laughed. 'He won't be coming back, Lupe. He'll be so goddamned glad that no charges were filed . . .' John shook his head about that. He said, 'Besides, he knows we'll kill him if he comes back.'"

Parker glanced over at me.

Lupe said, "I realized that Andre *would* kill the guy if he found out what had happened, and I begged them not to tell him. They understood, and promised they wouldn't. There was no use in Andre going to prison for the rest of his life over a rape that hadn't occurred.

"'And if we told him, he wouldn't let you cook for us anymore,' John said and hugged me again. Billy took me home, and after a while, things got back to normal. I came to the house and cooked for them, but I didn't attend any more parties."

Lupe smiled. "Billy took a special interest in me, and that was fine with me. He was *so* good-looking for a white boy . . ."

"You were his girlfriend?" I asked.

Lupe shook her head. "I would've been, if he'd asked me. I guess I loved Billy . . . *Everybody* loved Billy. And since he pretty much loved everybody back . . . He didn't want to get involved with me in that way. He didn't want to break my heart.

"He was like a big brother – like Andre, but not in that psycho, macho, Latino way. Billy knew I wanted the same things other girls wanted. He looked out for me, but he didn't preach to me about who I went out with or anything like that." She giggled. "Billy didn't pretend that he was anything other than what Max always said he was – *like a bad rumor, baby. All over town.* So how could he tell me to be a good girl and be in by nine?" She winked at Parker and grinned at me.

"I cooked for them – they were all so good to me. My college boys. Max and John and David and Billy." Lupe sighed heavily. "Then . . . it all ended. It started on a Sunday afternoon. Billy had been out *on the boulevard* – that's how Max put it – for a week or so. No one had seen much of him. So, when Max said he was coming back, he asked me to make a nice brunch. I thought it was supposed to be a little celebration because Billy was home again.

"But . . . Their moods were odd. Max seemed disgusted, pissed off about something, and David was sad and had a hollow, haunted look. John was in a good mood, smiling to himself, but he was unusually quiet. While we ate, Billy did all the talking, telling us about his new friend from Australia, and how he thought he'd like to visit there someday.

"We finished brunch. I went out to the kitchen and started doing the dishes. Max took off in a snit. He didn't say goodbye and slammed the back door on his way out. John came into the kitchen next. He winked at me; he grinned. He was obviously just as pleased as he could be about something. But he didn't say anything. He just gave me a friendly little hug and also left out the back door.

"A few minutes later, I heard . . . sobbing. I went down the hall to the living room. There were David and Billy, sitting on the couch. It was David that was crying. I guess I shouldn't have listened, but I thought of David as my friend, and if he was hurting, I wanted to – I thought maybe I could help.

"I hung back in the hall, waiting for an opportunity, I guess, waiting to *help.*

"David moaned, 'I don't know how this happened, Billy!'

"'The birds and the bees, little brother,' Billy replied. *He* wasn't crying. He was his regular cheerful self. He said, 'When mommies and daddies love each other . . . Gametes intertwine and create zygotes . . .'

"David whispered, 'She wants to get married.'

"Billy replied, 'It's the honorable thing, David. And who's more honorable than you? What's she like, anyway? John said she's from old money . . . She sounds like your perfect match.'

"I realized that they had to be talking about David's girlfriend. Jilly or Jenny or something."

"Ginny," Parker supplied.

Lupe nodded. "I'd only met her a few times. David didn't bring her to the house very often. I got the impression that she wasn't too keen on where he lived. She was okay with John, but I don't think she liked Max, and I don't think he cared for her, either. Billy hadn't been around much, so apparently, he'd never met her. She went out of her way to ignore me.

"David sobbed again. He said, 'She's great.'

"Billy asked with a touch of annoyance, 'Then why are you so upset, David?'

"I was shocked. I'd never known Billy to be annoyed with David before. John and Max, sometimes, but never David. He said, 'You know you've gotta do the right thing. What'll Edward J. Walker, Attorney at Law, say if his son abandons the debutante he knocked up? He'll cut you out of the will!'

"Oh shit, I thought. *The snobby girl's gotten herself caught!"* Lupe slapped her knee. "Oops!"

She was embarrassed by her own small show of vindictiveness, and continued quickly. "David whispered, 'I know. I'm gonna marry her. It's just . . . She wants to go back home. She's from Riverside, just like me.'

"Billy grinned, said, 'It's a small world after all.'

93

"David said, 'She wants me to transfer to UCLA . . .' He suddenly hugged Billy to him. 'But . . . I can't leave here! I love you!'

"I was surprised by this confession, but then it dawned on me. David's words made everything clear. I remembered all the times that he'd seemed distracted or even depressed – it was always when Billy was gone. John and Max would try to cheer him up, but he'd only become his ol' happy David self again when Billy returned. It wasn't some girl whose absence had made him sad and out of sorts. It wasn't Jenny.

"Billy said, 'I love you, too, David. But we all gotta grow up sometime.'

"And David cried, and Billy held him, just like he'd held me after he'd saved me from the rapist. But there was no saving David. He had to do what was expected of him. I snuck back down the hall to the kitchen. There was no help I could offer. I felt for David. I loved Billy, too. Everybody loved him." Lupe sighed.

"Max threw a big going away party. David and Jenny were going to elope, and then they were moving back to Riverside. I found out that John was going with them. Billy wasn't at the party. I heard that he'd spent the night somewhere else – maybe it was with his Australian friend. I assumed he'd already said his goodbyes to David.

"David left to get married; a week or so later, John had their stuff loaded into a U-Haul. Then he was gone, too. I never saw either of them again.

"After they were gone, Billy came back. Max remained in a bad mood for a long time – he had to interview new roommates, and I heard him yelling at Billy a couple of times, that they were never going to find anyone as *suitable* as David and John again."

Lupe paused and sighed once more. "As far as the rest goes – Andre's luck finally ran out. He was arrested for possession of . . ." She glanced worriedly at Parker and me. "Possession of . . . a controlled substance. He went to prison. Rosa took the baby and went to live with relatives, leaving me in kind of a bind. I didn't have a real job, and now I didn't have a place to live. That's when Billy stepped in.

"The whole marriage thing was his idea. It would allow me to get a green card. But we had to make it seem like it was a real marriage, so . . . We rehearsed. We quizzed each other. Where was our first date? Where had he asked me to marry him? What was his birthday, and what was mine? Where had each of us gone to high school? What were our parents' names, and our brothers and sisters, and where did they live? How many children did we want to have?

"There were interviews. Billy took great relish in *getting one over on the government,* so he went above and beyond. We opened a joint checking account, and got a credit card together. We bought a car in both our names. I had a little money set by – Billy added a little more to it, and we put the down payment on this house.

"It was a good thing that we'd prepared – the immigration people checked every document, bank statements and credit card statements, mortgage payments – I guess they keep a file on you for two years. Billy stayed here a lot – he slept in the spare bedroom. When the government people would drop by – he always made it seem like we were nothing more than a happily married couple. It was easy for me – I sometimes wished that it could be true, that he really was my husband. Eventually they stopped coming around.

"I got a job working in the restaurant at the same hotel where Rosa had once been a maid. The pay wasn't great, but it was enough to make the house note. I saw Billy often enough to keep up the appearance that we were married. We had noisy barbeques and invited the neighbors, in case any of them were ever questioned about our habits."

Lupe looked down at her knee and pulled at a loose thread on her dress. "Then my old boyfriend, Elonso, arrived from Mexico. I'd told him about my marriage, that it wasn't real . . . over the phone. I was afraid to put it in a letter.

"He had a good job waiting for him here, hanging drywall with his cousin. But he needed a place to stay . . . I'd missed Elonso. We'd been very much in love when we were teenagers. We more or less took up where we'd left off."

She sighed. "He believed that there'd never been anything between Billy and me, that we were just friends, that he'd just wanted to help me out . . . Or at least he tried very hard to believe it. But he was jealous. He didn't appreciate Billy visiting. Billy understood, and . . . stopped visiting.

"After a while, I showed old Mrs. Ramirez next door my new engagement ring. I told her that Billy and I had split up, and before you know it, the whole neighborhood believed that we'd divorced. He surely wasn't around anymore . . .

"Another one of Elonso's cousins was a pastor at a little church near Monterey. We had a wedding ceremony . . ."

"But you never actually divorced Billy," Parker said.

Lupe shook her head. "I'd lost touch with him. Elonso didn't want me to look for him, and there was all that governmental red tape to contend with. Going to court to get divorced and all. Elonso was sure I'd get deported. So he and I got married – in the eyes of God, and all of our friends and neighbors and family. But not in the eyes of the State of California. Elonso's cousin the pastor overlooked the formality of a marriage *license.* When we came back from our honeymoon, I was Mrs. Gonzales, and have been ever since. I'm listed that way on my children's birth certificates.

"Billy Munro saved me from a rapist, and he helped me to have a wonderful life here." Lupe smiled with a trace of sadness. "But I haven't seen him in thirty years, Officers. When you find him, please tell him how grateful I am."

****

We thanked Mrs. Gonzales and I called a cab to take us to the airport. I noticed that Parker didn't give her his card, but he did give her a hug.

Once inside the taxi, I said, "I think I should buy you a drink, *Officer* Parker."

He giggled in relief. "Yeah, I didn't think it was necessary to correct her on that. If it didn't go well, and she decided to call down to Riverside and complain – I figured I might wind up an officer again."

"And me, too," I agreed.

"I want to thank you for having faith in this, Jan," he said, with entirely too much sincerity.

I tried to deflect his heartfelt gratitude. "Well, we were already in town . . . Seriously, Parker. I think you're right – there's a case here. *Everybody* loved Billy. So how come nobody's heard from him in twenty-five years? We just have to find Adam Walker, first. Hell, maybe his mother'll be so happy about that, she'll get behind the investigation into his daddy's disappearance. Talk to her pal Paddy about pursuing it."

"Or maybe not." Parker frowned.

I didn't want to see his good mood fade, so I stopped talking about the Walker case. I asked him, "How did you know that Lupe and Billy's marriage was a sham?"

When he smiled again, my heart leapt; it positively rejoiced. Yeah, I needed a drink, if for no other reason than to put a lid on all the warm feels I was having for Parker. Or maybe to let 'em all loose.

He said, "From what we've heard about Billy, I didn't figure him to be much of the marrying kind. And I've got a buddy over at Immigration –"

"Parker! You didn't tell him about –"

"Of course I didn't, Jan. How fucked up would that be? *No wonder people hate cops.*" He smiled. "We all come from immigrant stock somewhere along the line.

"My buddy at Immigration had told me before about sham marriages. How citizens will sometimes marry aliens to allow them to stay here, but it's all really fake. When I saw the Spanish name on the marriage license, and after both of the ladies closely examined our badges to make sure *we* weren't from Immigration . . . I figured my guess was right, and I decided to just go with it."

"I thought she was gonna try to deny it at first. But you charmed her."

"That's because I'm charming, Jan." He winked, and this little display of ego from him made me smile. "Our flight doesn't leave for an hour and a half. I think we can have a couple of drinks."

****

When we settled into our seats on the plane, it became immediately apparent that the return trip wasn't going to be like our first flight. No tic-tac-toe – Parker ordered us another drink, even though both of us were a little tight from the ones we'd already had in the terminal. Once they arrived, he toasted my health and said, "You know, all the college stories we've been hearing lately have put me in mind of own of my own." His grin was mischievous. "Would you like to hear it?"

"By all means." Who wouldn't want to hear good-looking, slightly drunk Parker's not-too-long-ago college exploits, delivered with that intriguingly sly smile?

"Once upon a time, there was this guy. He was twenty-one, still a year from graduation. This guy was buddies with a grad student named Thom Wagner. Thom was twenty-six or so at the time. His field was archaeology. Thom and this other guy, who we'll call –"

"You?"

Parker grinned. "If we must. Thom and I were pals, like I say, and we could usually be found on a Saturday night, hanging out at one of the bars near campus. Being a more experienced drinker than myself, Thom usually picked where we went. He knew where all the good-looking women were, or so he always told me.

"On the Saturday that is the subject of my tale – it was in the late afternoon – our intrepid pair stopped at the Burger King there on University Avenue – you know the one I mean. The place was empty except for a couple of young gentlemen sitting in one of the booths. They had many tattoos and shaved heads, if you get the profiling picture. The girl that waited on us . . ."

To my utter surprise, Parker made the French finger-kissing gesture, as if he were talking about an exceptionally tasty crème brulee.

"She had it goin' on, as they say. She was a redhead, with beautiful, almond shaped brown eyes – her lashes were so thick and black that I was sure they couldn't be real – she'd just applied them with the rest of her make-up. She made that Burger King uniform walk and talk.

"Wagner glanced over at me and grinned, and I could tell he was hooked. When the girl – her nametag said *Gloria* – handed our take-out sacks to my friend, he asked her what she was doing after her shift. She giggled and said that her mother was expecting her home right after work; she said she lived just a few blocks away.

"Thom seemed to materialize a pen out of thin air and scrawled his name and phone number on the back of our food receipt. He told Gloria to give him a call the very next time her mother wasn't expecting her home right after work.

"He had a little dumpy apartment up there off of Elgin, and I saw Gloria at his place a couple of times over the next week. It was always in the afternoon, and she was always leaving when I was arriving, so it wasn't like I ever got to speak to her much. Just a pleasant hi, and then I'd watch her sashay on down the block." Parker wiggled his eyebrows at me.

"Come to find out, however, young Master Wagner had not, as yet, talked Gloria into any kind of . . . *romance* in the week that she'd been visiting him. She was only twenty, he said, and a little shy, and her good Catholic mother still kept a strict eye on her.

"Thom was not confessing his shortcomings, trying to get me to commiserate on a tough love life, however – he was telling me that he'd so far struck out so he could gleefully add that things were scheduled to take a turn for the better that very evening. Gloria had convinced Mama that she was staying overnight at a girlfriend's house, and would return to his place promptly at seven o'clock. Then *Carnival* would commence.

"I wished him luck with his gorgeous redhead. I went back home – I still lived at home at the time – and kicked around for a while, did a little studying, watched a couple You Tube videos, and so on. A little after six, my sister asked me if I might not go fetch her and her friends a couple of burgers. Since I didn't have anything else to do, and being the good brother that I am, I drove on up to Burger King.

"Gloria was not on duty, of course, and the place was crowded this time. Whilst I waited in line, I noticed the same two young skinhead gentlemen that had been there on the day Thom had met his dark-eyed beauty.

"With them was a girl who looked a lot like Gloria – she had the same on-fleek make-up, though she was a blonde. I couldn't help but overhear when she said, 'She's making a fool of you, Matt. All she talks about is that Indiana Jones college boy.'

"'I've seen her talking to him,' the other guy agreed. 'He's in here all the time. But I'm sure it's nothing, Matt. He's gotta be pushing thirty.'

"'You don't know what you're talking about, Brian,' the girl said and sucked on her straw. 'So you should just shut up. I'm telling you, Matt. Gloria's cheating on you. She showed me where he lives. She's going over there tonight.'

"'When?' Matt growled.

"The girl looked at her phone. 'Right now.'

"When Matt just casually ate another French fry, she said, 'Aren't you gonna do anything?'

"He smiled. 'We'll give 'em a little while to get all cozy. Then you show me where he lives. We'll use the fucking cops to our advantage for a change. You still got that burner phone, Brian? We'll call in a report that we heard a woman screaming at his apartment, and when they kick the door in . . .'

"'Why would they kick the door in?' Brian asked. 'If there's no screaming when they show up?'

"Matt smiled. 'Maybe they won't kick the door in. Maybe they'll just ring the bell. Say they had a report . . . And when they see old dude with a fifteen-year-old girl . . . Then the questions are gonna start.'"

Parker smiled. "Needless to say, I forgot about getting burgers for my sister. I went out to the car and called Wagner. As the gods were smiling upon him that day, he answered. I asked him if Gloria had shown up.

"He told me that she had, and they were just at that minute having a drink. 'Isn't that special?' I said, and told him of the conversation I'd just overheard. I said, 'You're feeding liquor to a minor, Tommy-boy.'

"There was a moment of stunned silence, then Wagner whispered, 'She can't be fifteen, Parker. How can she have a job if she's only fifteen?'

"I told him that they had things called work permits for the kiddies; my sixteen-year-old-sister had one. I told him that maybe his date wasn't fifteen – maybe the folks in Burger King had been talking about some other girl named Gloria and some other Indiana Jones-looking college boy. He wasn't the only guy at UCR that was studying archaeology, after all.

"I told him that it might all just be a big, unrelated coincidence, but it might also behoove him to err on the side of caution before the law showed up and the shit hit the fan. Wagner exclaimed a familiar Anglo-Saxon word of dismay and hung up."

Parker fell silent, and of course I asked, "What happened?"

"Wagner showed his teenaged almost-paramour the door. RPD did indeed arrive, and he invited them in, demonstrating that there were no women present. He told them that his neighbor down the hall was a screamer – he told me that he winked – and said perhaps it was she that had been overheard by the concerned citizen that had made the call.

"In the weeks that followed, Gloria tried to come back a few times, but when she found out that Wagner sincerely wasn't having any, she stopped hanging around. Since there'd never been any hanky-panky – only almost – he wasn't really too worried about any repercussions from hurting her feelings."

"And . . ."

"And we all lived happily ever after."

He could be so delightfully annoying. "So . . ."

"This wasn't just an amusing anecdote to liven up a boring flight, Jan. It actually has a bearing on our investigation." He winked and sipped his drink.

"Thom Wagner was *extremely* grateful that I saved him from a statutory rape beef, and whatever surprises Matt and Brian might've additionally had for him. Gloria was cute . . . But nobody's that cute. He was appalled that he hadn't realized how young she was. He told me that if he could ever do me a favor, all I have to do is give him a call."

"And how's he gonna help us with the case? Is he another IT geek?"

Parker grinned sheepishly. "Not the Walker case. The Billy Munro –"

"Christ, Parker!"

"What, Jan? We got absolutely zilch on Walker on this trip. No leads on how to track down his new identity . . . ." He sipped his drink again. "But we hit the jackpot on Billy. All that stuff Lupe said about his relationship with David . . . It confirmed what Stevens said. He said that David liked Max, but he *loved* Billy. Then Billy betrayed him. You said it yourself, Jan. He's gotta be under the folly.

"Stevens tells David about the affair. David somehow gets Billy to come to their office. Nobody's there because it's a holiday. David kills him . . . I wonder if we could still find some DNA . . . ."

"There's no way were gonna find any DNA after all these years, Parker! And even if we did, how would we prove it was Billy's? Are you out of your fucking mind? We couldn't even get a warrant to *look* for something so ridiculous! It's not even their office anymore!"

"Hold that thought, Jan. Warrants and such. We'll get back to that, momentarily. So, David kills Billy. Maybe slick Johnny helps him. They dig a hole out in the woods and put him in it, and then they build the folly over his final resting place. Sarah's playhouse." Parker frowned.

"And?"

His face brightened again. "I think *that's* enough evidence for a search warrant."

"It's hearsay, Parker, from Max Haycroft, a singularly unreliable source. Just because he says David killed Billy doesn't make it so. It doesn't mean we're gonna get a warrant to look for him."

"There's been no trace of Billy since that summer, just like Haycroft said." Parker shook his head. "That might be enough for us to get a warrant to look around the Walker estate. But you're right about one thing – there's no way were gonna get permission to demolish the folly and start jackhammering the slab, based solely on Haycroft's *hearsay.*

"This isn't a suspicious back patio that some do-it-yourselfer drug dealer threw up over the weekend, is it?" He looked at his phone, scrolled. "This is a structure *of such extravagant appearance that it transcends the range of garden ornaments usually associated with the class of buildings to which it belongs.* And it's at the chief's good friend's house. Not to mention that our probable cause is –"

"Weak."

"Our probable cause is nonexistent. Intuition and gut-feelings and hearsay aren't admissible in court, are they? This is where my good friend Thom comes in."

Parker grinned. "The archaeology game threatened to pay not much, so Wagner diversified out of all that National Geographic, finding-Troy bullshit. These days, he runs a place called California Subsurface Scanning. They use GPR – ground penetrating radar – to find all kinds of things. Underground concrete. Archaeological stuff. *Bodies.*"

"It's an election year, Parker. Paddy's not gonna okay the cost of ground penetrating radar."

"No cost, Jan. Wagner owes me a favor. He'll do it for free. And when the test shows a body under the folly, our probable cause goes way up."

"And a defense attorney's gonna ask why and how RPD got this valuable service for free."

Parker's grin widened. "This is how we'll do it. We'll get the warrant to search the estate. We don't even have to mention Billy yet – we'll say that we want to look for airline ticket receipts, or . . . I dunno. Something that Adam might've left behind, anything that might point to where he went. Mrs. Walker won't object to that.

"We get Wagner out there. When the test shows that there's a corpse under the folly, we take it to the chief, and he signs the invoice to pay Wagner for his valuable service, after the fact. *And* he gives us the go ahead to dig Billy up."

Even though I tried not to be, I failed: I was impressed. "You've got it all figured out."

"Here's the best part, Jan. We've got not a single lead on finding Adam Walker. Like his sister said, he probably doesn't want to be found, so –"

"When did she say that?" This came out sounding *way* too suspicious, but Miss Walker hadn't said anything along those lines in the interview, so it meant –

"She called. Said she wanted . . . someone to talk to about it. She said, maybe it would be best if we didn't find her brother. Maybe he doesn't want to be found."

"Why didn't you tell me she called?" Now I sounded like I was his jealous wife.

Parker ignored my tone. "To tell you the truth –"

Which is what people say when they're about to lie –

"– I'd forgotten about it. She didn't have any new info. She just wanted to tell someone that . . . that she was unsure about how she felt about us looking for Adam. It's not like she can say that to her mom."

"What did you say?"

Parker shrugged. "I asked her to tell me more about him. But she didn't have anything we haven't already heard, so with everything else that's been going on, I guess I just forgot that I'd even spoken to her again."

I couldn't escape the idea that Parker was lying in some way about his conversation with Sarah Walker, but I didn't get the chance to dwell on it, because next he said, "From the evidence – Christ, Jan. The kid faked his own death. That's proof right there that he doesn't want to be found."

"He's not a kid anymore, Parker. He's your age."

"The fact remains: we aren't any closer to finding him. The best part about my plan is – when we get a warrant to search the Walker place, it's gonna seem like it's all part of the Walker investigation. But when we find Billy under the folly . . . That's gonna take precedence. We'll just transition over to that investigation. In other words, we won't have to find Adam before we start looking for Billy, because it's gonna seem like we found Billy while we were looking for Adam."

"You're really not feeling the case we've been assigned, are you, Parker?"

He shrugged. "A rich kid takes off with his daddy. Like I said the first night – where's the crime in that? But the fact that daddy murdered his old college lover –"

"We don't know they were lovers, Parker."

"You must not've been paying attention to what Lupe said," he stated flatly. Before I could get offended, he continued. "Lovers or not, we're still pretty sure David killed him, aren't we? And if we turn up a body . . . I just think that's a far more important crime to solve."

103

A far more important wrong to right, you mean. Careful, Parker. You're just a cop, not a crusader, caped or otherwise. Being righteous is like wetting yourself in a dark suit: you get a warm feeling, but no one notices. Even if we find Billy – the guy you want to pin his murder on is dead. How much justice are you going to feel about that?

SARAH

Eric called to let me know he was back in town. He told me what the trip had been about, now that it was over: he and Detective Dunn had flown to San Francisco to look up some of Dad's old SFSU buddies, to see if any of them might have some inkling as to where he might've chosen to disappear.

I laughed before I could stop myself. "Wow, Eric. You guys are really reaching, aren't you? San Francisco for Dad was, what? Thirty-six years ago?"

The Bay Area was where I'd been conceived; the detectives were looking for clues from before I was born. That had been a long time ago, years before darling Eric had even been a twinkle in his father's eye. What had they expected to uncover from that long ago?

I asked, "Did you find my Uncle Billy?"

Eric seemed astonished; he stuttered. "Wha-at?"

"My Uncle Billy. I told you about him, remember? He was Dad's roommate in college. He stayed with us the summer before Mom and Dad got divorced. He went back to San Francisco, or so they told me."

"No. We didn't find him." Eric seemed to have recovered from whatever had surprised him. "We didn't find anything. The whole trip was a bust."

"Well, what did you expect?" Maybe that came out a little harsh. "It was a long time ago. And Adam . . . As far as I know, Adam's never even been to San Francisco."

"We've gotta follow up the leads we get, Sarah," he snapped. "This case is –"

"I know. I'm sorry, Eric. I know you guys are doing the best you can. I guess Adam *could* be in San Francisco."

"Adam could be anywhere," he said, still annoyed.

"So I guess that was a good place to start," I said, trying to sound hopeful, like Mom.

"It was a bust," he repeated. "Do you still want to have dinner?"

"I would like that very much."

Yeah, he made me feel like a teenager, maybe because it seemed like he could be petulant and moody like *he* was a teenager.

But maybe it was because he was a dedicated cop: his leads hadn't paid off, and he was frustrated about it.

We made plans to have dinner in a few days, and hung up.

I would see him before that, however. San Francisco might've been a bust, but apparently they'd gotten some new ideas from somewhere, because Mom called to tell me that they wanted to search the house and grounds.

"I did keep Adam's computer," she told me guiltily, that hope an undeniable spurt in her voice. "And all the papers he left in his desk. I . . . I put them in a box and shoved them into the closet. Maybe the police can find something useful . . . Maybe there's a clue or something on his computer."

I was surprised and maybe just the teeny, tiniest bit *wounded* that Eric hadn't told me he was coming to Mom's house to search. But then I told myself to jettison the teenage feelings, no matter how much some of them made me feel warm and squishy. Eric wasn't my prom date – he was a policeman, and he didn't have to check with me about the aspects of his investigation.

****

He was surprised when I opened the door at Mom's house. He stammered hello, then launched into his spiel about having a warrant to search the premises.

I interrupted him in the middle of it. "All this red-tape isn't necessary, Sergeant." I looked over his shoulder and smiled at Detective Dunn and the two uniformed officers beside her. "The police are always welcome in our home."

He handed me the warrant, anyway. I skimmed it, mostly because I'd never seen one before. There was Eric's name, and it said that he intended to search *the person, premises, location and any appurtenances thereto, the description of which is:* Mom's address. Several paragraphs regarding what they were searching for were available, but Eric had only checked two: they were looking for anything that *is or has been used in committing a criminal offense,* and/or anything that *would be material evidence in a subsequent criminal prosecution.*

Whatever. I read enough legalese at work. I handed it back to him. He tried not to be miffed that I hadn't read it minutely. It was just a formality, after all. Mom was seven thousand percent on their

106

side. She would've had the place burnt to the ground if she thought it would help them to locate Adam.

Eric handed the warrant to her. She didn't look at it at all. She set it on a side table and said to Detective Dunn, "I have Adam's computer for you, and a box of his papers."

"Thank you very much, Mrs. Walker," she returned with a smile. "If you'll show these officers . . . Sergeant Parker and I are going to have a look around the grounds. We didn't get a chance to do that when we were here before."

"Will you tell us where the folly is, Miss Walker?" Eric asked. He was all kinds of professional, as if we hadn't . . . Well, we hadn't. We'd just had one little good night kiss, and we had a date scheduled for dinner.

Mom asked why they wanted to see the folly. Eric said, "Your daughter said that Adam played there as a child –"

I had said no such thing. I'd said that *I'd* played there as a child.

"– and we just wanted to give it a once over to see if he might've left anything inside."

I told him to follow the path through the trees, just behind the house. "It's . . . *extravagant.* You can't miss it," I said with a grin.

I didn't go with them. I didn't want to interfere with the investigation or compromise the scene, or whatever, and I didn't think they were going to find much in the folly. I hadn't been out there in more than a decade, and contrary to Eric's assumption, I don't think Adam ever *played* in it. It was pink and white and frilly and girlish, and it was something the father in whom he'd never been interested had made for his daughter. Mom never visited it, either, even when I was little. It was my space. But they had a search warrant, so they were going to search everywhere. I imagined that the garage would be next.

JANET

Young Parker must've never seen *Jaws*, because his friend Thom Wagner reminded me not of Indiana Jones – not in the least – but of the shark researcher portrayed by Richard Dreyfuss in the famous fish tale. Though he wore workingman's clothes – old jeans and a faded California Subsurface Scanning t-shirt and steel-toed boots – and though he sported long hair and a scraggly beard – his round, librarian-style, wire-rimmed glasses and the very expression on his face screamed *academic*. If Max Haycroft had resembled a homeless guy when he'd showed up for his interview, one look into his sharp and cynical eyes had broadcast his intelligence. It was the same with Parker's college buddy – when he snuffed out his cigarette and offered me his calloused hand, regardless of that or his blue-collar attire, I could tell that this was no run-of-the-mill construction worker.

He'd parked his truck behind the uniforms' patrol car, and from the passenger side, he removed a tiny box with little wheels and a handle in the middle. He said it was called a Structure-Scan Mini, and it contained all the necessary components for the job – the control unit, the antenna, and the survey encoder – in one dedicated system. He explained that he was going to run it along the concrete slab of the playhouse, and through electromagnetic this and the amplitude of that, the machine would penetrate through the surface to reveal what lay below. When he started to go into different frequencies and dielectrics of cured concrete and clay soils, I sort of zoned out. If he could detect a body with it, that was all that mattered.

The structure was probably ten by twelve or so, but the simple dimensions don't describe how lovely it was. It had dormer windows with little flower boxes, and curlicued eaves, as Sarah had said. But there were no flowers in the boxes, and the pink and white paint had faded. It put me in mind of a forgotten gingerbread house, or maybe Grandma's cottage, waiting for a visit from Little Red Riding Hood.

But the Big Bad Wolf believed that there was a body buried beneath it, so he frowned at me when I exclaimed over how cute it was. He and Wagner decided to run the little machine around the perimeter of the structure first, so I opened the door.

I didn't need any kind of forensic alternate light source to see the line of footprints in the otherwise uniform, undisturbed dust. They were clearly visible in the shaft of sunlight from the open door. Someone – I'm no shoe expert, but it looked like they were about a size 9 or so – had walked across the floor of the polly, paused at a desk built into the wall, and had then turned and walked back again.

Procedure stalked through my mind – the interior of the structure should be secured, the footprints should be forensically photographed, the desk dusted for prints. But no crime had been committed here – someone, maybe a woman with big feet or a man with average feet, had just *walked* across the floor recently. And Parker and Matt-Hooper-from-*Jaws* were going to be in here momentarily to run the GPS box across the floor.

I didn't want to get into an argument with Parker about securing a crime scene where no crime had taken place, and then waiting for a forensics team – he might not be able to get his boy with his subsurface whatchamacallit out here again. So, I made a detective's decision: I took a close-up picture of one of the footprints with my cellphone, and walked through the dust to the desk.

I took a pair of gloves out of my pocket, and gingerly opened the top drawer by its corner instead of the knob, preserving any fingerprints. I'd just tell Parker not to touch it and we could get it dusted later, if need be.

Remember the scene in *Pulp Fiction* when Jules opens Marcellus's case and all we see is an awe-inspiring, golden glow? We're never told what it is that glows like that, and fandom theories rage to this day. When I opened the drawer to that little girl's desk in now-grown Sarah Walker's playhouse, there wasn't actually a glow, but I knew what I was looking at – the evidence that might just solve our case.

Not the unauthorized, disappearance-of-Billy-Munro case, the one that Parker had such a hard-on of righteousness to solve, but the one we'd been assigned. I'd just discovered precisely what we needed to find Adam Walker.

Unlike Marcellus Wallace's belongings, my evidence didn't require a big, bulky case. I put it into an evidence bag and put it in my pocket. I closed the drawer firmly – no dusting for fingerprints was gonna be necessary.

Parker and Wagner appeared in the doorway, ready to run their little gizmo over the slab. "Proceed, gentlemen," I said airily.

There was no need to ruin Parker's big day, his high-tech murder investigation. If he found Billy's body, that'd be great. When he was done congratulating himself about that, I'd just whisper in his ear that we were also gonna solve the Walker case.

****

The two uniforms back at the house called to tell me that they'd found nothing of any use amongst Adam's papers. A few old school reports, a few print outs about cars and motorcycles; that was it. I was surprised when they told me the laptop was brand new; Mrs. Walker had failed to mention that it was still in the box. Only factory software was on it; Evans said he didn't think it had ever even been booted up. Whatever computer Adam had actually *used,* it had apparently disappeared with him. I told them to go on back downtown and write up their report, because it looked like Parker and I were going to be here for a while yet.

The electromagnetic survey took all afternoon. I saw Wagner shake his head a few times, say, *Inconclusive;* then he'd run the funny little machine over the floor once again, because Parker was his friend, and if there actually was a body under the polly, he wanted to find it for him.

Finally, he said the machine's battery was getting low, and shut it off.

"There's nothing showing, Eric. But . . . Let me take it back to the office and look at it on the big monitor. And Sammy's there." He smiled at me, because he didn't want to look at Parker's frown anymore. "Sammy's the brains of California Subsurface Scanning. He's better at interpreting the data than I am."

But it's your company, I thought. Until we heard a revelation from Wagner's genius partner, I was gonna go with his original findings: inconclusive. He hadn't found Billy's final resting place.

The three of us walked back to the house; Parker shook hands with his friend and thanked him. Wagner said he'd have a definitive report to him first thing in the morning. He told me it'd been nice meeting me, then got in his truck and departed.

Parker glanced up at the house, then rather abruptly got into the car. I didn't comment. It wasn't necessary to say goodbye to our cooperative hosts, but it surely would've been polite, and it might've been prudent.

But Parker was having a mood. He drove in silence, and I felt like asking him, *So, you never ran into any brick-walled, dead-ends in Orange County? You never had any hunches that didn't come through?* I thought about saying, *Thank Christ we didn't get this GPR thing okayed ahead of time, huh?*

But I didn't say any of that, because Parker was a good cop and he didn't deserve any derision at the moment. I still agreed with the original idea: Billy Munro was dead, and David Walker had undoubtedly been the one that'd killed him. But without a body, all of Parker's efforts in his secret investigation had been for nothing. His investigation was gonna stay secret until we found Adam Walker, and even after that . . . I was pretty sure that Iglesias wasn't going to be persuaded to open a look into Billy's disappearance. We had not the oft-mentioned shred of evidence; not one physical clue as to where to even begin. All we had was Max Haycroft's logic and Parker's belief, neither of which was enough. There wasn't going to be any justice for Billy.

So I didn't make fun of Parker. He didn't deserve it – this wasn't a cop show where the good guys always get their man in forty-three sarcasm-laced, commercial-interrupted minutes. This was real life, and stewing in his own disappointment . . . I figured that was enough for Parker. It might even be good for him.

Regardless, he was gonna forget all about Billy Munro and his perhaps not-undeserved fate once he saw what I'd found inside that drawer. So I didn't feel too bad for him. As soon as we got back downtown, the minute he was sitting down, I'd wipe that whipped-pup look off his face. I'd see that great smile again.

****

John T. Stevens, Attorney at Law, was standing in the lobby when we arrived at the station, however. I sighed. My awesome evidence would have to wait.

With that shark's smile, he greeted us, shook our hands, apologized for not having an appointment, and asked if he might have a private moment of our time. Parker glowered, mumbled *okay,* and led the way down the hall until he found an unoccupied interrogation room.

111

"What can we do for you, Mr. Stevens?" I asked pleasantly, to offset Parker's unprofessional petulance.

"I was just wondering what you were looking for at the Walker estate, that you felt it necessary to employ ground penetrating radar?" I must've looked surprised, because he explained. "I'd called to see how Ginny was doing. Sarah answered the phone and she mentioned something about a search warrant. She said that you'd just left. And she said something about a truck with California Subsurface Scanning written on the door, and that you'd gone out to the woods. She had no idea what it was all about, so I thought I'd inquire."

Parker took his copy of the warrant out of his pocket and slid it across the table without comment.

Stevens's gaze flicked over it. "This isn't very specific." When we said nothing, he grinned. "And since it doesn't appear that you're going to enlighten me, I'll speculate. Let's see. Ground penetrating radar. Hmmm. Treasure, perhaps? Do you think David buried clues to his whereabouts out in the woods? Or . . ."

Stevens guffawed and slapped his knee. "Have you resurrected your theory that David disappeared from that boat only to bring Adam back to his childhood home, murder him, and leave him in a shallow grave in the woods?"

Stevens studied Parker minutely, as if he were a hostile witness on the stand. "That's it, isn't it? You think Adam's buried in the woods! No wonder you didn't tell his mother and sister what you were looking for! No wonder your warrant is so vague!" He slapped his knee again, the picture of amusement. "Tell me, Sergeant, did you find him?"

Parker said, "We weren't looking for Adam's body, Mr. Stevens," and a little alarm bell went off in my head. Parker was angry, he didn't appreciate this smarmy lawyer laughing at him –

"Who then, Sergeant? Because surely you weren't looking for underground lairs or a suitcase full of buried clues. They wouldn't even trot that out on *CSI.* So it had to be a body you were looking for. Who –"

"You know, the Walkers weren't the only ones that disappeared without a trace," Parker said slowly, and I opened my mouth to tell him – I dunno, to tell him to shut up, I guess. But I was too late. He was too pissed off to think about investigative protocol, about need-to-know, about keeping his mouth shut.

And the goddamn lawyer saw that he had my young partner right where he wanted him.

"Interesting," he said, still studying Parker, his body language, his obvious bad mood. "People disappear without a trace every day, but I don't think you're going to go looking for all of them between the Walker house and the golf course. It has to be someone specific to this case. We know where David is, so . . . if it's not Adam . . ."

"Max Haycroft said –"

"Parker!" I growled, but it was too late. He ignored me. He'd said too much on purpose, hoping to goad Stevens into . . . What? A spontaneous confession, like on television? *Jesus, Parker, I thought you were smarter than that!*

Stevens narrowed his eyes. "Someone else that disappeared . . . Max said . . ." The lawyer's eyes widened, but it wasn't with guilt. It was with further amusement. "Oh my God! You were looking for Billy!

"Being the thorough policemen that you are, you must've gone to see Max already. And he must've told you – I remember that he called looking for Billy, that autumn. I told him what'd happened, told him David had paid Billy off. Next thing I know, two cops are at the office, wanting to speak to David. I told them I was David's attorney.

"They said, 'Close enough,' and explained that their brethren in San Francisco had received a vague, completely worthless report of a missing person. The cops up north hadn't thought it merited a trip down from Frisco, so the boys from RPD were there as a going-through-the-motions formality on their behalf. I told them when David and I had last seen Billy, they wrote it down in their little cop notebooks, and that was the end of it."

"We went to Frisco."

For Christ's sake, Parker!

"You did?" It was like Stevens was talking to a little kid. "And who did you talk to there?"

"We talked to Lupe."

Absolutely no recognition. "Who?"

"Chef Lupe. Your cook in college. I understand she makes a mean Chili Verde."

"She said she was friends with Billy," I added quickly, before Parker could tell this lawyer every *single* thing we'd learned, as if Stevens had administered some kind of true serum to him.

Stevens laughed. "Billy had a lot of friends."

113

For the space of another heartbeat, I was sure that he had no idea who Lupe was, then those old college memories returned.

"Right! Lupe, the little Mexican girl! She *was* a great cook!" Stevens grinned. "She was Billy's *special* friend. He saved her from a particularly ugly situation once, and after that, she had rather a crush on him."

"She said everybody loved Billy," Parker said. "So, it strikes me as odd that no one's heard from him in more than twenty-five years."

Stevens ignored *what struck Park as odd,* concentrating instead on how *everybody loved Billy.* "You saw his picture, Sergeant. And he was thirty-something then. In school . . . His hair was as black as the River Styx, and his eyes were as blue as Lethe. His glance made you want to forget what you knew yourself to be, and become whatever *he* wanted you to be." Stevens laughed wryly. "If you loved Billy, he'd let you. He'd even love you back for a little while. Until the next person came along that had a mind to love him. Then you had to get back in line."

"And you . . ."

Steven's eyes danced with mirth. "Oh, I had my turn, Sergeant. It was college, as I said, and he was a lot of fun. But I was immune to *falling in love* with him. There were entirely too many fish in the sea in those days, girls and well as boys. A veritable smorgasbord.

"And I saw how Billy was immediately, how he took advantage of his looks and his charm, because . . . Billy and I weren't that different in the taking-it-where-it-was-offered arena." He winked at Parker, and even offered me his killer smile. Lost in remembering for a split second, he added, "Yes, sweet Lupe was always there, quiet, like a fly on the wall. I'm sure she knew about all manner of secrets."

"Lupe said David was in love with Billy."

The lawyer grinned at Parker again. "But you didn't have to go all the way to Frisco and unearth our old housekeeper to find that out. I told you myself. I told you – the hardest part about leaving SFSU and coming back to Southern California, the hardest part about assuming the mantle of loving husband and doting father – was that David had to leave Billy.

"I'm not saying that David didn't love Ginny, because he did. Truly, madly, deeply, and all that. But just as I told you before, there are many different flavors of love, Sergeant. David's love for Ginny didn't *replace* what he felt for Billy. It was just a different kind of love. So he was overjoyed when Billy showed up, unannounced, after ten years. And he was crushed when both of his loves betrayed him."

"And since you and David were also friends, maybe you felt for him enough to help him get rid of Billy," Parker suggested.

"And bury him in the woods?" Stevens sneered. He looked balefully at me. "You should rein in your hot-headed partner, Detective Dunn. I don't think he realizes the peril in accusing an officer of the court of first degree murder without any evidence." Then the grin returned; he wasn't actually an angry shark, just an amused one. "Or do you have evidence? Did you find Billy's body in the woods?"

I was inordinately proud of Parker: he didn't look down and give himself away. He held Stevens's gaze and said, "We'll have the report tomorrow morning."

"Let me tell you what it's going to reveal, Sergeant. Absolutely nothing. Allow me to give a statement concerning your alleged first degree murder. Write it down if you want, though I doubt that my friend the DA would touch an investigation into it for anything. I saw David hand Billy twenty large in cash American. I saw Billy pick up his suitcase and leave the office. I never saw Billy again.

"It's entirely possible that David thereafter murdered Billy. It is purely speculation on my part, of course, because if he did it, he didn't tell me. But he was intensely angry about Billy's betrayal for the space of about forty-eight hours. Then he was over it, adopting the grown-up attitude of *easy come, easy go*. He felt that way about Billy *and Ginny*.

"He divorced her, we moved to LA, found places to live, opened a new office and got on with our lives. But I can tell you one thing with complete certainty, Sergeant. David Walker was a brilliant attorney, a clear-minded, methodical thinker. If, in a moment's uncontrolled rage, he murdered the old friend that had cuckolded him – I can tell you beyond a shadow of a doubt that he wouldn't've been so monumentally stupid as to bury the body in the woods behind his house. If David did get rid of Billy, you're as apt to find Jimmy Hoffa in Ginny's backyard as you are to find him there. David just wasn't that stupid."

Stevens shook his head. "You watch too much television, my young friend. If David killed Billy, you're never going to find his body. Like I said, thousands of people disappear every day, and not so much as a hair or a fiber is ever found. In this case, it's been twenty-five years; the trail's not merely cold, it's nonexistent."

115

Stevens sighed. "While you've been chasing ghosts all over the West Coast, did you turn up anything that might lead you to Adam? The case that the good taxpayers are actually expecting you to investigate?"

Parker opened his mouth, but I pre-empted him. "As a matter of fact, we have a very promising lead. You'll be the first to know – along with the rest of the family – if it turns up anything. Was there anything else you wanted to discuss with us? If not, I'm afraid we'll have to say goodbye. Time is the taxpayers' money, and all."

Stevens grinned at my curt dismissal. "I wish you all the luck in finding Adam, Detective. It would make his mother so happy." He rose and shook my hand. He gave Parker another *No hard feelings* slap on the back and left the interrogation room.

****

When the door closed behind him, Parker shook his head and murmured, *"That* guy . . ."

I wasn't going to upbraid him about the embarrassingly inept interview, because I had, as Granny used to say, other fish to fry. But Parker read my displeasure, even though I didn't speak it.

"Hell, Jan. I know – it's not even an authorized investigation. We don't have any evidence. Wagner's scan didn't turn up anything. He was just being nice, saying he had to go over it again. Billy's not buried under the folly.

"But I'm still sure he's dead, and that slick Johnny was in on it, even if we can't prove a goddamned thing. It's just like Haycroft said – I wanted to see him sweat."

"He didn't sweat, Parker. He laughed at . . ." Not *you*. I was his partner, and I'd let him run his mouth off. "He laughed at us."

Parker shrugged, repeated, "I'm sure he was in on it. Even if we can't prove it – now he knows he's not as smart as he thinks he is."

I wanted to tell him that a lawyer that got away with murder – even if he was only an accessory – was indeed as smart as he thought he was. He was smarter than the blind justice that he and David Walker had taken an oath to protect, not too differently than we had. The justice that demanded motive, means, and opportunity, not to mention *corpus delicti.*

I wanted to tell Parker that making unsubstantiated accusations of *murder in the first degree* was something for angry, vengeful tough guys on the street corner, not law enforcement. I wanted to tell

116

him that he'd made a mistake – he'd made a powerful enemy here today.

But I didn't tell him any of that. I asked, "Do you have an Android charger handy, Parker? Or do you still use one of those overpriced –"

"You're a peasant, Jan." He didn't smile. "An IPhone is so superior to an Android, let me count up the ways . . ." He looked over at me. "What's wrong with your charger?"

"I guess we could use my charger." I smiled. "But it's not for my phone. It's for David Walker's phone." I took the evidence bag out of my pocket and slid it across the table to him. "Or, Kevin Bennett's. See the driver's license there?"

Nonplussed, Parker moved the phone around inside the bag until he could see the driver's license with David Walker's picture on it. There was also an American Express card and a Bank of America ATM card, all in the name of Kevin Bennett.

"Where . . .?" Parker was having a little trouble with his words.

"You were probably too busy running your scan to notice the built-in desk inside the polly."

"Folly, Jan."

"What, as the man said, ever, Parker. I knew this had to be somewhere. That whole empty-wallet-with-just-a-picture-in-it thing had to . . . I dunno, it had to *mean something.* Maybe David'd had that picture sandwiched in between a driver's license and a credit card for all these years, and had forgotten it even existed. Maybe it had just stayed stuck in his wallet when he'd removed his identification, because . . . I thought maybe he took everything out of his wallet before he went up the house to confront his ex-wife. Maybe he thought she might have him arrested for trespassing or breaking and entering or something, and it would take us longer to identify him – by whatever alias he'd assumed – if he didn't have any ID on him. If he did get arrested, he could use his phone call to warn Adam, so he could stay missing.

"I don't know what his exact motivations were, Parker, but I knew he didn't just materialize in his ex-wife's bedroom. He had to travel there, pay for gas, pay for a room, pay a cab. I knew there had to be ID somewhere." I snatched the bag from my astonished partner. "Now, I'll just hand this over to Forensics . . ."

"Forensics?"

"For fingerprinting, and so on . . ."

"The hell with that, Jan. We don't need prints."

"The phone guys'll want to –"

"The hell with them, too. We don't need a forensic inspection of Mr. Bennett's phone. That'll take forever. Are you fucking kidding? Go get your charger."

He was so adorable when he was making detective decisions.

****

While we waited for David's dead phone to charge, Parker examined the driver's license. "Sherman Way? Isn't that from *Finding Nemo?*"

"What?" I didn't think I'd seen *Finding Nemo.*

Parker scrolled on his own phone, to check his sources, no doubt. "No. It was *P. Sherman* and *Wallaby Way.*" He set his phone down, and held Kevin Bennett's driver's license up to the light, turned it every which-a-way. "This is the best fake ID I've ever seen."

I rubbed my fingers together, the universal gesture for *money.*

"Where's Anza, anyway? Is there really a Sherman Way there?"

"Google it, Parker. I'm gonna go get the file."

In the hall, I ran into Iglesias, told her that we might have a break in the Walker case. "That's great, Dunn," she said, not asking for specifics. "The chief'll be happy. Tell me when you've found the kid. I've got a meeting." And she was gone. I wondered vaguely if she missed real police work, or if she preferred the endless string of meetings that constituted administrative life.

When I returned with the file, Parker took it from me wordlessly. He opened it and found Billy Munro's photograph; he set it beside David Walker's now revived cellphone.

"I am astounded," he said simply. "What about you?"

Luckily for us, there was no lock on the phone. Otherwise, we would've had to call in the forensics boys to get into it for us, after all. But this break wasn't what astounded Parker.

In the picture on David's phone, a young man was smiling for the camera, a beer in his hand. He had longish, wavy black hair and blue eyes. Set beside the old shot of Billy – however much he'd looked like his daddy as a teenager, Adam's resemblance to Billy Munro seven years later was indeed astounding. They could be the same person.

"Blood will tell," I said.

Parker picked up David's phone again, swiped. He swiped a few more times. He enlarged, using thumb and forefinger. Then he looked up at me and grinned. "I know where David's car is."

He reduced the screen and showed me a blue line on a map, and in his best instructional tone said, "Here he was in Anza." Parker again enlarged the screen, and I had time to admire his long, shapely fingers before he said. "And here he was at Mrs. Walker's house. As you know, he didn't leave there . . ."

"What app is that?"

"This is Google Location History. It shows everywhere the phone's been."

"Why would David have a tracking app?"

"There's all kinds of tracking apps, Jan, for keeping tabs on possible cheating spouses, and so on. But this isn't one of those. It probably came with the phone."

"So . . . Is that . . . Is that on my phone, too?"

"Probably." Parker smiled at me. "Have you been somewhere you don't want anyone to know about?"

I took the phone from him and studied the blue line. It will never cease to amaze me how much of our lives are contained on our cellphones, and how much I still don't know about the little tracking device I carry around with me every day.

"How do you know – so, where's the car?"

Parker took the phone back and scrolled. He showed me another blue line, below the map. It listed the Sherman Way address, then a short line to the Canyon Crest Towne Centre, and then another short line to the address of Mrs. Walker's house.

"He was at the Canyon Crest Towne Centre for twenty minutes," Parker said. "Unless he was grocery shopping – I'm willing to guess that he called a cab from there, to take him up to the house. Unless it was towed . . . I'll bet his car's still there."

"We don't know what kind of car –"

Parker giggled. "One that looks like it's been sitting there for a while."

I called and sent a couple of uniforms up to the Canyon Crest Towne Centre to start running plates. "The registration'll be in the name of Kevin Bennett."

Parker continued to scroll through the phone. He turned it around: here was David, standing beside the Billy lookalike. Adam. His partner in crime.

Parker swiped again, showed me another picture. This one was of David and Adam, standing beside an old couple that put me in mind of the farmer and his daughter from *American Gothic*. They didn't really look like that famous couple, but I got the same old-timey vibe. The old man was wearing overalls. The four of them were standing beneath a faded sign that said *Weaver's Market*. The numbers to the address were plainly visible.

"You reckon that's in Avalon?"

"Anza, Parker. Avalon's on Catalina Island."

Unconcerned with his geographical faux pas, Parker continued to examine the evidence. "Here's David's last text. It's from the night he was killed, to someone named Mark. *I'm at the house now.* Mark writes back: *Good luck.* Then a few hours later, Mark says, *Is everything ok?* Then, the next morning: *When r u coming home?* A few more: *R u ok?* again and, *I'm getting worried!* Then . . . nothing. Maybe he figured out that there was no reason to keep texting if he wasn't getting any answer." Parker scrolled. "There aren't any other texts, to anyone. Let's look at . . . He doesn't have very many numbers in his contacts. This Mark person. Something that says *Doctor.* Some guy named Marty. *Weavers.* "

As Parker read off the few people David Walker had called often enough to've saved their numbers, I felt a wave of sadness. Poor Adam had been left with nothing but a string of unanswered text messages, for almost ten days now. He had no idea what'd become of the man he thought was his father. He must be distraught; he had absolutely no means with which to find David. What was he going to do, ring up his mom's house?

"There's a few pictures of that market, and a house, and some deserty landscapes, but all the other shots . . ." Parker held up the phone again. The home screen was that old Halloween picture of seventeen-year-old Adam in his cowboy get-up, the one Sarah had shown to David. The one that'd started it all.

"Maybe I should just ring *Mark* up," Parker said, his finger hovering over the screen. "Tell him we'd like to have a little talk with him."

"Don't, Parker!" I said with way too much urgency. Then, calmer: "You'll spook him. By the time we get to Anza, he'll have taken off again."

Parker continued to look at me, waiting for some further explanation of my unexpected show of emotion. He hadn't really intended to call the person listed as *Mark* in David Walker's phone, this person that was undoubtedly Adam. The element of surprise was an invaluable advantage in our line of work . . . I knew Parker wasn't going to hit *Call,* so why had I gotten all freaked out about it?

I obliged him with an answer. "You've heard of the Black Dahlia murder?"

Parker nodded, wondering what one of LA's most famous unsolved homicides could possibly have to do with the matter at hand.

"I read about it when I was a little kid. Like twelve years old. I was fascinated by it, years before I was old enough to understand anything about sex crimes or anything like that. All I knew was that this beautiful girl had been snatched off the street and brutally killed. My dad always said my interest in that ancient homicide case had to be what led me to want to be a cop."

I shook my head – the nature of the crime, the murderer's motivations; my dad's theories about my choice in careers – these were not the reasons I'd brought it up.

"The police were a lot chummier with the press back then. After she was identified, LAPD gave her name to the papers, and some reporter located her mother back East. He called and told the woman that her daughter had won a beauty contest, and asked for all kinds of personal information. Only after he had his *scoop* did he tell the woman that her daughter had been murdered."

I stopped, and Parker waited without comment for me to continue. I sighed. "I remember that this one detail stood out to me – how incredibly cruel that man was. He calls her mother, all the way on the East Coast, at a time when cross-country phone calls were a rarity. He tells her this good news, this complete fabrication. Only after Mom proudly and happily tells him all the details of her daughter's life does he give her the awful truth. I always wondered – how did he say it? *Oh, by the way, I lied, they found your kid sawn in half and dumped in a field?*

"The way she must've felt . . . It stuck with me. Past all the other horrific details of the murder, the things I would come to understand more as I got older – the way that reporter had lied to her mother – that always seemed like one of the worst things about it.

"If Adam's phone rang, and he saw the call was from David . . . All the worry he has to've been feeling . . . He would be so relieved . . . And then to find out that it was just some cop, calling on David's phone to him to tell him that his dad is dead . . . It would be just like that reporter calling the Black Dahlia's mother. Unbelievably, inexcusably cruel."

Parker didn't say, "You know I wasn't really going to call," because he knew I knew that. He just continued to look at me silently.

"Have you ever had to tell somebody?" I asked. When he shook his head, I said, "Regardless of what David and Adam did . . ."

Adam Walker wasn't a criminal – the fraud he'd committed to become someone else was a crime, true, but it was a crime of paperwork, of numbers – victimless, really – causing your mother and sister heartache wasn't a factor in the laws he'd broken.

"Adam deserves more than a phone call."

"We have to find him first," Parker said.

****

The rest of the pieces fell into place after that, just like on *Law & Order*. We already had an address and a map to David's residence, in the homey little burg of Anza, California. I knew vaguely where it was, and Parker's always efficient internet search clarified: it was about 80 miles from the station, and it should take us an hour and a half to get there.

"If there's zero traffic," he commented. "I'd say no less than two hours."

"RSO has jurisdiction, I do believe."

I was curious to see if Parker had anything derogatory to say about the Riverside County Sheriff and his deputies, like he had about the cops from the beach. He gave me the same look as when I'd suggested turning over David's fake ID and cellphone to Forensics. It communicated that he didn't feel it was necessary to coordinate with RSO at this juncture. I had to agree with him – it wasn't like we were gonna swoop down upon the house on Sherman Way, guns drawn, and needed back up for it. The two of us would be sufficient, jurisdictional protocols be damned.

Kevin Bennett's residence address informed our search – he was listed as the owner of that property, and it didn't take long to uncover his purchase of another property, at the address we'd seen in the photo of him and Adam and the old couple. Dropping the little Google Maps man in front of the place confirmed it: David Walker was the owner of Weaver's Market. As the fake Mr. Bennett, he'd set up housekeeping and gone into the grocery store business in Anza a little over two years prior to his appearing in Virginia Walker's bedroom on what would turn out to be the last night of his life.

"Let's go to the market first," I suggested.

Parker's cellphone *whistled.* It was a relatively new sound from his device, and again I wished he'd change it, or put his phone on vibrate. Of the five or six text-announcement noises he had programmed, this one was the most annoying. Whoever she was – I assumed it was a woman – she'd been texting a lot lately, and I didn't appreciate the intrusion of Parker's private life into my professional life with him, via a *whistle.*

He held up his finger, checked the message. He smiled, but didn't text anything back. Then he looked up at me blankly and said, "Do you really want to go this minute? We're gonna hit all the traffic in Temecula if we leave now. The place'll probably be closed by the time we get there." He glanced at the clock, then winked at me. "It's almost shift change, Jan."

It was 4:10. We didn't really have a shift, per se, and this had always been Parker's little smug nod to the fact that he wasn't a patrol cop. This and the mention of *quittin' time,* whenever things were going nowhere on a particular day.

"I think we should drive up there first thing in the morning," he added. "We've waited this long . . . Why not be fresh when we wrap this thing up?"

I wasn't in the mood for the two hour drive, that was true. Parker's lady friend's texts – hell, maybe it was his mother texting, but I didn't think so, by the way he smiled when he looked at them – her thoughts would no doubt continue to whistle for him all the way up there. I felt bad about leaving Adam Walker to wonder what had happened to his dad for another night, but on the other hand, he'd let his mother believe he was dead for seven years, and I wasn't a social worker.

"First thing in the morning," I said to Parker, and told him to have a nice evening.

SARAH

Eric was all smiles at dinner. He said there'd been a major break in the case – he said they might locate Adam as early as the next day. He said he wished he could tell me more about it, but there was that police protocol – he said if everything worked out, my brother might be coming home very soon.

That was all well and good, but I didn't press him for more info, because Adam coming home and everything that was going to open up because of it was not foremost in my mind. Eric's standing on the precipice of solving his case made him ebullient; he was of a mind to jump, to cut loose, to celebrate. His good mood made him even more attractive.

I suggested that we go dancing after dinner, and he was heartily down. I was thinking of a couple of places I knew of in LA, but Eric said we didn't have to go that far. He took me to some place I'd never even seen before called Club Sevilla, tucked up close to the freeway off ramp, right downtown. It was dark and loud, stuffed with people his age. It was great.

Eric knew the bartender at this place, too, so I was never for a moment without a drink in my hand. When he kissed me hungrily in the middle of a slow song, I responded with all of a teenager's eagerness – this good-looking young cop made me feel half my age. I looked forward to Act II with an adult's anticipation, however.

I led him out to the car and we pawed each other for some time, again like high schoolers. Then Eric seemed to remember his place in the world – he laughed suddenly, a little shakily, and told me that RPD often cruised bar parking lots, lights off, looking for drug doing and . . . he didn't say, *sex having,* but that thought was definitely in his eyes. He gently pushed me back over into my seat and started the car.

The seatbelts and the center console were in my way, but I kept my hand on his thigh for the entire drive to my place. I didn't think that this was the sort of thing *Sergeant Dudley Do-Right* did on a regular basis, and I didn't want him to remember that I was part of his investigation; I didn't want him to start to consider what kind of forgiveness he might have to beg for, as he hadn't asked for permission.

Don't worry about the future, honey, I thought. *Just do what comes naturally tonight.*

I needn't have fretted. The liquor he'd consumed and all those victorious feelings he had because he was going to solve his case on the morrow made Eric heedless. There was no small talk when we arrived at my apartment. *I* was what he wanted for a celebration; he felt that he *deserved* me.

The alarm on his phone went off at 8 in the morning; he glanced around my bedroom with a faint air of surprise, then looked at me with a more pronounced expression of guilt. I was sure of it then: Sergeant Parker was not in the habit of engaging in one night stands. It wasn't as if I was an anonymous bar pick-up, but maybe that made it worse. He knew me, and now he was wondering if all this was gonna have to *mean something.*

I smiled at him, offering reassurance. I wasn't twenty-two or even twenty-six. I wordlessly let him know that I didn't assume that we were now a couple, that he was going to have to take me to meet his parents, that he was going to have to endure Virginia Walker's dubious and not-surprised appraisal, just because of one drunken and well-earned escapade. I wiggled my eyebrows at him, casting how-we-were-gonna-have-to-act-in-public-now to the wind. Everything was okay. No commitment had been made. He relaxed and kissed me.

He didn't have time for breakfast – he told me that he had to meet his partner at nine, and before that . . . The idea that he couldn't go in to work wearing the same clothes he'd had on the previous day was stamped upon him like the scarlet letter. He had to get home, take a shower, change, make himself presentable . . .

He was adorable.

He kissed me goodbye quickly, and running out the door, he promised that he'd call me as soon as they'd located Adam.

JANET

Parker was late. I was annoyed. When he finally showed up, he was uncharacteristically disheveled, and even though I loved the scent of his cologne, he was wearing too much of it this morning. *I had a helluva date last night* was written all over him, so I was further annoyed.

On the other hand, he was only twenty minutes late, and he'd brought me a Starbucks. And if he'd had a date, it wasn't any of my business, now was it? If I wanted to have a date with him, I should just open my never-before-reticent mouth and suggest it.

But I still wasn't so sure I wanted to do that. I liked Parker a lot; he was smart and sexy, and if I gave into my desire to find out just how smart and sexy he might be . . . Well, that could end badly. I wasn't ready to risk the bad ending for a great beginning and an awesome middle. Not yet. I wasn't ready to risk our good professional relationship for what I was sure would be a better personal one.

Yeah, I was sure he'd be down, that we'd be great together . . . But maybe I wasn't entirely sure. If I made the suggestion, maybe Parker would feature me with a boyish, embarrassed kind of smile, and turn me down. This growing warm I had for him – I didn't mind keeping it secret for the moment.

And since I was exceptionally fond of him, I couldn't stay annoyed with him for very long. The fact that he'd silenced that irritating whistle – he hadn't silenced *his phone,* because it still made other noises, but whoever the whistler was, she wasn't texting him this morning – this further reduced my annoyance. I told myself that maybe it'd just been his mother, after all.

Since I wasn't annoyed with my partner anymore, the drive to Temecula and then up the winding road to Anza was pleasant. Because David had been gone for some time now, we figured that Adam was probably looking after things at the store. Or maybe not. It was as good a place to start as any, and it was on the way to the residence address.

Parker came off the blacktop into the parking lot of Weaver's Market a little too fast, and the car slid rather cinematically to a stop in front of the place.

I said drily, "What d'ya know? The cops are here."

"I didn't know the lot wasn't paved," he replied, with just that embarrassed kind of smile upon which I'd been reflecting earlier.

I waited for the dust to settle without comment.

The market was dim and cool inside, after the morning heat outside. The old lady that we'd seen in the picture with Adam and David was standing behind the scarred wooden counter. She smiled and asked us how she could be of service to us on this lovely day that the Lord had made.

Parker smiled in return and showed her his badge, introduced himself and me. "We're looking for Mark, Mrs. –?"

"Weaver."

"Of course." He gestured in the direction of the sign outside. "Mark's not in any trouble or anything. We were told he might've been a witness to a traffic accident, and we'd like to have a few words with him about it."

I thought of the lying Black Dahlia reporter.

"Is he here?"

Mrs. Weaver smiled. "You didn't have to tell me that Mark wasn't in any trouble, Officer. He's a good boy. You just missed him, though. He goes to DaVita on Wednesdays."

"It's Thursday, Mrs. Weaver."

"Is it? How silly am I? He said he was going to the doctor's – if it's Thursday, he must've been talking about Dr. Perez."

"Is her office here in town?"

"Oh, no. Her office is at the Temecula Valley Hospital. Back down the hill. Just ask for her there. Dr. Amelia Perez. I've met her a few times. She's just the sweetest thing. Not standoffish like most doctors."

The old man from the picture came in. He scowled at his wife as he joined her behind the counter, than turned and scowled at us. Flustered by his sullen stare at law enforcement, Mrs. Weaver quickly explained, "These are policemen, Henry. They're looking for Mark. He was a witness to a traffic accident and they need to speak to him about it. Take a statement, I imagine?" Parker nodded. "I was just telling them that Mark's gone off to see –"

"I heard you," the old man growled. "You're always running off at the mouth, Linda. Like a broken faucet. Don't tell 'em anything else." His eyes narrowed. "What is it you want with Mark, exactly?"

"It's just like we told your wife, sir. He was a witness to a traffic accident –"

"This was here in town?"

"No, it was in Temecula."

"Lemme see your badge." Parker complied, and the old man's scowl intensified. "You're not Temecula PD."

"No, but we're coordinating with them." My partner's lie was unraveling in the face of this old party's suspicion, but he recovered effortlessly. "I can't discuss the details. You understand."

Parker smiled and Mrs. Weaver smiled back, but her husband was unmoved. "If I see Mark, I'll tell him you're looking for him."

"Do you expect him back today?"

"I don't *expect* him at all, *Officer.*" The word sounded like a curse coming from Mr. Weaver. "I'm not his keeper. He makes his own hours. This time of day, he could be anywhere." He glanced witheringly at his wife.

"Well, thanks for your time." Parker turned to go.

"I'll be sure to tell him you're looking for him," Mr. Weaver promised darkly. "If I happen to see him."

"That'll be fine, sir."

We left the market.

****

"You want to go out to the house?" Parker asked, when we were back in the car. "Or do you want to try this doctor's office? We might be able to catch him before the old guy warns him we're here."

"Might as well. Mrs. Weaver seemed pretty sure that's where he is."

I asked the GPS on my phone to direct us to Temecula Valley Hospital. It told me that the trip would take about forty minutes, but Parker straightened the curves and made it in twenty-five.

On the way, he said, "Old Mr. Weaver was downright hostile, wasn't he? Do you think he knows the score, that Kevin Bennett and his son aren't who they say they are? The cops arrive – do you think he knows the gig is up?"

I frowned at his phrasing. "I doubt it. Some people just don't like cops, Parker. Especially old people that live out in the boonies."

The hospital was a four-story affair, long, but not very wide. We were directed to the appropriate module; Parker smiled at the nurse on the other side of the glass.

"I was wondering if it might be possible to see Dr. Perez?"

"Just put your paperwork in the box," she replied absently. Parker discreetly pressed his badge against the glass. Now he had her full attention. "Oh! Hold on just a minute. She's with a patient."

A few minutes later, the doctor appeared in the doorway to the waiting room and looked questioningly at us. She was in her mid-fifties, somewhat austere looking, but what did I expect? Another angry, ancient hippie, like Mr. Weaver?

She led us through the module to her office, and after another round of introductions and showing of identification, she offered us seats in front of her neat desk. She went around behind it and sat down. She steepled her fingers, and asked us what she could do for us.

"We understand that you have a patient called Mark . . ." I hesitated. We didn't know that Adam was using the same last name as David. The doctor looked at me doubtfully for a split second, so I just went for it. "Mark Bennett."

"Yes." She eyed the both of us for, oh, I dunno, a good, solid, ten seconds. "Is he is some kind of trouble?"

Parker trotted out the witness-to-a-traffic-accident story. Dr. Perez didn't ask to examine our badges again because maybe she believed my partner, but she remained just as tight-lipped as old Weaver had been. The slap of someone putting a file in the holder on the wall outside of her office broke the silence, but still the doctor just stared at us.

"Mrs. Weaver told us that he was coming to see you today," Parker said.

Dr. Perez let that one slide right on by. "You say Mark was involved in some kind of accident?"

"He was a witness to an accident," Parker said. "You understand that we can't disclose any information about an ongoing investigation." He glanced around the office. "What's your specialty, Doctor? What are you treating Mark Bennett for?"

"My specialty is orthopedics, Mr. Parker." She smiled expansively. "But I'm afraid I can't disclose the specifics of Mr.

Bennett's treatment to the police without a court order. HIPPAA regulations and all that."

Dr. Perez looked at the computer on the desk in front of her; she typed, clicked the mouse. "Unless of course Mr. Bennett is . . ." She read from the screen, ". . . *a suspect, fugitive, material witness or missing person.*" She looked up from the computer. "And since he's none of those things . . ." She smiled, paused. "Since you say you only want to talk to him about a traffic accident, I can tell you that Mrs. Weaver was correct. He was in to see me today. You just missed him, in fact. But I can't tell you any more than that."

"Thank you very much for your time, Doctor," I said quickly.

She nodded and showed us out of the module.

As we got into the car, I said, "I know what you're thinking, Parker. Adam Walker is all of those things, to one degree or another. A suspect, a fugitive, a material witness. If nothing else, he's most assuredly a missing person. But we don't have any kind of paperwork stating that he's any of those things. She would've wanted to see that."

A phone rang; I didn't recognize the tone. Parker took David Walker's phone out of his pocket. "The *Doctor* is calling David. When she doesn't get an answer, she'll probably call her patient next." He grinned. "We didn't really need any info from Dr. Perez. This was just a time-killing trip, right? Because helpful Mrs. Weaver said she knew Adam wasn't at home?"

"You read my mind, partner," I said, wishing again that he could really read my mind. "Let's see if we can catch Adam before the whole world warns him we're coming."

Maybe I'd buy Parker a drink after we *wrapped this up.* Maybe I'd just tell him exactly what I'd been thinking. I wouldn't waste any more time hoping for him to telepathically guess what I wanted.

****

We turned off of Highway 371 onto a dirt road. Sherman Way was also dirt.

"Aren't any of the streets in this town paved?" Parker complained as he slowly maneuvered the car over the ruts.

"It's the boonies," I repeated, looking out the window at the scrub. "The perfect place to disappear."

The mailbox at the end of the long driveway said *Bennett;* the dwelling wasn't a house at all but a triple-wide mobile home. We

130

again waited for the dust kicked up by our arrival to settle around us, then I said, "Let me do the talking on this one, Parker."

I didn't look at him – it was kind of a bitchy order. It was also unnecessary: whenever we approached an important subject together, I always did the initial talking. But the way Parker had accused Stevens of being an accessory to murder when he had no evidence was still fresh in my mind. That had been an emotional thing, *just to see him sweat,* and it had been entirely unprofessional, and totally worthless. Last great acts of defiance have no place in police work.

Parker was excited that we were at last going to *wrap this thing up,* but this was an excruciatingly delicate situation. It didn't matter what name Adam Walker was calling himself these days. Whatever fraud he'd committed to become someone else also didn't matter. Even if we had a warrant for his arrest regarding that fraud, which we did not have – none of it mattered *right now.*

Right now, Parker and I were there to tell him that his father was dead, and that his mother wanted him back. I needed to do the talking.

We knocked; he answered the door. As Parker had been, I was struck by his resemblance to Billy Munro. I asked, "Are you Mark Bennett?"

He nodded slowly. I introduced Parker and myself; we showed him our shields. I asked if we could come in and have a few words with him. Again he nodded wordlessly. The squeak of the screen door seemed like a scream in the silence of the hot afternoon.

Once inside, it was impossible to tell that this was a mobile home. The days of Grandpappy's twelve by sixty aluminum and wood-paneled trailer were passed, at least for people with money. The little living room was neat and tidy; Adam led us through it and offered us seats at the kitchen table, then took the one that was left.

He remained silent, watchful. If I didn't know better, I would've thought he was mute. Maybe the old man or the doctor had reached him. Maybe he knew it wasn't about any traffic mishap.

"We're so sorry to have to bring you this news, Mr. Bennett. There's been . . . an accident. Your father's been killed."

A small tremor shook him, and tears welled up and fell from his blue eyes. But his gaze remained locked with mine, and still he remained silent.

I didn't see the clock in the kitchen, but I knew it was there somewhere, because I could hear it ticking. Next would come sobs; he would cry out, "How?" Or he would whisper it.

131

The clock continued to tick; the quiet was unbroken. Parker reached across the table and gently took the bereft young man's trembling hand.

I wasn't getting to the point quickly enough, so Parker decided to take over, despite what I'd told him in the car. It was just as well. I'd pretty much lost the procedural need to be the bearer of this bad news.

Parker said gently, "He went to your mother's house in the middle of the night."

The tears coursed down his face, but Adam's expression didn't change at the mention of his mother.

Parker continued. "She mistook him for a prowler. She . . . she shot him."

Adam tried to cover his face, but Parker held tightly to his hand. "She was terrified, but somehow, she found the courage to turn on the lights. Once she saw that the man she'd shot was someone she knew . . . She sent us to find you. She misses you very much."

"We know who you are, Adam," I added softly.

He inhaled a great shuddery breath, and now the sobs came. Parker released his hand and scootched his chair around the corner of the table. He hugged Adam and held him whilst he cried out this first shocked and unutterable pain.

I knew that more tears would come, for days and weeks, months, maybe years, but it was not for the entirety of Adam's grief that I felt my own tears well. It was because, at this unbearable first moment of loss, he had no one to comfort him except strangers, because he had cut himself off from all those that loved him to disappear with a man he hardly knew.

Why?

Eventually, Adam stopped crying, for the time being. He disengaged himself from Parker's arms and rose, pulled a paper towel from where the roll hung from a cabinet. He wiped his face, blew his nose. He braced his hands on the sink and stared out the window. Parker rose and again laid a comforting hand on his shoulder.

I knew it would go one of two ways. It was always the same when a person was confronted with the news of the death of a loved one. Some people would feel a kind of embarrassment at their naked vulnerability, and wouldn't want to further display their helpless grief before strangers. These people always thanked the police for their condolences and showed us the door.

If Adam did that, we'd have no option other than to go. We weren't there to arrest him.

When he again hugged Parker, grateful for his simple, physical show of sympathy, I knew it would go the other way. Sometimes, the shocked next of kin wanted to talk, to remember. Especially if, like Adam, they had nowhere else to turn.

He asked us if we'd like some coffee, and while he prepared it, he began.

"You say you know who I am, Detective Dunn?" He raised his hand, stopping my reply. "You know my name, but you don't know who I am. Nor who David Walker . . . was. I guess I owe you an explanation."

"You don't owe us anything, Adam," Parker said softly.

"I owe it to somebody," he whispered. "Maybe after you've heard it . . . You can help me figure out what to tell my mother and sister, because I don't have a clue as to how I'm gonna do that."

He sniffled and swiped at his eyes and waited in silence until the pot filled, and we also waited. He poured us each a coffee, offered cream and sugar, which we both declined, then sat down. He stared unseeing at the brown liquid in his cup, and once he'd attained some semblance of composure, he again spoke.

"The first time I talked to David, I didn't even know it was him. I got a text from an unfamiliar number. *You don't know me. I saw your picture on your sister's phone. That's where I got your number. Don't ask her about it – it's not like she knows I copied it down.*

"Sarah lived at home at the time," Adam explained. He looked up at me. "I guess she doesn't anymore?"

I shook my head. "Not for some time now."

"Mom moved into her old room? Upstairs? That's where she . . . . Where she shot David?"

I nodded.

"He wasn't there to see Mom, Detective. He was there to see Sarah . . . I guess it never occurred to either of us that she might've moved out again." Adam shook his head; Sarah's part would come later. "Anyway . . . I got this odd text. I figured that it was from someone I *did* know – one of my friends' sisters or girlfriends or something, someone that I'd already met but didn't remember. She'd seen Sarah's phone lying on the table unattended and had copied down my number from it because she wanted to get to know me better. But she wanted to be mysterious about it . . . Maybe she was shy.

"I asked her what she wanted, and she said she just wanted to talk to me. I was seventeen. I thought it was cute. I told her I'd make a game of it; if she told me what she looked like and where she went to school and stuff like that, I'd try to figure out who she was.

"He corrected me right away. He repeated that I didn't know him, and that he wasn't a teenage girl. He said he was a man – quite a bit older than me, actually. He repeated that he'd seen my picture, and that he was . . . *interested* in me."

Adam paused and gazed steadily at Parker, and again I was proud of my partner: he showed no surprise, no judgment. Only a neutral attentiveness.

"He asked me if I was okay with that, or did it make me uncomfortable." Adam continued to hold my partner's gaze. "I was seventeen. I'd had my share of girls . . ." He smiled at Parker, demonstrating why he'd had his share – he was strikingly attractive, and he knew it. Parker returned his smile.

"There'd been an . . . *incident,* however, when I was almost sixteen. Sarah had an invite to a wedding. It was one of her old friends from high school or college or something. It was to be a huge, lavish affair, months and months in the planning, but when the date rolled around, Sarah was once again single."

Adam asked if I knew whether or not Sarah was single now, since she wasn't living at home anymore. The question took me off-guard. I'd assumed she was, since she'd made eyes at Parker, but I couldn't really say *that,* now could I?

"I'm not sure. I think so. She wasn't wearing a ring when we interviewed her."

"Sarah was always single," he said. "Except when she wasn't. It was hard to keep track.

"Anyway, she'd been going with some guy when she'd accepted the invitation to her friend's big wedding, but now he was gone, so at the last minute, she asked me if I wanted to go. I had a nice suit that I didn't get to wear very often, so I figured, *why not?*

"The ceremony was pretty boring, but the reception was a giant, outdoor thing at the bride's parents' house, some huge place over there in Indian Hills. There were tables and chairs set up outside, a tent with a buffet, and a little stage with a band and a DJ. Lots and lots of people.

"At one point, I caged a glass of champagne, and ducked around the back of the buffet tent to drink it. There I found another kid with the same idea. We got to talking . . . His name was Jeremy, of all godawful things.

"He played football for his school's team; he was exactly four months older than me. He'd just gotten his driver's license; he'd driven Dad's Porsche to the reception. He was impressed that I'd skipped the seventh grade and was a year ahead of him in school.

"Jeremy and I hit it off. We hung around together for the rest of the afternoon, stole a few more glasses of champagne. We talked . . . Sounded each other out, so to speak. When it started to get dark, I asked to see Dad's Porsche. We took a ride, parked, took a walk in the dark in the woods. To make a long story short, I made the suggestion, and after a few moments' hesitation, and after extracting my promise not to tell *anyone,* Jeremy agreed."

Adam smiled slyly at Parker. "The girls had been pawing me since I was fourteen, and that was fun, but this was the first time it'd been totally *my* idea. As you might expect, I was a little surprised at myself. Jeremy was also surprised – at me, at himself, at the fact that it just seemed like the thing to do. I saw him a few more times, but he lived on the other side of town and wasn't allowed out in Dad's Porsche very often, so it didn't last very long.

"I'd also had a . . . for lack of a better word, I'd had a *relationship* with an exchange student named Rolf. This was during my senior year in high school, which had just passed when I received this mysterious text. We'd kept it quiet – it wasn't anybody's business, and as we knew there was no future in it – he'd be going back home to Germany when we graduated, which he'd done, the previous June . . . Well, it just wasn't anybody's business. Like I say, I'd gone out with my share of girls . . . Nobody knew about my other . . . *proclivities.* Not my friends, or my sister . . . Certainly not my mother."

Wow, I thought, *and he hadn't even made it to college yet – John Stevens's excuse for exploring such* proclivities.

"But apparently this enigmatic male texter knew, just from seeing a picture of me. This aroused my curiosity, so I told him that his interest didn't make me uncomfortable in the least.

"We texted, emailed, talked on the phone. I told him about myself, and he told me about himself – he told me his first name, that he was divorced, that he was a lawyer, that he had a practice in LA. I mentioned that my father was also named David, that he was also divorced, and a lawyer, and also had a practice in LA."

Parker stirred, and I could read his mind as clearly as if he'd spoken his question aloud. He wanted to ask when and how David Walker had finally revealed that he was indeed Adam's father. But Parker didn't speak. He was a good cop, and this wasn't an interrogation. It was a confession of a sort, an explanation, and he knew, as I did, that it was best to allow Adam to confess and explain in his own good time.

Like Parker, Adam was intuitive, and he guessed my partner's unspoken question. "My new friend asked me to tell him how I felt about my dad – how I felt that he'd abandoned me before I was even born, how I felt about the fact that I'd never even had occasion to meet him. These were *his* interpretations of what I'd already told him about my life. I'd never used the word *abandoned.* I told him that I didn't feel that way at all.

"Some things just don't work out – that was all my mother had said about her marriage to the man I'd never met, and, well . . . I'd never really thought much about it. My childhood, my life, had been full and complete and happy – I had a great mom and a great sister and great friends. I'd had great . . . *experiences.* I hadn't thought about being fatherless . . . How could I miss something I'd never known? I'd never missed anything, or so I felt, except . . ." Adam trailed off, sipped his coffee.

"We talked about everything, politics and religion and current events. Eventually, we talked about other, more intimate things." Adam ignored me when he said this – he didn't care about my reaction, only Parker's, someone who was of an age with him. A *man* who was of an age with him.

"I realized that what I'd been missing in life was something like this – someone I could talk to about . . . anything. I was fascinated with him – this stranger, this voice on the telephone. His thoughts, his ideas . . ."

Sarah Walker had told us that her brother had met someone online, someone that'd *intrigued* him. Parker met my eyes. It hadn't been a girl that had captivated Adam, and they hadn't met online. There'd never been any girl. The person with whom he'd shared secrets and talked till the wee hours had been David.

"I pressed for a meeting," Adam said. "He hesitated, reminded me that he was a lot older than me. 'You don't even know what I look like,' he said. I told him to send me a picture, then, and he finally did."

Parker couldn't help himself. "Did you recognize him?"

Adam shook his head. "I thought there was something vaguely familiar about him, but I didn't connect it. I'd seen a photo album of my parents' wedding just once, when I was maybe six years old. My mom was so young, I barely recognized her. Her groom – my dad – and the rest of the people in the pictures were strangers to me. It bored me.

"So, finally, reluctantly, he agreed to meet me. It was pedestrian, ordinary. I parked in a lot across from the Staples Center in LA and met him at the Starbucks around the corner. It was on a Saturday afternoon, in broad daylight, a week or two before Christmas. Nothing at all like a thrilling, dangerous assignation with a complete stranger, someone older than me, which is how I'd thought of it.

"I recognized him immediately from the selfie he'd sent: he was indeed older, but striking nonetheless, his hair *a sable silver'd.*" Parker smiled at the allusion, and Adam returned his smile. "He was about my size, trim; entirely more attractive than I'd imagined he'd be. We shook hands, then hugged, without any awkwardness. I felt as if I knew this man . . . I felt as if he knew me.

"Though it was a little chilly, we went outside and sat on one of the concrete benches in front of Starbucks. It wasn't any more private than inside the coffee shop – crowds of people, holiday shoppers, walked to and fro, talking to each other, talking on their phones. There was the noise of the traffic . . . I was excited to be finally meeting him . . ."

Parker was on the edge of his seat with anticipation: how had David broken the truth to his eager son? Adam sensed Parker's own eagerness and he grinned.

"He took his wallet out of his pocket, not breaking eye contact. He slid his driver's license out and handed it to me – with some reluctance, I looked down at it and . . . I laughed in surprise. 'My dad's name is –'

"'No,' he said. 'It's not. I was married to your mother, and I'm definitely Sarah's father. At least, I'm pretty sure . . .' He shook his head. That wasn't important. 'But I'm not your father, Adam.'

"I'm sure my mouth fell open in astonishment. I was devastated. All the things we'd shared . . . I whined, "But I thought . . . You said you were *interested . . .*"

He held up his hand, said, "What did I just say, Adam?" And I saw Sarah in him then, or I guess it was *him* that I'd always seen in

137

Sarah. She'd say that to me when she was annoyed, if I bothered her repeatedly about something. *What did I just say, Adam?*

"'I'm not your father,' he said again. 'I'm not blood to you in any way. We're . . . strangers.'

"He took something else out of his wallet. It was a small snapshot of my mother – young and beautiful. On the piano at home, there's a larger, framed photo of her, wearing the same dress. It must've been taken the same day. David passed one hand in front of it, like a magician doing a trick, then unfolded it, voila! He set it on the bench between us.

"'That's your father,' he said, pointing to the man standing beside Mom. He grinned. *'Not I, said the fly.'*

"I was still nonplussed, uncomprehending, so he laid it out for me. Mom had had an affair with this guy, David had found out about it and divorced her. Not long after, I was born.

"'That's why you never saw me, Adam,' he said. 'I knew that you weren't my son.'

"'But Mom's always said . . .' I stammered. 'She's never mentioned . . .' I gestured at the picture. 'My name's Walker.'

"'I'm listed on your birth certificate,' he agreed. 'There was no use making a big deal about your true paternity.' Now *he* gestured at the picture. 'It wasn't like this guy was ever gonna come back and claim you. He took off, before you were even born. No one knew about your mom's . . . *actions*. Why make a big deal about it? You're your mother's son and your sister's brother, Adam. Everyone just assumed that you were my son, too, so why not just go with that? Your real father had taken off, so I let your mother give you my name.'

"I asked him if Mom had asked to have it that way, and he shook his head. 'I haven't spoken to your mother since I filed for divorce. There was never any kind of discussion. We were married when you were conceived; so it just followed that you were my son. Maybe Ginny assumed that you *were* mine . . .' He shook his head again. 'I don't know. But I'm sure that the moment you were born, she couldn't help but know.' He gestured at the picture again. 'You look just like him.'

"He continued, 'We were already divorced when you arrived. I didn't want anything to do with your mother. I figured, if you *were* my son, she would've demanded that I have some kind of input into your life, but she never did. So I knew that what I'd suspected all along . . . It was true. We've got the same last name, Adam, but this is your dad. Not me. And I never would've contacted you, except that – '

"I was angry then, bitter, *so* disappointed, and I cut him off. 'Why *did* you contact me, then? What was the point of any of it? Your mysterious text, saying you were *interested* in me – all the things we've discussed – was it all just so you could give me this ridiculous, maudlin speech? What am I supposed to do now, go on some great quest to track down my *real father?* I don't care about any of this!'

"My voice had risen. I was *so* upset. All the anticipation I'd felt, to finally be meeting the man whose conversation had fascinated me for the last month or so – the bottom had just dropped out of all that. I was angry, hurt. I was practically shouting. A couple stared at us as they walked past, and David stared back at them until they looked away and hurried on.

"He wasn't angry or even upset. He smiled and said, 'You can go on a quest after your real father if you want, but I don't think you'll find him. I doubt if he wants to be found. And anyway, what would be the point? You don't know him any more than you know me.'

"I looked down. I was *so* disappointed. I said, 'I thought I knew you, David. I thought we had some kind of a connection.'

"He grabbed my wrist, squeezed it, so I'd look up at him. He said softly, 'None of that's changed. What I told you in the beginning – that was all true. When I saw your picture on Sarah's phone . . . I . . . I had to talk to you. I *had to.* You got inside my head . . . I had to find out what you were like, if you were . . . like me. You're . . . unforgettable.' He touched my cheek tenderly . . ." Here Adam extended his hand, as if he would similarly touch Parker. But he didn't.

"Then David immediately dropped his hand. He said, 'A part of me hoped that you'd tell me to get lost . . . That would've been so much easier. To just let it go. Not only is there the appalling age difference – '

"I told him I didn't care about that. He smiled. 'I should care about it, but . . . I don't. I should never have contacted you, but I did. Woulda, shoulda, coulda. Life is short. I had to meet you." He shrugged. *"What's done cannot be undone.* Regardless, before anything else, you had to know about all these unfortunate . . . *ties* between us.'

139

"'What am I supposed to do now?' I demanded. 'Am I just supposed to forget about all the things we've talked about?'" Adam grinned abashedly at Parker. "I was almost hysterical; another passerby stared at me.

"David said again that there was no blood between us, and I said, 'But there is. You're Sarah's father, and Sarah's my sister . . .' It was all too much to process at once.

"He said he was sorry; he again said that he never should've texted me. I said no, I'd enjoyed our talks so much, I'd *so* looked forward to meeting him . . .

"He said, 'I want you to go home and think about it, Adam. You're practically an adult, but you're not an adult yet. It's not like we could . . .'

"I started to protest that I certainly was a goddamned adult, cutting him off again, and I thought, *It's not like we could what?* We could do whatever we wanted! We weren't related.

"But he just shook his head, and said, 'I'm a lawyer remember? You're a minor. I can't be . . . *influencing* a minor. Go home and think about it. If you see it for how it is, how it could be, then maybe in a couple of months . . . Go home and think about it.' He squeezed my wrist again. He stuck the picture and his driver's license back in his wallet, then stood up and walked off into the crowd.

"I sat there and thought about it. I drew a family tree in my head: there was a line from him to my mother, with another line to Sarah, with dates from before I was born. Ancient history, as unrelatable to my life at that moment as the story Mom likes to tell about how Grandpa or Great-grandpa had almost married one of the North daughters. Or maybe it was one of the Gage daughters." Adam shook his head. "Things that happened before I was born didn't matter.

"I drew another line on my imaginary family tree – from my mother to this other guy – I didn't even know his name – and then a line to me.

"But it was just like David had said: there was no line from him to me. No blood, no familial relationship of any kind. We weren't even related by marriage anymore; he didn't even qualify as my stepfather. He'd been married to my mother once, but wasn't married to her anymore, hadn't been, even before I was born . . . . All this, despite what my birth certificate said.

"I didn't have to go all the way back to Riverside to come to a decision. I wanted this man in my life. I texted him, told him I

140

wanted to see him again. I said that we'd figure some way around all the things that were written down in black and white, birth certificates and names and false lineages. I said we'd just ignore it all if we had to, these things that *seemed to be,* but were really not."

Adam smiled. "I babbled to him in text form, just like I'm babbling to you now. I sat on that concrete bench in front of Starbucks, around the corner from the Staples Center, and the crowd quick-walked and slow-walked and ambled by me, unnoticed. I waited for his answer.

"He didn't make me wait long. *Okay,* he texted. *We'll think of something.*

"We spent Christmas Eve together – I told Mom and Sarah I was spending it with friends, like I was a naughty middle school kid. It wasn't like I had a curfew – I was almost eighteen, and I'd stayed out overnight before."

Adam smiled; the tears were still wet on his cheeks, like a child, but he was caught up in the memories of happier times. That we were the ones with whom he was sharing them, because an explanation was necessary and because he didn't have anyone else – it touched me.

"Mom had emotionlessly delivered *the talk* when I was about fifteen, after she noticed the frequent phone calls I was getting from the girls at school. She'd explained rather clinically what they wanted from me, and told me what my responsibilities were in giving it to them. When she was sure that I had a firm grasp on these most important biological aspects of the birds and the bees, she let me go my own way. It wasn't long after that when I met Jeremy, but of course, *he* wasn't allowed to stay out overnight. But Rolf was allowed." Adam grinned. "As long as I called and let Mom know I was all right – she trusted me to stay out overnight and not get myself or anyone else in any trouble.

"But I didn't spend the night with David. He made me go home in the early hours of Christmas Day. He said I should spend it with Mom and Sarah, and . . . He also gave me this big speech. He said he knew what I wanted – what I *thought I wanted.* He said that he wanted it, too.

"'But allow me to be a little bit parental just this once,' he said, and when I made a face, he smiled and said, 'Okay, if you don't like that, let me put it another way. Once upon a time, when I was just a couple of years older than you are now, I thought I was in love. I jumped head first into all the things that being in love entails, and the person that I thought I loved – the person that I *worshipped* – he just went ahead and let me do it.

"'And yeah, it was all sunshine and daffodils for a little while. He was everything I'd imagined he could be, and blah, blah, blah. But after a very short time, I discovered that he wasn't *entirely* what I wanted him to be. It's a great big world, and he was a lot of things to a lot of people – my ideas of happily ever after weren't realistic in the framework of *his* life. I still loved him, but . . . I also suffered. Disillusionment, heartache.

"'I'm telling you this cautionary tale for this reason, Adam. Perhaps, if I would've hesitated, just a little bit . . . If I would've waited and watched, I might've seen the truth, that this person wasn't a god, made especially to my order. He was just a guy. If I would've waited – I still would've loved him. Everybody loved him. But maybe it wouldn't've hurt so much when I had to tell him goodbye and he didn't care in the least, and maybe it wouldn't've hurt so much . . . I would've realized that the things he did were just the things he'd always done.'

"I wasn't getting what he was trying to tell me. It must've showed on my face, because he said, 'I'm just asking you to wait a little while before you jump into this with both feet. There are *so many* obstacles – there's the difference in our ages, and all this other bullshit. Things'll never be easy for us.' He laughed suddenly. 'I'm gonna sound like a pervert – because that's how it'll seem to people; I'm not your father, but I'm surely *old enough* to be your father. But I have to say it anyway, like a pervert would: if we get involved with each other, it's gonna have to be *our little secret.*'

"I grinned, and stepped closer to him. I told him I was good at keeping secrets, and I knew what I wanted. He held up his hand and said, 'I want you to think about it. This has all the possibilities to become an incredibly big mess. Look at all the angles. The truth of *Oh, sweet Jesus, what'll happen if Mom and Sarah find out?* Give yourself the benefit of your intellect – which is something I never gave myself.' He kissed me goodbye, and I reluctantly went home."

Adam sighed, and a shadow of the grief that would soon overtake him crossed his face. "During the week between Christmas and New Year's, I heard that one of the girls I'd gone to school with had committed suicide. I hadn't known her past saying hi, and I didn't know the precise reasons that had led her to take that irrevocable step. I wondered all the things that everybody always wonders: could anything have been said, could anything have been done, that might've stopped her, might've changed her mind? I talked to David about it; he just restated the obvious. 'Some people find their lives unbearable, and they feel like they have to escape.'

"We talked about other things, but that idea of *escape* stuck in my head. I wasn't depressed, I certainly wasn't suicidal – I saw new vistas of life opening up for me, as soon as David felt that I'd *thought about it* long enough. I didn't have to think about it anymore – I was already in love with him, just from the conversations we'd had, the thoughts and feelings we'd shared. I was just like he'd been, I guess – I couldn't see any way that he would hurt me. That's probably how he'd felt about the guy that had wound up hurting *him*.

"I didn't want to wait anymore, but I used my intellect, like he'd told me to do. I didn't want to kill myself, but I realized that life *would* become unbearable, if Mom and Sarah ever found out that we'd met. We'd have to pretend the kind of relationship that was . . . Well, it was an utter lie.

"David was vibrant and sexy, and the fact that he was thirty years older than me didn't matter to me at all." Adam frowned. "Do you see what I'm trying to say? Sooner or later, Mom was gonna wonder where I was going and who I was seeing. If I let her know that I'd been palling around with my "dad," if she ever saw us interact, eventually she would figure it out, and then the shit would hit the fan. I couldn't pretend to be David's son. The situation was untenable; it would become unbearable, just as it had for that poor girl that had killed herself. But I didn't want to give him up. We had to think up some solution.

"On New Year's Eve, I went to see him in LA, and I drew for him the parallels between the dismal prospects of our future and how that girl had also seen no other way out of her problems. He said, 'So you're set on a future with me? You've known me for what? Less than two months? And you're ready to risk everything you've ever known? Christ, Adam, what will people say?'

"I reiterated that it was just how someone contemplating ending it all must feel. There was nothing to be done. But something had to be done. I told him I loved him, but of course, death wasn't the answer."

Adam finally looked at me, then back at Parker once again. "David laughed. He said, 'Maybe death is the answer.'

"I must've looked frightened then, because he laughed again, and hugged me. 'I don't mean actual death, Adam! Jesus, since I've met you, I've never felt more alive! I want to . . . *eat you!* It takes every ounce of self-control I possess . . .'

"He hugged me again, kissed me . . . I said, 'About that . . .'

"He shook his head, stepped away from me, but I could see the desire in his eyes. He went over to the couch, as far away as he could get. He picked his laptop up from the coffee table; after a minute, he read, *'The age of consent in California is eighteen. It is illegal for anyone to engage in sexual intercourse with a minor (someone under the age of eighteen), unless they are that person's spouse.'*

"I sat down next to him on the couch and put my hand on his knee. I said, 'Let's get married, then.'

He smiled at my attempt at seduction, then got up and sat in a chair. 'That's all under appeal in high court at the moment,' he said. 'But maybe we could become the spokesmen for the cause, right? It would certainly grab headlines. *SoCal lawyer wants to marry his minor son. Claims DNA test will refute biological paternity.* Christ, Adam! I'd be disbarred. Your mother would die of embarrassment.' He set the laptop back on the coffee table, ran both hands over his face, and declared, 'I need a drink.'

"'All right,' I said. I'd never had more than a couple of beers with him in the past, but I knew where he kept his liquor.

"'Not here . . . alone,' he said. 'It's New Year's Eve. We should go out, celebrate.'

I told him jokingly that he was afraid of me, and he grinned and said that he was afraid of himself. He told me he had to make a few phone calls to find a party, and in about a half an hour or so, we were on our way.

"David's confession that his willpower was nearing the end of its tether made me feel smug." Adam winked at my partner, and Parker smiled back at him. "In the car, he slapped my hand off his knee like an offended schoolgirl. He said, 'Once you're eighteen . . .'

"I wouldn't be eighteen for another six months, and I told him that I didn't want to wait that long.

"'We'll go to Vegas for your birthday,' he promised. 'As reward for your patience and my . . . *stoicism.'*

"I could tell he was steadfast, at least for the moment, so I stopped trying to touch him and asked where we were going.

"We're going to learn how to disappear,' he said.

"I thought he meant it in some kind of metaphorical, *get wasted on New Year's Eve* kind of way; I thought he was telling me that he'd surely stop saying no after he'd had a few drinks.

"I contemplated that idea in silence, and when I didn't make further conversation, he said, 'Do you think you could do that, Adam?' He smiled with a touch of grimness. 'For *our love?'*

"'Do what?' I asked.

"'Give up everything. *To die: to sleep; no more.* At least to all the people in our lives. I know a guy . . . He could make us disappear.' Then David laughed it off, like he was kidding, and added, 'Regardless, he throws a mean party.'

"We drove for a long time; almost all the way back to Riverside. Then we got off the freeway and David had me read the directions he'd written down. We arrived at some little house. It was still early – maybe only nine o'clock – but the party was already in full swing.

"David said the party-thrower was some friend of his from college, but when the guy opened the door, he was positively gobsmacked to see David standing there. Speechless. David gave him a hug, said, 'This is Adam,' and we all went out on the back porch where it wasn't so loud."

I noticed that Parker was holding his breath. Adam was about to implicate the third party in the scam. Would it be Max or Charlie?

"David's old college buddy stared at me like I had three heads, but he didn't talk much, so after a few minutes, I went inside to get a beer. I wasn't in a hurry to go back outside and be started at, so I mingled with the other people at the party. After a few more minutes, David also came back in.

"He asked if we could have a private word with this Asian guy that had been talking me up. The guy was a little drunk – he looked at David, then he looked at me, then back at David again – then he smiled and said, 'Okay, why the hell not?'

"He was surprised when David went back outside to the car. I guess he thought we wanted to . . . It was New Year's Eve and all . . ." Parker didn't get the picture Adam was trying to paint, so he continued quickly, "Well, never mind what he *thought* we wanted. We sat in the car and David got immediately to the point. He said that a little bird had told him that this guy was the man to talk to if a person was in a bind and needed to . . . to become someone else. Without batting an eyelash, the guy said that such a thing could indeed be accomplished, if the price was right. He gave David his number and said if he was still interested after the party – he said he was anxious to get back to the party, since *we* didn't want to party with him – then David should call him about it.

"We drove back to LA. I asked David for details about what he had in mind. He said he would lay it all out for me later, after he talked further with the Asian guy. Then he said to forget about it for the time being – or to think about it, whichever I wanted. It was New Year's Eve, he said, always his favorite holiday. 'All the sins of the previous year can be forgotten; all the sins of the new year have yet to occur.'

"I took this as the invitation I'd been waiting for, but again I was mistaken. David didn't even make me a drink. We watched the replay of the ball dropping in New York, and after one kiss at midnight, he told me he loved me." Again Adam smiled at Parker, and again Parker smiled back. "Then he said, 'Drive safe,' and kicked me to the curb."

Now Adam's smile faltered a bit. He arose, asked if we wanted more coffee, freshened our cups and his own, and returned to his chair.

"For the next five months, we continued to meet in secret. We talked about disappearing – finally gave a name to it –"

"Faking your own deaths," I said, and was surprised at the sadness in my voice. I cleared my throat.

Adam nodded.

"Did you see Charlie – the Asian guy – again?" Parker asked.

Adam's eyebrows went up in surprise. "Is that his name? Did he tell you how to find me?"

Parker shook his head. "We got his name from David's old college buddy. The one from the party. But we didn't . . . get to talk to Charlie."

"I never saw him again. David and I didn't discuss any specifics – not about the names we would assume, or anything like that, not about how we would actually go about it. Nothing was concrete at first.

"The thing he was most concerned about, of course, was how I thought I was gonna handle giving up Mom and Sarah and everything else in my life."

"What about what he'd be giving up? His law practice? His friend, his partner, Mr. –?" Parker looked at me – if I hadn't known better, I almost would've believed he'd forgotten John Stevens, as if he was just some random family acquaintance we'd talked to. Parker was good. I supplied his favorite attorney's name, and he asked Adam if he'd ever met Mr. Stevens.

Adam answered the question with a question. "Have *you* met him?"

"We interviewed him in connection with the case –"

"And what was your impression of him?"

Parker opened his mouth, but no words came out. *He* was supposed to be the one asking the questions. Again Adam smiled. *Boyishly,* I thought, though he was surely no boy. He was twenty-five, Parker's age – and the stories he'd already told about adolescent trysts, always at his instigation, about his desire for David – plus, he looked too much like Billy Munro for me to mistake him for a boy.

"I met John a few times," he said, relieving Parker of the necessity of describing his own *impression.* "I found him to be stand-offish, almost . . . unfriendly. Watchful. John stared at me, just like David's other college pal did. It wasn't . . . I didn't find him in any way *welcoming,* I guess."

"How did David feel about leaving John?" Parker wanted to know. "And their law practice?"

Adam shrugged. "He said he knew John would be sad – but then they were all gonna be sad. John and Mom and Sarah. Everyone we knew. They were gonna think we were dead, and David wanted to know how that was gonna sit with me. 'It's going to break your mother's heart,' he said.

"'Either way, it's gonna break her heart,' I said, because I knew it was true. She'd never be able to deal with the insanely novel idea that her son was in love with her ex-husband, her daughter's father.

"And at that moment, David suddenly couldn't deal with it either. He said, 'This is nuts, Adam! I never should've started this. You think you want to give everything up for me – you don't even know me!'

"This made me angry. I was ready, and now *he* was having second thoughts. I sneered. 'I know you, David. You're the guy that says he loves me, but won't show me. Maybe you're right. Maybe it *is* crazy, me thinking about abandoning everything for someone who won't even let me touch him.'"

Adam smiled with a touch of embarrassment. "David wasn't like me, always flying off the handle. I've always been that way. But he was never one to even *react,* nonetheless *overreact.* He'd *act,* but always calmly. From what he'd told me about his life – he'd said that there hadn't even been much of a scene when he'd found out that Mom'd been cheating on him. He'd told me that there hadn't been any screaming or reproachful tears. He'd just told her he wanted a divorce, moved out, and let his lawyer handle it. He was an evolved, thinking kind of person.

"So he didn't react to my smart-assed remarks then. 'I've lived a pretty tame life, Adam,' he said slowly. 'My wild days were definitely wild, true, but they were brief. Then I was the doting husband for ten years, and then . . .' He gritted his teeth in a flash of bitterness so complete that it surprised me. Then it was gone, and he said quickly, 'That got me Sarah, whom I love. But Sarah's a grown woman now. She won't miss me too much.

"'In the years since the divorce . . . A recital of the few women I've dated – there were no men – that peccadillo had gone dormant, or so it seemed, until I saw you.' He smiled. 'A listing of the ladies I've known wouldn't raise a single eyebrow. All in all, a pretty sedate fifty years.'

"He shook his head in disbelief. 'But now . . . Now I'm seriously considering chucking it all, everything I've been, everything I had left to be . . . for you. I love you. But you gotta give me this one thing, Adam. If I ever have to stand before the world's stern and incapable-of-understanding judgment about this crazy, wonderful thing, I want to be able to say, "Well, your honors, *my princes and my noble peers,* at least he wasn't underage."'

"I wasn't amused. I was angry and frustrated and suddenly, unwillingly, doubtful. I said, 'That sounds like bullshit to me, Counsellor. It's only another couple of weeks. Maybe you should sequester yourself and *think about it* till then. Maybe you'll change your mind and decide you want to chuck *me.*'

"I turned and dramatically stalked out, without looking at him. I didn't want to see his reaction. If I'd hurt him, I didn't want to know it – I'd *wanted* to hurt him, but even as I left, I knew it was childish impatience that had driven me, and if I saw pain in his eyes, I'd hate myself later when I thought about it *with my intellect.*" Adam frowned. "And if I hadn't hurt him – if this was all just some kind of meaningless, unfathomable *tease* on his part, some kind of game to him – I didn't want to see that either.

"I didn't hear from him for two days. I was just about to text him – *Hey, David, wtf? I* literally had my finger poised over the *Send* button, when my phone beeped with a text from Mom, asking me to come downstairs.

"Her eyes were big and round with a kind of disbelieving surprise, but as usual, she got directly to the point. 'There's someone outside that wants to meet you. He didn't want to come into the house.'

"I had no idea who it could possibly be, someone who wanted to meet me, someone whose arrival had made Mom look like she'd been told the greatest riddle in the universe and just couldn't figure it out. She opened the door.

"David was facing the other way – just to be theatrical, I think. He turned, smiled, extended his hand. 'Hi, Adam. I'm David Walker." He looked down, scuffed the porch with his toe like a remorseful schoolboy. 'I'd like to say, *We met at the hospital,* but we all know that isn't true, so . . .' He looked up, looked *through* Mom, like she wasn't even there. 'So I thought maybe it was time we did meet. I was wondering what plans you had for college.'"

"Your mom said you were surprised to see him," Parker said.

Adam nodded. "I was *utterly* surprised. He hustled me out to the car before I could make a sound. It didn't seem like he was going to say anything, either, but then he stopped the car at the end of the driveway and grinned at me. 'David Walker is taking his soon-to-no-longer-be-a-minor son to Las Vegas for his birthday.' He handed me a piece of paper that listed reservations at the *Bellagio,* still two weeks away, when I would indeed be eighteen. He said, 'I thought your mother should know about it.'

"We drove back to LA, and had dinner with John, to celebrate the successful conclusion of some divorce case. So pleased was the ex-Mrs. Whoever with the verdict, John said, she'd invited him to go to Europe with her to celebrate her newly single state. David was in a great mood – he congratulated John, and told him that he was planning a little vacation of his own, that we were going to Vegas in a couple of weeks. John looked dubiously at me and said, 'Then I guess you won't miss me.'"

"Do you think he knew?" Parker asked suddenly. "That you and David were . . . That yours was more than a father-son kind of . . . friendship?"

Adam shrugged. "Maybe. I don't know. If I'd had to guess, I would've said that Mr. Stevens also . . . ." Here he smiled broadly at Parker. *"Played for both teams,* as the charming idiom states. It was just something about the way he looked at me. So he undoubtedly knew that David was also a . . . *switch-hitter.* They'd been friends for a long time." He shrugged again. "David didn't talk about John very much, past mentioning that they'd all gone to college together, he and John and Matt –"

"Max," Parker corrected, before he could stop himself.

Adam smiled apologetically. "If you say so. I've never been very good with names, and it's not like David talked about these people all the time. He'd told me that he'd gone to SFSU for a little while, before he met Mom, with John and . . . *Max,* and the guy he'd been in love with."

"Do you remember his name?"

Again Adam smiled in apology. "I wanna say . . . Donny? Bobby, maybe? Like I say, David only mentioned him once or twice."

Adam sipped his coffee, and I thought about what a singularly poor witness he'd make in court. He couldn't recall any names. I pictured the attorney: "When you say *Matt,* Mr. Walker, are you referring to Max Haycroft?"

"Objection! Leading the witness!"

This wasn't ever going to go to court, at least not with any kind of examination and cross-examination. I imagined that if the whole identity-fraud crime didn't just get swept under the rug entirely, the most Adam would be in for would be some kind of fine, maybe some back taxes, all adjudicated and paid off quickly. I wasn't sure – I'm a cop, not a lawyer. All I knew was that Virginia Walker had powerful friends: they'd kept David's resurrection and second demise out of the papers; surely the general public would never learn that her son had also faked his own death. If he had to pay for it, legal-wise, he'd pay for it quietly.

So it didn't matter what kind of witness Adam would make. His need to explain, to *tell someone,* and our sitting here listening while he did so was tying up a lot of loose ends. It was solving the case.

Adam continued. "But to answer your original question, Sergeant, uh –?"

"Parker."

The kid that was bad with names then used the common mnemonic, the correct etiquette. He repeated my partner's name back to him. "To answer your original question, Sergeant Parker – maybe John did know about *the nature of our relationship.* Maybe he guessed. I don't think David would've told him – I was a minor and all that. But . . . I dunno. They'd been friends for a long time. David trusted John – maybe he trusted him with *our little secret.* All I know for sure is that John certainly didn't like me."

Adam returned to his explanation. "After dinner, we said goodnight to John and went back to David's place. He said, 'I'm going to demonstrate for you the brilliance of this disclosure. You're gonna call your mom, tell her you're having a great time talking to your dear old dad, and that you'll see her in the morning. She won't object.'

"I smiled and tried to hug him, but he shook his head. 'I love you, Adam,' he told me, 'but you have to sleep in the other room. It's only for two more weeks.'

"Of course I pouted about that – it was *really* getting tiresome. But I realized that he'd made it possible for us to spend all the time we wanted together, without sneaking around. That had also begun to be tiresome. And we were going to Vegas soon . . .

"In the meantime, he acted exactly like a father newly acquainted with his abandoned son would act. He even had Sarah come down and hang out with us in LA a couple of times. We were just a big, happily reunited family, patriarch and adoring children. I told Mom that I'd always been curious about him – she just looked blankly at me. I'd never mentioned this curiosity to her before, but what could she say? Wasn't it natural for a son to want to get to know his father?"

Adam paused. He swirled the dregs of coffee in his cup, and didn't look up from it when he spoke again. "Vegas was . . . phenomenal. Transcendental." He giggled, still not looking at us, and stated conversationally, *"Oh sweet mystery of life at last I've found you.* When the clock struck twelve on June 1ˢᵗ . . ."* Now Adam sobered, and a tear dropped into his coffee cup. *"Nothing in his life became him like the leaving* of this ridiculous, artificial stricture that he'd placed upon himself. I was officially an adult, a man like himself, and David cast off all reticence, *as 'twere a careless trifle."*

Adam cleared his throat, embarrassed at his borrowed poesy, and finally looked up at Parker, then at me. "Needless to say, after Vegas, we were agreed. We would disappear, go somewhere where we could be what we were. It took another four months to prepare, to finalize things. I guess David had been making the arrangements all along, with . . . what's his name?"

"Charlie," Parker supplied. *"Charles Xavier Wang."*

Adam blinked. "Really?"

Parker nodded, smiled.

Adam continued. "We set the boat adrift, actually *swam* back to shore –"

"How did you – someone was waiting to pick you up?" Parker asked.

"It was a Mexican guy. Some friend of David's, from San Francisco or San Jose or somewhere. From college, maybe? I'm not sure."

Here was one of the joys of police work, when another one of the disparate pieces of the jumbled puzzle fits into place. I imagined Andre, Lupe's brother, incarcerated on a possession charge, lo, those many years ago. There he was, in prison – whatever public defender he'd been assigned surely hadn't helped him. He'd kept in touch with his sister – Lupe would've wrote him letters to keep his spirits up, told him the gossip, that law-student David had knocked up the prissy sorority girl, and that they'd had to get married. Maybe Lupe told her brother that John and David had transferred to UCLA.

Maybe somewhere along the line, after he was paroled, Andre again had need of a mouthpiece – maybe he'd looked up his old pals, John and David. John probably wouldn't have taken his calls – immigrant ex-cons were not his type of clientele – but maybe David had helped him out, maybe kept him out a prison a second time. And when David had needed a ride away from his old life, maybe he'd asked Andre to return the favor.

Maybe it was all bullshit; maybe the Mexican guy that Adam had mentioned wasn't Andre at all. It was an insignificant detail – I wasn't going to ask Adam if he remembered the guy's name, because surely he didn't. Still, it felt good for me to assume it was Andre, because if police work teaches you nothing else, it teaches you that people maintain connections over the years.

Adam was saying, "We just stepped into our new identities. David handed me a driver's license with the name *Mark Bennett* on it. Though I've never actually seen them, he said there was also a social security card, and a birth certificate –"

"And it lists Kevin Bennett as your father?" I asked.

Adam grinned. "No, Detective. We were trying to get away from all that, now weren't we? My father was some guy name George, David told me. I guess George was supposed to be his cousin . . . So that's what we were, too, if anybody asked. We were cousins, a few times removed. The same last name thing would help if there was . . ." Adam's face clouded over and he paused. "If there was ever any kind of . . . emergency. In a pinch, he or I could claim that we were more closely related.

"We lived in Phoenix for a year or so, then when ASU started their undergraduate program in Lake Havasu City, we moved there. I took the majority of my classes online, though. Got my Business

Administration degree and all, and hasn't that helped with running a grocery store?" Adam grinned. "In Havasu, we rented a little trailer, right on the river."

The thought crossed my mind that David Walker, who'd *never been on a boat in his life,* according to John Stevens, had developed an affinity for the water after "dying" in a maritime mishap.

"David got a job at some hole-in-the wall personal injury firm. He worked as a paralegal."

"And that paid for your tuition to ASU?' Parker asked in surprise.

Adam was smug. "David had plenty of money, Sergeant. He'd transferred a bunch of his . . . investments, I guess, before . . . He had money in overseas accounts."

A shadow crossed Adam's face again, and I wondered if he was thinking about what was going to happen to all that money now. David Walker was dead, twice, and Kevin Bennett hadn't actually ever existed, so any kind of inheritance – he was still legally David's son – any kind of inheritance was liable to be held up in court for years.

But then I realized that I was just thinking like a poor girl. The scion of the Walker family – in name if not in blood – had never worried about money a day in his life, not when his name had been Walker, not when it became Bennett. His mother's fortune had always been there when Adam was young, as unconsidered as the air he breathed, and David had successfully transferred enough of his own not unsubstantial assets to foot the bills for their new lives.

Adam underlined this point. "David didn't actually have to work at all, and surely not at this little nothing place – but he said he had to do something, and after years of estate law and millionaire's divorces, it amused him to pretend to be nothing more than a paralegal working for an ambulance chaser named Marty, in Lake Havasu City, Party-Town, USA.

"After I graduated, David asked me what I thought about moving back to California. We'd been dead for almost five years, he said. We were forgotten. But he didn't want to move back to LA or any other big city. He asked me if I was okay with that – some little town – and I said that I wanted to be wherever he was.

"He told me that he'd looked at property here in Anza before, when he was married to my mother, as a weekend getaway and a tax write-off. He said he liked the quiet, and that we get a little bit of a change of seasons. It's not Big Bear, but it snows sometimes. So we picked this place. 'Now we have to find a hobby,' he said with a laugh. 'Maybe get us a little shop or something.'

"David's shyster boss in Arizona also dabbled in bankruptcies; he sometimes flipped real estate in foreclosure. He said he knew a guy who knew a guy, right here in town. *That* guy said he had just the place.

"This realtor told us that Weaver's Market wasn't in foreclosure, however. The old couple owned the patch of ground outright. They lived in a little trailer behind the store. But through a stubborn unwillingness to change with the times, Mr. Weaver had run his business into the ground." Adam pantomimed an incoming bomb and an explosion. "The bright and shiny new 7-11 just down the road hadn't helped. The old man had finally decided to cut his losses and put his lot up for sale, but nobody was buying for the price he was asking.

"David told the realtor he wasn't interested, then we drove out and looked at the place anyway. The *For Sale* sign was torn and faded; the store was dark. The freezer and cold cases were empty; the power had been shut off because the Weavers couldn't pay the bill. They were sitting out in front, selling vegetables from their garden on a table. The wolf was literally at the door.

"David fell in love with the place immediately. Always a master of the delicate art of negotiation, he succeeded in talking cagey old Henry Weaver down from his ridiculous price. In exchange for this reduction, David said he'd let them stay on in the home they'd known for decades, rent free. He'd pay them to man the store for him, but he'd handle the business end of it."

"The Weavers are very fond of you," I told Adam.

"Yeah, they're great people. The salt of the earth." He frowned in sorrow. "I don't know what's going to happen to them now."

He looked carefully at us for a long moment, then sighed once more. He spoke quietly. "We'd only lived here for a few months. Everything was wonderful. We were *so* happy. Mr. Weaver was grateful for David's kindness and impressed with his business acumen. I frequently overheard him bragging to the old-timers about how *that boy from Arizona knows his shit,* how he was turning the store around. Mrs. Weaver mothered David and grandmothered me. Everything was perfect.

"Then, one Saturday afternoon, I slipped and fell off a step ladder. It wasn't from any great height. I landed on my clumsy ass, bumped my arm on a shelf. . ." Adam unconsciously rubbed his left elbow. "Anyone else would've been okay, but not me. The pain was . . . intense. David took me down the hill to Temecula Valley Hospital. Of course we didn't have any insurance, but David had cash, which was quite good enough.

"They took x-rays, discovered I'd fractured my elbow. Dr. Perez would later tell us that she was puzzled as to why someone like me – someone who seemed healthy – she was puzzled as to why my bones had splintered like so much driftwood from a simple fall. She ordered a bunch of lab tests – blood and urine and all that. A few days later, she called and asked us to come in, when the test results came back. She was very solemn when she told us the news. My bones had begun to thin because I was in a rather advanced stage of kidney disease. She asked if I'd noticed any other symptoms – chronic tiredness, swollen ankles, shortness of breath and so forth – and I said yes, I'd experienced a few of those."

Adam shook his head. "Dr. Perez tried to be upbeat. She told me – and David, whom she assumed was my father – he'd indicated that he was on the paperwork for expediency's sake. The disease shouldn't progress too much farther, now that we'd caught it, she said. We could control it with diet and medicine . . ." Again Adam shook his head. "But it didn't go quite like that. I didn't get any worse, symptom-wise, but last year I started dialysis. It was once a month at first. Now it's once a week."

"How do you . . . pay for it?" Parker whispered.

"Like I said, David's got plenty of money. But money wasn't the issue. We'd thought of damn near everything when we'd become the Bennetts . . . Everything but this. I've got a college degree and a social security card, a driver's license and a birth certificate. What I don't have are any medical records.

"Where did this disease come from? Had I showed any symptoms, been treated for them in the past?" Adam smiled grimly. "Who was Mark Bennett and where was his shot record?

"Luckily, when they called in the orthopedist to consult in the ER, we got Dr. Perez. She was more concerned with getting my arm set than with answering any of these questions. Many blanks on many forms are often over looked when one is paying cash for services. But once the test results came back . . . She had to know."

No wonder the good doctor was so uncooperative, I thought. *She's another party to this fraud.*

"You told the doctor that you weren't really Mark Bennett?" Parker blurted in undisguised, unprofessional amazement. He was usually cool, but sometimes he reacted to amazing statements. "You told her that you'd faked your own deaths?"

He couldn't believe that the doctor had lied so completely, that she'd so calmly read off all those things from the HIPPAA regulations, knowing all the while that Mark Bennett was indeed not who he claimed to be. Yeah, Parker was usually cool, but sometimes the cop-show drama of a consummate liar like Dr. Perez gripped him. And he was way too fond of that expression: *faked your own DEATH??*

Adam shook his head. "David concocted a tamer, less . . . *illegal* story. He told her that he truly was Kevin Bennett – he wasn't the one having to produce any medical history – but I wasn't actually his son.

"He made up a *little hometown jam* for me, as Bruce was wont to say . . ." The Springsteen reference went completely over Parker's head. "Again, nothing illegal. I'd messed around with the wrong girl, and her father and brothers had threatened my life. David implied that these men were in a position to make good on their threats, so I'd had to get the hell out of Dodge for my own safety. David told Dr. Perez that we'd been friends in Arizona, and since he was moving to Anza anyway, he'd manufactured a son for his deceased brother George, so my girlfriend's vengeful kin wouldn't be able to find me. Kinda like witness protection." Adam smiled winningly.

It was exactly the scenario that Parker had once imagined as the reason that Adam had contacted David, based on vague hints given to him by Sarah Walker about Adam's fascinating (non-existent), online girlfriend. In spite of this fact, Parker was still incredulous. He said, "And the doctor bought it?"

Adam shrugged. "Two things. Dr. Perez didn't really care about who I was or where I came from, or even my medical history, for that matter. She wanted to make sure I got treated for the disease I was afflicted with – I guess how I'd come to have it wasn't really that important, medically speaking. And secondly . . . From almost the first moment she met him, Dr. Perez had developed a rather extensive . . . *crush* on David."

Parker still didn't believe it. "So he's been stringing her along for what? Almost two years? All the time she's been treating you?"

Adam shrugged again. "Dr. Perez became our family physician. She still makes recommendations, but I see a specialist at a place called DaVita for dialysis. Dr. Perez laid the groundwork. She lowered all those red flags about my non-existent medical history, stuff like that. I've even got a little medical insurance, thanks to her. David expressed his gratitude to her for all that . . ." This thought twisted in the wind for a brief second, then Adam let it die. "Sometimes, we have dinner with Dr. Perez and her daughter, Angela. She's a few years younger than me. Sometimes we all go out to the movies together.

"Dr. Perez would like to see Angela and me become more than friends." Adam offered his best boyish smile again. "And we really are good friends – we have an understanding. She doesn't know . . . what I am, but I know what she is. I act as her beard. I go down to Temecula to pick her up for "dates," which makes her mom happy. But then I drop Angela at her girlfriend's house, and she assumes that I go and check out the action at the local bar. Sometimes I just go back home; sometimes David and I have a night out on the town. Then I go back and pick Angela up and take her home to her mom's. Her dad lives up north somewhere. Angela says that she's not yet prepared to come out to him or her mom." Adam frowned. "I understand that completely."

He saw from Parker's expression that he wanted further explanation of David's *gratitude* to Angela's mom. "As far as how friendly David was with Dr. Perez . . . Well, I guess you could say that he was friendly enough. He didn't make her any promises, but he went over to see her when she asked him."

"And that was okay with you?" I asked.

Adam smiled. "David loved me, Detective. He'd given up everything for me. His occasional visits to a lonely woman – kind, helpful Dr. Perez – it helped to keep our secret intact. It was okay with me.

"With the dialysis, my condition has more or less stabilized. But I'm tied to it. I have to go once a week. So, a few months ago, Dr. Perez and the doctors at DaVita started talking about a transplant.

"There's a screening process, and it was up in the air as to whether my sketchy medical history would hold up to it. Another reason I didn't mind David's visiting Dr. Perez, Detective – she got herself checked to see if she could be a donor. If she loved David . . . Well, I guess she loves me, too. But she wasn't a match. Nor was Angela, nor David himself.

"The next likely candidate was my mother, but she's really too old to be giving up a kidney. And to approach her would mean . . . When she found out that we weren't actually dead . . ." Adam sighed; again he looked down at his coffee cup. He set it on the table abruptly and met our eyes once more. "David was sure that Sarah would keep our secret, at least for long enough to find out if she was a suitable donor."

"That's a lot to ask," Parker murmured.

Adam nodded. "His plan was to sneak into her room . . . He was going to convince her to leave the house with him, tell her that I needed her. He was going to explain what we'd done by making up some lie about a criminal enterprise . . . Embezzlement from the firm or some other claptrap. He'd had to disappear because of it, and I'd volunteered to go with him.

"He said that she'd be outraged, at first, but he was convinced that she'd keep her mouth shut. She wouldn't want to see her father go to prison for . . . grand theft, or whatever story he was going to tell her. He was also convinced that if she was a suitable donor, she'd be willing to give me a kidney, if it meant saving my life."

Adam shook his head, and the tears welled again. "As you can see, it's not like I'm bedridden. The dialysis . . . A transplant isn't vital right now. My life doesn't need saving." He sobbed, and Parker held him again.

Adam cried into my partner's shoulder for a time, then once again got ahold of himself. "I guess I gotta go back and face the music now. Try to un-break my mother's heart." His beautiful blue eyes, dark with sorrow, red-rimmed with grief, pleaded with us. "What should I tell her?"

Parker smiled kindly. "I'd go with the embezzlement story, Adam. Anything else –"

"Anything else . . . She wouldn't understand. She *still* won't understand. Going on the lam with Dad – that sounds . . . I dunno."

"Like an adventure," Parker suggested. "Something an intelligent, eighteen-year-old kid might be down for. You can say that you really didn't consider all the pain it would cause . . . She's gonna be so glad to have you back, she's not gonna be thinking too much about *why* you left. It's a good enough reason."

Adam considered. "I'd have to talk to John, first." He grimaced. "Get him to back me up. Admit to Mom – say, yes, some money had disappeared . . . He didn't say anything before, because what was the point? David was dead . . ."

I was amazed at the lengths to which Adam Walker had gone for love; at the further lengths he was willing to stretch. He'd faked his own death to be with David, and now he was willing to invent another lie, to collude with John Stevens, whom he was sure didn't like him – to save his mother from the truth of the real reason he'd run off with David. The love they'd shared – Virginia Walker would never understand it.

I thought that perhaps Adam underestimated his mother on that score.

Adam asked Parker, "Do you think John'll go for it?"

"It's worth a shot. Either way, it's your word against his. If he won't back you up – maybe he was just too dumb to notice the embezzlement. Like I say, I don't think your mom's gonna care, anyway."

****

As we were walking out the door, I got a text from one of the uniforms I'd sent to look for David's car. He told me that the management of the Canyon Crest Towne Centre routinely had anything that'd been there for more than a few days towed. He and his partner were currently at the impound yard, looking for a vehicle registered to Kevin Bennett. He said the place towed a lot of cars, from all over town, and their record-keeping was poor; they were going to be there for a while.

Adam said he'd just take his own car and follow us back to Riverside. I told him that we'd call on the way and see if John Stevens was available for a meeting.

"If not, you can stay with me until you're ready to see your mom," Parker volunteered.

I was surprised at this largesse, but on the other hand, I was not in the least surprised. Because of Adam's grieving vulnerability, Parker wanted to help the kid. I corrected myself again: if I didn't think of my partner as a kid, I couldn't think of Adam that way either. It was only his loss, his *lostness* – the love of his life was gone – that made him seem fragile and childlike to me, and Parker as well.

But it wasn't entirely Adam's sadness that had moved my partner to make this beyond-the-call-of-duty offer. I could tell that after only this short period of time, Parker had developed a genuine fondness for the bereft young man. After the trying times to come – Adam's meeting with John Stevens, his reunion with his mother and sister – I could picture Parker and Adam as friends, palling around together.

It wasn't love – despite any veiled comments to the contrary during the course of this investigation, I was pretty confident that

Parker was a heterosexual – at least I most fervently hoped that he was. No, it wasn't a *crush* that Parker had suddenly developed for Adam. He just *liked* him. Everybody liked him. I recalled Mrs. Weaver's smile at the mention of his name, Mr. Weaver's protectiveness. And there was also Dr. Perez's willingness to incur God-only-knew-what kind of professional censures – manufacturing a medical history so one's patient could obtain health insurance is also fraud. Yet she'd risked that for him.

It occurred to me that nature trumped nurture in Adam Walker's case. If there was a *likeability gene,* he'd surely inherited it from Billy Munro, and it'd been advantageous to his life, without Billy ever being present to instruct him in its use.

****

I decided to drive this time. When we were back on the road, my partner said, "I really feel sorry for him, Jan. If David Walker was still alive –"

"I know, Parker. But he's young. He'll grieve for a long time, but surely someone else'll come along someday. Someone that he'll love as much as he loved David."

Parker frowned severely at me. "What I was gonna say is, if David Walker was still alive, I'd like to punch him in the mouth. He took advantage of Adam. He was just a kid, and David – David was just like Max Haycroft. He took advantage of his more powerful position. He was an old man, confident, familiar with life, and Adam was just a . . . a boy."

This statement *astonished* me. "You're kidding, right? Adam's devastated right now, but from the things he's told us, he's no boy."

"Not now . . . But he was only seventeen when David contacted him."

"Adam wasn't a boy at fifteen, Parker."

"That's not what the law says, Jan."

"Ah, yes. *The law.*" I frowned. "Here we have one of the great thorny conundrums of modern life, Parker. David saw it himself – he was painfully aware of it, in fact. Since he's not here to speak for himself – I guess I'll be his advocate about this age thing."

But who'll be my advocate, Parker? You're not thirty years younger than me, true, but you are almost a decade younger. In some circles, that would draw as many frowns as the disparity between David and Adam.

160

But I'd opened my big mouth; Parker was waiting impatiently for my defense of David. Maybe after I'd spoken it, I'd have a clearer understanding of his opinions on May-December relationships. So far, it wasn't looking too favorable.

"Here's David," I began. "He sees Adam's picture, and he's attracted to him. He texts him, talks to him on the phone. Maybe he thought it wouldn't go any farther than that."

"Maybe he shouldn't have even done that," Parker growled.

"Maybe he thought it wouldn't go any farther than that," I repeated. "Adam responds, asks to meet him; David demurs at first."

"He didn't demur very much."

"This is the point I'm trying to make, Parker. In the history of the world, it's only recently that we've stretched out this concept of childhood. Once upon a time, a woman could be married and have children at fifteen."

"They also used to believe in witchcraft, Jan. They used to draw and quarter people. I think we've evolved from there."

"I'm not suggesting that fifteen-year-olds should start to get married and have kids." *Although it still happens, every day,* I thought, *right here in our* evolved *United States.*

"Then what are you suggesting?"

"Let me ask you a question, Parker. At what age does childhood end, in your estimation? At what age is a person capable of making his own decisions, for good or for bad? At what age is he responsible for the consequences of those decisions, also for good or bad? In California, legally, that age is eighteen, just like you said. David waited until Adam was eighteen."

"That's all just semantics, Jan. Words. Adam was only seventeen when David approached him."

"I've met sixteen-year-old drug dealers, Parker." I laughed without humor. "Schoolboys that aren't old enough to shave yet, running neighborhood syndicates. They're practically criminal masterminds. It's usually some stupid *adult* customer that gets them busted. And I've seen forty-year-old men that still live at home, still have Mom and Dad paying their cellphone bills. At what age are we mature enough to be responsible for our own actions?

"It seems to me that Adam was sure of what he wanted, from the beginning. David made him wait until he was allowed, under the law, to make the decision. Until he was legally allowed to think for himself." When Parker still seemed unconvinced, I asked, "Do you think Adam regrets anything he's done? He's the same age as you –

do you think, if he could go back to his not-hardly-innocent underage days, that he'd now think better of his decisions, from the wisdom and experience of twenty-five? Do you think he'd change anything?"

Parker didn't reply, so I said, "I'm not saying that relationships with a big age difference are always as . . . *equitable* as this one was. But on the other hand, there are power plays among people of the same age, too. You don't have to be a lot older or a lot younger than someone to take advantage of them. Give Adam some credit for maturity, Parker. David didn't seduce an innocent boy. Adam recognized what he wanted. From the beginning, he was adult enough to know his own mind."

Parker still frowned, but I could tell that he knew I was right, because really, Adam's own statement backed up my words. When David first contacted him, he hadn't been an innocent. His smile had been sly when he'd told us of all the girls that had *pawed* him, when he recounted his enjoyment of his encounter with Jeremy, and his relationship with Rolf. But he'd used the word *love* only when he was talking about David.

"The heart wants what it wants I guess," my poetic partner finally admitted. "If there hadn't been this . . . this family thing that made them feel they had to disappear, they probably would've lived happily ever after."

The cynical cop in me spoke before I could stop her. "Or maybe Adam would've woke up on his thirtieth birthday and decided that there was more to life than a boyfriend twice his age. We'll never know. *Adam'll* never know."

"Shit, Jan. Just when you get me to see all the tragic romance of the thing, you gotta go and say something like that." But Parker smiled; there was more than a little bit of the cynical cop to him already, even if he was only twenty-six.

"Why don't you ring up your buddy Counsellor Stevens?" I suggested, ending our discussion of tragic romances. I didn't want to think of age disparities any more at the moment, and besides, there was still a little more work to do on this case. "Tell him we need to see him this afternoon?"

Parker frowned again. "You call him. I don't think he'll take a call from me."

I smiled. "Dial it."

Parker did so and put his phone on speaker. When the receptionist at Stevens and Walker answered, I said, "Detective Dunn for Mr. Stevens, please," and winked at Parker.

The attorney came on the line immediately. "Ah, Detective! Are you calling to tell me you've cobbled together some evidence in your homicide case? Do you have a warrant for my arrest?"

I said, "Not at all Mr. Stevens."

Parker quickly scrawled, *He still was in on it, tho,* on his notepad, and held it up for me to see. I smiled. He'd never change his mind about the lawyer's complicity in Billy's disappearance. It was monumentally too bad that he couldn't prove it.

"We've had a break in the case the taxpayers are expecting us to investigate," I told Stevens. I glanced in the rearview mirror. Adam was right behind us. "I was wondering if you might have a moment this afternoon to discuss it."

There was a heartbeat of silence, then suspicion. "What has this break to do with me?"

"It's not something I want to discuss over the phone," I returned officiously. "Can we drop by your office, in, oh, about two hours?"

Stevens didn't hesitate now. His curiosity had him. "Of course, Detective. I'll see you then."

****

I'm no lip-reader, any more than I'm a shoe expert, but when John Stevens came out of his office and saw Adam, he was positively astonished, and I'd swear on all the Bibles in all the courtrooms in all the world that, from the way he put his lips together, the word that he almost spoke out loud was *Billy.*

I don't know if Parker noticed it, and Adam surely didn't. He didn't even know his daddy's name. He extended his hand and said, "Do you remember me, Mr. Stevens? I'm Adam Walker."

"Of course I remember you, Adam."

You're unforgettable. Wasn't that what David had said about him?

"Mr. Walker would like to have a few words with you before he goes to see his mother," Parker explained.

Stevens's surprise was palpable, but he didn't give it voice. He gestured toward his office.

Adam turned to us, shook our hands. "Do you have a card or something?" he asked Parker. "I want to call you . . ."

Parker handed him a card, and the thought crossed my mind that Adam wanted to call us to make sure we all were on the same page. Whatever story he was gonna concoct with John Stevens – he wanted

163

to tell us its details, and make sure it was the same story we related to his mother and sister, if the opportunity ever presented itself.

Yeah, Adam was no boy. He was these days *an evolved, thinking kind of person;* I thought that maybe he'd picked up these traits from David Walker.

****

Twenty minutes later, we were sitting in Iglesias's office. Or, more precisely, I was. We'd passed her in the hall, and I'd told her that we'd found Adam Walker. She'd said, "Give me ten."

Parker had sat one of the chairs in front of her desk, scrolling through his phone. He'd given our supervisor about three, then said, "I'll be right back, Jan. It was a long drive." He set his phone on the corner of Iglesias's desk and scooted down the hall.

I waited, looked at the photographs and read the commendations on the wall, as I'd done a thousand times before when the boss had said, "Give me ten." I speculated about what aftermath of human failings we'd be assigned to investigate next. Yeah, it was a little maudlin, but I was feeling that way. I tried to think of the Walker women's joy at Adam's return, and not dwell on the sadness of what he'd lost. Surely, seeing his family again would help him through it.

Parker's phone whistled.

No one else was in the room; I could finally satisfy my curiosity as to who had been texting him so much lately. I leaned forward – the text said, *Did you solve the case yet?* ☺ The contact name said *Sarah.*

Well, I'll be damned. It was *Sarah Walker* that'd been whistling at him for days now? It had to be her. How many Sarahs could one person know?

I'd guessed it was a woman, had felt a little spurt of unentitled jealousy about it. What right had I to be jealous if Parker was getting texts from a woman? It was none of my business. If I wanted his phone to whistle when I texted him, then I'd have to speak up . . .

But this wasn't so bad, after all. Adam's sister was part of the investigation; she was concerned about its progress. Of course she'd be texting Parker, requesting updates.

The smiley face was a little much, though.

Parker's phone whistled again.

I've been trying to make that Espresso Martini, but I've run out of vodka ☺ Stop by after work if you want. I'm grilling steaks. You can tell me if your lead paid off.

So much evidence in one little message. *That* Espresso Martini. Parker would know which one. He'd obviously shared it with her. *Stop by the house if you want.* He knew where she lived.

My heart plummeted. My partner was *seeing* Sarah Walker, in more than just an investigative capacity. He hadn't wanted to drive up to Anza at *shift change* yesterday, because she'd just whistled for him. His date last night, the one that had made him late for work, had caused him to apply too much cologne – it had been with her.

Apparently he hadn't discussed the case in too much detail, however. That was clear from her texts. If he had, she would've said, *Did you find Adam in Anza?* or something like that, instead of, *You can tell me if your lead paid off.*

At least he had some professionalism.

I scooted my chair over, so his phone wasn't in my direct line of sight, just as Iglesias strode into her office.

"Well? Where is he?" She picked up a random file from her desk and started looking through it. Always busy is my boss.

"He had to go to the . . . You said ten minutes."

She looked up from the file and blinked in annoyance. "Where's Adam Walker, Dunn?"

Oh, yeah. Not Parker.

My perfect partner appeared in the doorway, right on cue. "We dropped him off at his lawyer's office."

Now Iglesias blinked at *him.* "No shit? Before he went to see his mom? Does he think that she's gonna sue him for being a heartless little bastard?"

My partner let that one slide. "The guy's an old family friend. They're gonna go up to the house together." He picked his phone up off the desk and put it into his pocket without looking at it. I know because I watched him.

Iglesias put the first file down and chose another one. She was so busy, she couldn't even give her full attention to the case we'd just solved. Thumbing through this second file, she asked, "Did he tell you why he and his father faked their own deaths?"

The question was directed at both of us, but I looked at Parker to reply. Adam's embezzlement lie – Parker had supported him on that. Why Adam and David had decided to disappear was of course the lynchpin of the investigation, but the truth of it was that the *why* wasn't a crime. The empty boat – the *how* wasn't a crime, either. The only crime was the fraud of the forged documents that they'd used to become Kevin and Mark Bennett.

Where did Parker's loyalty lie? With his new friend, or with the question that was on everyone's mind?

"He wasn't surprised to see us," Parker said.

That was true.

"He hadn't heard from his dad in more than a week. He figured something had happened to him."

True . . . *enough.*

"He said he wanted to talk to his lawyer before he gives a statement about their disappearance."

A complete fabrication.

"But he did tell us why David went to Mrs. Walker's house."

Now Iglesias looked up. David's going to the house had gotten him killed.

"Adam's got kidney disease. David was going to ask his mother to donate a kidney."

"Why didn't he give the kid his kidney? Aren't both parents usually a match for that kind of thing?"

Parker shook his head in believable consternation. "Not always, I guess. Not this time. The ol' man wasn't a match."

He wasn't betraying Adam with the truth about David's motives. Virginia and Sarah and John Stevens would want to know why he'd come back, too, so I was sure that the kidney-donation issue would be the very first thing that came up after the initial joyful reunion. There was no need for Parker to lie about the reason that David had returned. The reason why he'd left – Parker had successfully sidestepped explaining that.

Iglesias picked up a third file. "Well, you guys are done with it. It's up to the DA now, if he wants to file on the fraud." She offered a rare, toothy smile. "Good job. I expected nothing less. You can take the rest of the afternoon off."

Wow, a smile, praise, and a joke, too. Will wonders never cease? It was almost five, *shift change.* We had the rest of the afternoon off, anyway.

Parker said, "Thanks, Boss. We'll have a report for you by the end of the week."

"What's the matter with you, Dunn?" Iglesias asked suddenly. "You look like you swallowed a bug."

"It's been a long day," I replied lamely.

"Go on home, relax. You're gonna need the rest. There was a homicide on Victoria last night. More rich people. You guys can join the team on it in the morning."

She tapped one of the files on her desk, and I inexplicably thought of a Three-Card Monte dealer. Was this the file on the new murder, or was it one of the *other* files? Could I follow the shuffle?

I shook my head. It had been a long day, a successful one, though sad. Sadder still, to me anyway, was the fact that Parker was dating Sarah Walker –

"Go home, Dunn. Take a nap or something. Sheesh."

Yes, she actually did say *Sheesh,* and that got me on my feet and out of her office.

Parker was waiting in the hall, looking at his phone. "Let's go have a drink, Jan. To celebrate."

I realized that he wouldn't be grilling steaks with Sarah Walker tonight after all, because she'd be having that joyous reunion with her brother. Maybe it was taking place at that very moment.

I was immediately cheered. "Mickey's?"

"By all means." He offered his arm like an old-fashioned swain and we left the station.

My mood had lightened because of this wonderful knack I have for rationalization. Maybe we all have it. I told myself, so what if Parker's *seeing* Sarah Walker? They'd only known each other for ten days, so he surely hadn't *seen* too much of her – even if he had so obviously spent the previous night with her. So what? He was only twenty-six, good-looking, single. He probably went home with women all the time. It was one of those examples of youth being wasted on the young.

I was sure that there couldn't be anything serious between Parker and Adam's sister, or she would've invited him to the family reunion. I was freaking out over nothing.

I'd enjoy having a drink or two with him. I might even tell him how I was starting to feel about him.

****

Parker and I did a lot of drinking at Mickey's that night, but we didn't do it alone. The first round had just arrived when O'Hara and Michaels from Homicide walked in.

O'Hara was a transfer from San Bernardino PD, and he thought of himself as a minor celebrity: he claimed to've worked on a few cases with that cop that had dynamited the girls' school a few years back.

I thought the guy was insufferable, a bragging boor, but O'Hara amused the hell out of Parker. "How can you dislike my idol, Jan? I hope that someday, I'll be just as tenuously connected to a headline grabber – one so big, it's all I ever talk about, even years later. Just like O'Hara."

The Walker case isn't going to be it, I thought. If Parker'd been able to solve Billy's disappearance, if he'd found a body, and thereafter been able to pin the murder on David and slick Johnny – he might've bragged about that for a while. But finding Adam Walker had been routine; once we had David's fake ID and his cellphone, it had been nothing but a records search.

Parker knew better than to talk about it, anyway.

I rolled my eyes when I spotted O'Hara and Michaels, but Parker smiled and enthusiastically motioned them over to our table. "The next round's on you if I get him to mention it in the first five minutes," Parker said.

"You're on. But you can't just ask him about it. That's cheating."

Parker nodded and we high-fived to seal the bet. He was sincerely too cute to be believed.

We greeted our colleagues. Parker signaled the waitress for a round of beers for all of us. He said, "I hear you guys are lead on this thing on Victoria." He had heard nothing of the kind. He'd simply threw it out there.

"Yeah, we were first on the scene," Michaels said. "So I guess that makes us lead."

Parker studiously avoided looking at me when he said, "Tell me, O'Hara. Is this a gruesome one, or what?"

"Nah, not really. There wasn't really even much – you wanna hear about gruesome? Let me tell you about the case that led to the bombing in Berdoo. *That* one was gruesome."

"He's heard it, O'Hara, for Christ's sake." Now Michaels rolled his eyes. "Everybody's heard it."

"Everybody has *not* heard it," O'Hara replied emphatically.

"Detective Dunn hasn't heard it," Parker said and held out his hand. I put a twenty and a ten into it for the next round.

"If you walk into the office up there, it's not like you can look it up in the database," O'Hara told me darkly. Confidentially. "The file's disappeared. I'm the only one that knows –"

168

"That's bullshit, O'Hara," Michaels said. "When was the last time you visited your old pals in San Bernardino? You don't know what's in their *database* anymore."

Of course, Michaels was right when he'd said that everybody had heard about O'Hara's ties to the bomber. I'd heard about it, or rumors about it, anyway. It went like this: O'Hara had drawn some stabbing case – the exact details about the first crime were vague. The victim hadn't died, and it was supposed to be open and shut; there were a bunch of witnesses. O'Hara was just about to go out and interview them, when this other cop asked if he and his partner could handle the interviews instead. O'Hara handed over the file, and that was really his only connection to the guy. A few days later, this cop bombed a private girls' school.

That was how I'd heard it, anyway.

But now there was apparently a new wrinkle. O'Hara was talking cover-up. I had to believe that such a thing was definitely possible, now didn't I?

But *cover-up* is such an unpleasant word. Like all cops, I believe that complete transparency to the public isn't always necessary; nor is it always fair. It simply feeds the press's desire to sell news, and the public's desire for the prurient. It's my opinion that the man on the street doesn't always have to know everything that happened to a crime victim. Some details are just not everybody's business.

So I didn't want to hear about the cover-up. I didn't want to listen to O'Hara at all, because a) I didn't particularly care for him; b) I already knew all I wanted to know about the Mad Cop Bomber of San Bernardino; and c) I wished that the boys from Homicide would both take their free beers and go drink somewhere else, because I wanted to be alone with Parker.

So before O'Hara could rehash the *gruesome* stabbing, before he could whisper about the cover-up, I asked about the *end* of the story. I *cut to the chase,* as it were.

"Why did he blow up the school again?"

"Why does anyone do something like that?" Michaels said. "He'd lost his fucking marbles. His wife and his partner –"

"There was more to it than that," O'Hara interrupted. "But the guy *was* crazy. That's true enough. There was a confession. A tape. I heard it. He *emailed* it to his boss, before the timers ran down."

"Yeah, you heard it," Michaels said. "You heard *of it*. Or maybe you made it up. You're so full of shit, O'Hara. There wasn't any confession. The guy just went nuts."

O'Hara glared at his partner's disbelief. Parker was bored. He's won his bet, and really, he didn't care to listen to O'Hara's legend again, any more than I did. He changed the subject. "What about this new thing? On Victoria?"

Michaels shrugged, then unknowingly echoed Iglesias. "Rich people. Great big house. Dead body. Not much else to say, yet."

We talked of other cases, solved ones, mostly, and a few cold ones. We drank many cold ones, hee, hee. Parker, coming from *behind the Orange curtain* as he did, was a bit of a snob – he thought his cases were more interesting than our drab Inland Empire capers, and the evening soon devolved into the cop equivalent of a pissing contest. It wasn't really my kind of thing, so I only contributed a few stories, and spent most of the time just watching Parker, listening to the sound of his voice.

O'Hara and Michaels, thoroughly drunk, decided to roll on up out of Mickey's at around ten-thirty. We bid them farewell, told them we'd see them again in the morning, at Iglesias's meeting concerning the new case. There were a few grumbles about that, then they were gone.

"I guess we should be taking off, too, Jan," my partner said, adding, "9 am comes mighty early."

It was another cliché, but still, I couldn't help but think of him as an original. He was perfect. All I'd have to say was, *You want to come back to my place, partner?* and I could discover the bounds of that originality.

But then a little voice in my head said, *Wouldn't it be* really *original if you just wait until* he *asks* you?

I thought suddenly of David Walker, and Parker's opinion of him: *He took advantage of his more powerful position. He was an old man, confident, familiar with life, and Adam was just a boy.* I'd convinced my partner that Adam was surely no boy, that he'd known his own heart and mind, but it suddenly occurred to me that maybe our situation wasn't so different than theirs.

I knew what I wanted, as David had, but if Parker was interested in me . . . Maybe I should allow him to express it, give him time to think about it, as David had given Adam time.

I was drunk, he was drunk. We had to be to work in less than twelve hours. Tonight was not the time to begin anything.

****

I showed up for Iglesias's meeting with a puffy face and a pounding head. I was a few minutes early – I'd learned years ago that not enough sleep to erase the effects of drinking was not enough sleep, whether it be a good eight hours or a solid ten. I was gonna look and feel like hammered dog shit regardless, so why be late? It would've taken a good twelve hour coma to feel myself again, and I just didn't have time for that today. I noticed that O'Hara and Michaels were looking a tad bleary and worse for wear, also.

Parker arrived bright-eyed and bushy-tailed at nine am sharp, demonstrating yet another aspect of youth being wasted on the young. He could still drink and be alive the next morning. He squinted at my run-down countenance and handed me a Starbucks. I wondered if he'd seen Miss Walker last night after all, then decided I'd kept him out too late for that. They'd probably just shared a few cutesy texts before nighty-night, or maybe a phone call. *No, you hang up first.*

With the hangover came the sour mood, or at least that's what I told myself.

Three or four others came into the room and sat down; a veritable task force. I figured that someone important had gotten iced, and there clearly were no suspects yet. Iglesias entered, stood before the podium. She scanned the gathering, then zeroed in on me and nodded.

I obediently rose and approached. Taking in my appearance, she said quietly, "I thought you were gonna go home and take a nap, Dunn?"

She wasn't a bad supervisor, I reflected. She could've said, "I thought I *told you* to go home and take a nap," which would've immediately put me on the defensive, as coming into important meetings hungover was not my usual M.O., and she knew it.

She added, "I guess you deserved a little celebration," which was almost a nice thing coming from her, and, "It's not like the people're gonna pat you on the back for this, huh? The chief sends his thanks, though."

I nodded. Thanks from Paddy was good enough.

171

"There's a memorial service for David Walker this afternoon." When I blinked in surprise, Iglesias said, "Not a public thing. Mrs. Walker asked Paddy to come, but he reminded her that he was chief of police, and as such, the press might wonder what he was doing over there in the middle of the day –"

"Do they really follow him around like that?"

Iglesias shrugged. "I dunno, Dunn. I guess he doesn't want to take any chances. So, he again gave Mrs. Walker his condolences at the death of her ex-husband, communicated his joy at the return of her lost brat, and said he'd send his finest detective to deliver these sentiments to her personally. That's you."

I was speechless, like a little kid. I was Paddy's *finest detective?*

"So wear a nice black suit," the boss was saying. "It's at two, at the Walker estate. I understand they had the ol' man cremated." She grinned with no shame. "I guess that way, he'll stay dead this time."

I nodded again, heedless of her gallows humor, still thinking about being a *fine detective.*

Iglesias started the meeting immediately, so I didn't get a chance to tell Parker until afterwards.

"You're gonna have to write up the Walker report on your own this afternoon," I said smugly. "They're having a memorial for David, and since the chief can't make it, he asked that I go in his place."

Parker smiled mildly. "I'll see you there, Jan. I'm . . . Adam invited me."

That little hesitation – had Adam invited him, or had it been Adam's sister? It had probably been both of them: Parker's new buddy and his new *girlfriend.*

****

The urn containing David Walker's earthly remain sat, surrounded by exquisite flowers, on a tall table in the library of what had once been, in happier days, his house. Mrs. Walker greeted me effusively, thanking me for my efforts, telling me she'd be sure to tell the chief of her satisfaction. The old gal practically gushed with joy – she didn't care that her ex-husband was dead. Hell, *she'd* killed him. She was regally clad in an incredibly expensive black dress, and tried to put on a somber face for the occasion, but she couldn't quite pull it off. She was too happy about her son's return. I passed on saying *I'm so sorry for your loss.*

I said it to Adam, though. He gave me a warm and genuine hug, and said that he knew that I was. His grasp of the depth of my sympathy touched me. I knew that no one could ever replace David, but again I hoped that he would find another love someday.

He introduced me to a frail, sorrowful old man: his grandfather, Edward Walker. I shook the retired attorney's gnarled hand gently, and he also thanked me for my part in returning Adam to his family.

"Ah, Detective Dunn!" John Stevens materialized beside me, seemingly out of thin air. "I'm so sorry that it's under these sad circumstances that I see you again."

He'd seen me yesterday.

"You'll excuse us for a moment, Ed?"

David's twice-bereft father nodded, frowned, and shuffled away. Virginia put on a sad face when he spoke to her.

Stevens guided me by the elbow into an adjoining chamber, where a buffet was set up. He confided softly, "Ed doesn't care too much for me. He never has. But he's happy that his heir, once removed, has been restored. The dynasty lives on. He'd have a coronary if he knew that not a single drop of Walker blood courses through his beloved grandson's veins."

It occurred to me that it wasn't empty air, exactly, from which the attorney had materialized. Wherever he'd been before he'd greeted me, there'd been plenty of liquor. As he was whispering in my ear, I was close enough to smell it on him. John Stevens was more than a little bit loaded.

He walked around the buffet table until he was facing me, and again referenced David's father. "Yeah, old Eddie never did like me. He thought it was my influence that led David astray, dragging him off to Frisco for college, allowing him to get that Leeds girl in trouble. Now he's sure it's all my fault – his sainted boy, an embezzler! Oh, the shame!"

Stevens studied me carefully across the canapes and caviar, and to avoid his gaze, I glanced at the painting on the wall over his shoulder. I wasn't in the mood to be cross-examined by a drunken lawyer at a memorial service for his dead partner.

There was a doorway in the wall beside the painting, and movement in the room beyond caught my eye. The room was fairly small, a cloakroom or something, like a large closet – what do I know about the floor plans of big, old houses? I didn't have time to reflect on what it was, anyway.

Parker was standing there, looking exquisite in a well-cut, dark suit. Sarah Walker was with him, wearing a sleeveless black dress – I had time to think that it was a little showy for a funeral – then she put her head on Parker's chest. He embraced her gently, stoked her hair, offering comfort for her sorrow.

That was okay. Parker was a kind, comforting kind of guy. Only a heartless monster would've failed to hug a woman that'd just lost her father, for the second time. I surely couldn't feel any jealousy –

Sarah looked up and smiled at my perfect partner. She put her arms around his neck and kissed him, and neither her kiss nor Parker's response had anything to do with grief or its condolence. This seemed to go on for a lifetime, but I couldn't stop watching them, taking in every detail of their – yes, I'll say it – of their passionate clutch.

Finally the truth of what I was witnessing stabbed at me – there was more to Parker and Sarah then some quickie one night stand; there was affection, *connection*. Thanking all that was holy that I hadn't made a drunken pass at him the night before, I tore my gaze from the happy scene, and found John Stevens staring at me.

The shark's grin. "Oh, yes. Then there's *that*. Sarah told us all about her *fondness* for Sergeant Parker. Her mother's unsure about her daughter dating a policeman, and one so young, but what can she really say? David was ten years younger than her. Of course, Adam approves."

"Hey, Jan." Parker stepped out of the closet-whatever-thing. He didn't know that I'd seen him making out with Sarah – would he care, regardless?

Sarah followed a hot second later, and also said hello. Unlike Parker, she studied me carefully. But I haven't been a cop for fifteen years for nothing. Like Adam had said of David, I don't *react*. I was quite cool. It wasn't any of my business, after all. I told her again that I was sorry for her loss, as it seemed like the appropriate thing to say. I was spared making further small talk – Virginia Walker summoned us back into the library at that moment.

There was a small circle of chairs, and one by one, David Walker's family members rose, stood beside his ashes, said a few words, and sat back down again. Virginia's was a brief, *though we parted years ago, I still always loved him* speech, and I thought that it was probably true. She had allowed herself to love more than one man at the same time, custom be damned, and was not ashamed of it, especially since she was sure that those of us that knew about it would keep our mouths shut.

Edward Walker croaked a few unintelligible syllables of sorrow, but ended on a happy note: his last years would still contain joy because of the return of his grandson – just as John Stevens had said. Sarah was dry-eyed as she spoke of the man who not just her dad but also her best friend; Adam was also composed when he said he was thankful for the time he'd shared with his father, though it had been brief.

John Stevens, drink in hand, didn't hardly slur at all when he spoke of his lifelong friendship with David, a good man, *faithful and just to me*. He didn't ask us to bear with him whilst he paused until his heart came back to him, but his eulogy was poetic enough. He ended it on a similar note to Adam's grandfather: though he would also mourn David's loss to the end of his days, he took great solace from the fact that Adam was now back in their lives; he'd be able to remember David whenever he saw his son.

Parker glanced over at me at that one.

****

I was spared any chit-chat with the new couple, as the grieving family had plans to take David's urn and quietly deposit it in the Walker mausoleum. Grandpa Walker gingerly shook my hand and again thanked me for my assistance in the past and my discretion in the future. Virginia did the same, and gave me a hug. Sarah also gave me a hug, and I had time to wonder if she'd learned her watchfulness from John Stevens. The attorney himself gave me a boozy, sloppy, wordless squeeze, his gray eyes broadcasting a kind of smug pity – I desperately hoped that my yen for Parker wasn't as obvious to everyone else as it was to slick Johnny, and I vowed to conceal it better in the future. Parker told me he'd meet me back at the station.

I'd never in my life been so glad to get back into my car and flee.

****

My report on the Walker case was brief, and it didn't take long to finish it, as I had Parker's neat, thorough notes from the file. Iglesias wasn't in her office when I dropped the report into her *IN*

175

basket; she was probably enmeshed in another meeting, or had at last gone home for the day.

I returned to the cubicle I shared with Parker, and stared at the wall, waiting for him to show up. After about forty-five minutes, a little voice in my head said, *Oh, fuck this,* in a very succinct and forthright manner. Why was I waiting around for him? It was past dinnertime; Virginia Walker had probably asked him to stay and get acquainted with the family on a more personal level, now that their professional relationship had so successfully concluded.

I realized with a kind of dazed surprise that Friday night had just snuck up on me. I didn't have to go in to any meetings at the crack of dawn tomorrow. I was off. So at the suggestion of that voice in my head, I decided to drink dinner. It wasn't something that I did often; it had been many years, in fact. But my somewhat comically unhappy mood, coupled with the lingering effects of the previous night's alcohol consumption, made a little hair of the dog seem like a stellar idea. I could sleep it off for the whole damned weekend, and maybe I wouldn't therefore spend the whole damned weekend thinking about Parker and how I'd missed my chance with him.

I left my car in the lot – at least three bars were within walking distance. I'd just call an Uber to take me home after I was done feeling sorry for myself, at least the part of it that I planned to do in public.

There was Mickey's – not a cop bar, by any means, but there was always a chance that I'd run into Michaels and O'Hara again, or maybe even Parker and his new woman. Pass. There was The Noodle, tiny and beery, which catered to the just barely twenty-one crowd. No – I didn't want to sit around and watch young people pick each other up, and I surely didn't want to run the risk of one of them trying to pick *me* up. *O, that way madness lies; let me shun that.*

Across the street from The Noodle was The House of Ale, catering to a cross-section of drinkers of all ages, at least until the band came on. I'd just choose a booth in the back and cry in my beer(s) until then.

The place was fairly empty, but solitude was not to be my fate for the evening. I ordered a drink at the bar; the young woman was quick and efficient, and when I turned to find a booth in the corner in the dark, who should I see waving and smiling at me? None other than John T. Stevens, Attorney at Law. Apparently, he'd skipped dining with the Walkers this evening.

I sighed and trudged reluctantly over to his booth. If I didn't already have my drink, I surely would've gone elsewhere, but there was no escape. There was no reason to be rude, I supposed. He'd already been half in the bag when I'd seen him earlier; it might even be amusing to watch him climb the rest of the way into it.

He stood, wobbly. Yeah, this might be funny. He gave me a friendly hug, then signaled to the waitress. He asked what I was drinking, told the tired-looking girl to bring me another one, and another Seven and Seven for him.

I sat in the booth across from him; he inexplicably launched into verse:

"God pity them both! and pity us all,
Who vainly the dreams of youth recall.
For of all sad words of tongue or pen,
The saddest are these: 'It might have been!'"

I raised an eyebrow and said, "I have no idea what you're talking about, Mr. Stevens."

He smiled. "Of course you don't, Detective."

The waitress returned and set our drinks down. Stevens smiled at her, said thanks, then turned to me again. "Please, call me John. People drowning they're sorrows together should be on a first name basis."

"At least while their drinking," I allowed. "But I'm not drowning anything."

"Of course you're not, Detective," he repeated. "What is your name, anyway?"

"Janet."

He shook the ice in his drink, drained it, and picked up the fresh one. "I've been in a reflective mood since you dropped Adam off yesterday, so I feel fortunate that you're here. What good is reflecting if you can't share it with someone?"

I gulped my drink and did a little reflecting of my own: the storied counsellor wanted to talk – I might be here for a minute. On the other hand, what else did I have to do but listen to him?

I told him just that: "I've got all night, Counsellor."

"And I surely couldn't hope for a more experienced-with-life yet sympathetic ear than that of a policewoman." He winked. "And in the spirit of that, I have to say that I wasn't entirely truthful when you and your intrepid sergeant interviewed me about David's boating accident." He paused, then said, "I wouldn't worry too much about him and Sarah, by the way."

177

"I'm not concerned with –"

He held up his hand. "Sarah is . . . How shall I say it? She's . . . flighty. She's thrilled entirely one moment, and bored utterly the next. In the seven years since I've been back in Riverside, she's had several boyfriends. About one a year. She'll tell me enthusiastically about this one's wonderfulness, then by the next time I talk to her, he's down the road. The good sergeant's youth may appeal to her for a while, but the footsteps in which he follows . . . I can't see him faring any better than those that came before him."

"Our investigation has concluded, Counsellor, so Parker's free to . . . His relationship with Miss Walker is none of my business," I stated flatly.

Stevens grinned. "I'm willing to maintain that falsehood just for the pleasure of your company, Janet. But you can't fool an old student of human nature. Young Parker is attractive, and you're a single woman –"

"How do you know I'm a single woman?" I asked in surprise, but once the words were out of my mouth, I thought I already knew the answer.

"You mean, besides the absence of a wedding ring?" The predatory smile that was so dangerously charming on him was not in any way compromised because he was drunk. "I employ a very good investigator, Janet. He found Max Haycroft for me in an afternoon, and Virginia Walker couldn't have just any lady cop looking for her declared-legally-dead-but-now-obviously-not-deceased boy. A very high level of confidentiality would have to be sustained . . . Your partner is as squeaky clean as a soapy squeegee, and you have not one single skeleton in your closet. Your divorce was amicable, on paper, anyway –"

"If your investigator is so good, why didn't he find David and Adam? Right when they disappeared? When the trail was fresh?" I was more than a little outraged that he'd had me investigated, although not surprised; I surely wasn't going to discuss my divorce with him.

"I didn't put Jesse on it because he'd just started working for us at the time; I didn't know him as well as I do now. And . . . I wanted to believe that David and Adam were dead. It was a very painful time for me . . . Still . . . What I started to say – I wasn't entirely truthful when you asked me if I'd had any doubts that David and Adam were indeed really dead, when the accident occurred. So I'm telling you now – the thought *did* cross my mind that it might be a scam, but I buried the thought. I paid the searchers and grieved with Ginny and Sarah, and I buried the thought so deeply that it stayed buried. David was dead, body or no body."

He sipped his drink. "But now, after everything that's happened . . . I've been reflecting, like I said, upon the incredible lengths to which we go to delude ourselves. The things we bury, and so deeply, because if we ever let them stand and continue to exist in our minds . . . they would destroy us."

Stevens shook his head. "I've been examining the delusions that I once held as gospel truths; I've been deconstructing David's delusions. I'd been friends with him since junior high. I was thinking about how I'd once been so sure I was gonna be a rock star, when we were sixteen. I was so convinced of my talent . . . It was a girl named Melinda that convinced me.

"I'd also known her since junior high – she was skinny, pretty, then. In junior high. And so she was the last time I'd seen her – Charlie Brown's little red-haired girl with a tomboy twist."

Stevens's fond smile turned into rather a leer. "But when Melinda came back to school in the fall for sophomore year . . . I'd honed my musicianship over the summer, and Melinda had turned into a woman. A woman that liked guitar players. A woman that liked me.

"Everything I love about the female body, I first learned to appreciate from hers. In my humble opinion, *there's nothing like a dame,* Janet, just like the song says. *Nothing in the world.* And Melinda was soft, round, firm perfection. Her scent made me forget my own name. The way she would sigh and coo . . ." Stevens sighed himself.

"Unfortunately, Melinda was just as crazy as a shithouse rat. One day she'd be down – *down on the ground* – she couldn't get enough of me. I was manhood personified; I was Clapton and Eddie Van Halen and Ernie LaBelle, all rolled into one. She would take my guitar and set it on its stand and drown me in her body to the point of exhaustion. And it takes a lot to exhaust a sixteen-year-old boy.

"The next day, she'd be up on her high horse, untouchable. She'd tell me I was a talentless pussy, and she was going down the block to check out Jerry Blaustein, a real man. He was also sixteen; he played the bass. I had nothing against Jerry, and he had nothing against me. We'd talked about starting a band a couple of times.

"Melinda would spend the weekend or a week with Jerry, no doubt telling him he was better than Bella Fleck and Roger Waters and Lenny Whitly. Jerry and I would wave and kinda shrug at each other if we passed in the hall at school, communicating, *This crazy chick* . . . Because both of us knew that in a little while, Melinda would be back, knocking on my window in the middle of the night, ready, willing, and able to wear my ass out again. Sometimes, she'd take a break from both of us and go and worship Scott Feldman. He was a drummer.

"This was all a conundrum to me, and Jerry as well, and probably Scott, too: a) that Melinda behaved this way, which is not the way we'd been told that girls behaved; not just girls . . . It wasn't the way that *anyone* behaved; and b) none of us were that broke up about it. We were musicians, acquaintances if not friends, and Melinda . . . *Love me when I'm here, miss me when I'm gone* . . . But I didn't miss her that much. I got a little rest when she wasn't around. And I knew she'd be back. Eventually, she didn't come back. She threw me and Jerry both over and devoted herself entirely to Scott.

"The thing I discovered that I missed immediately was that intimacy; the laughing and cuddling and sex, the times you spend in bed with a person that you never forget. I looked around for another girl, and of course I found one. I was a musician after all." Stevens winked. "The girl's name was Darla; her best friend, Katie, was a year older than us, and she was dating David.

"We were at my house one night – Dad had converted the basement into what in later years would be called a *man cave*. There was as big a color television as Dad could afford, which really wasn't very big in those days, and a little bathroom, and a little kitchenette, a couch that folded out into a bed. The young ladies were always impressed." Again Stevens winked.

"This was in the late seventies, decades before *Netflix and chill*. If one was staying in with one's date in those days, you simply watched whatever was being broadcast on television. Darla and I had been in the other room making popcorn, and when we stepped back, whatever was being broadcast was being ignored, as David and Katie were making out on the couch. I cleared my throat, and David shot me that classic, *Your timing sucks, bro,* look.

"From out of nowhere, the thought occurred to me that perhaps we all should trade."

Stevens wiggled his eyebrows at me, and Ludacris shouted in my mind, as if in empty, quiet room, *Tag team, off the ropes!*

"Katie's face was flushed, her lips swollen. She was beautiful with interrupted desire." The old attorney drained his drink, then set it down, not taking his eyes from mine. "But to my complete surprise, I found that it was *David* that was quite inexplicably more attractive to me. His black hair was disheveled, curling carelessly over his brow; his blue eyes glowed in the light reflected from the forgotten show on the TV. Like I say, I was surprised at how *good* my friend suddenly looked to me, and I smiled at him, no doubt showing this surprise. He smiled back.

"Since we were not old nor experienced enough to realize that if we folded out the bed, there would've been room for all four of us to do whatever came naturally, decorum reasserted itself. We sat on the couch like civilized children – neither Darla nor Katie were as wild and unfettered of social mores as much-missed-at-that-moment Melinda had been. We watched TV, ate popcorn. Darla had caged a few beers from her of-age sister, and we drank those, except for Katie, who was driving.

"It was not as much fun as we'd imagined it would be, this double-date-in-the-basement-of-Chez-Stevens, and after a few more uncomfortable minutes, even though it was still early, Katie said she had to be getting home. Darla wasn't going to sit there alone with the two of us; David and I reluctantly bid the ladies goodnight. So the evening wouldn't be a total loss, we smoked a few bowls, as I had a small but of a fine variety stash –"

"Being a musician and all," I interjected. Stevens smiled and I smiled back.

"At one point, I looked over at my friend, and the thoughts I'd had earlier in the evening returned. I'd been missing all the warm intimacy I'd shared with Melinda, and I was just stoned enough to dwell on the fact that Melinda was not coming back, Darla was way too much of good girl to in any way take her place anytime soon, and David was right there. I said something to the effect that, owing to the left high and dry, disappointing outcome of the evening, I was of a mind to kiss him."

There was a cymbal crash and a drum roll, a quick, ear-shattering guitar riff. I looked over and was astonished to see that while I'd been listening attentively to Stevens's *reflections,* The House of Ale had filled up with people, and the band had taken the stage.

"Hello, Riverside!" quoth the long-haired kid on the mike, and the crowd cheered. The singer looked to be about fifteen to me, and I just had time to argue with myself – that's ridiculous, this is a bar, he's got to be a least twenty-one – before he and his band blasted into their first seismic number.

I looked back, but my garrulous drinking buddy was gone. I searched and found him at the bar, handing his credit card to the bartender, paying his tab. He glanced over at me and motioned toward the door.

By the time I pushed my way through the crowd, Stevens had concluded his transaction and was already out on the sidewalk. He was on his phone. The music leaking out from the bar was so loud, I could see his lips moving, but couldn't make out any words.

He concluded his call, and taking me by the elbow, he led me up the block to where it was quieter. Smiling, he said, "Would you like to come back to my place, Janet?"

Over the noise from The House of Ale, I still heard a sound in my head like prison doors clanging shut: I'd only had two drinks – my guard went up immediately. But I had had those two drinks, so I didn't laugh in the old mouthpiece's face. I said, "You're much too drunk to drive, Counsellor."

He smiled. "This is undoubtedly true, but the band –"

"Not a fan of modern music?" I said with a smile. "A musician like yourself?"

I saw no need to be rude to him. There was no way I was getting into a car with a smashed lawyer behind the wheel, even if he'd been . . . *eligible* in some way. I'd just walk back toward the station and call myself a cab on the way. Chances were good that Stevens wouldn't get popped for DUI, and when he sobered up in the morning, he could debate with himself the outrageousness of propositioning a cop, twenty years his junior. There was no need for me to be rude. I expected he might even call and apologize, but maybe not.

"Oh, new music's all right, but I'm not in an overly festive mood tonight." He studied me for a heartbeat, then said, "Oh, I get it." He laughed. "Trust me when I tell you that I'm not of a mind to seduce you, Janet. While you're a beautiful woman, and I'd surely jump at the chance some other time, I'm more than a little bit toasted right now. *Drink, sir, is a great provoker of three things* – but in my current mood, lust isn't one of them. The night's still young, however, and I'd still enjoy your company."

He gestured at a white limousine that had just stopped beside us. It was blocking traffic; someone honked.

"Courtesy of Edward Walker," Stevens said. "He called it for me this afternoon when he thought I might be a drunken boor at dinner. He doesn't understand that different people grieve differently, I guess. It's at my disposal till I retrieve my Jag from the Walker manse." Stevens opened the door to the sleek car. "My good friend Andy here will take you home after we finish our conversation. I promise he won't make a pass at you, either."

I hesitated; the car behind the idling limo was apparently in a hurry, and honked again. I couldn't be standing on the street corner all night waiting for John Stevens to take no for an answer, whilst the traffic backed up around the block. I thought, *What the hell, why not?* and climbed in. I was confident that I could easily fend off any overtures from him, anyway. He was *very* toasted. And I wanted to hear the rest of his story about David Walker.

The door clunked shut and Stevens said, "Home, James, and don't spare the horses."

The driver grinned in the rearview mirror. "Your wish is my command, Mr. Stevens."

"Andy's a great guy," the attorney confided. "Old Eddie's used this limo service since we were kids, since before Andy had his driver's license, since before he was born. But I'm more fun than Mr. Walker, isn't that right, Andy?"

"You certainly are, Mr. Stevens."

It wasn't a long drive to the attorney's condo, and I realized that maybe the reason why friendly Andy had been so prompt when summoned, the reason that he thought waiting around for a drunken lawyer to summon him was *fun,* was because John Stevens told him a joke and slapped him on the back and handed him fifty dollars cash American when we arrived. Ol' man Walker no doubt had the limo service under contract; he probably never felt the need to tip.

John Stevens's immaculate condo was impressive in an expensively understated way; I was more than a little surprised that it resembled the minimalist and trendy bachelor pad that I'd often fantasized for Parker. Perhaps to underline his lack of ulterior motives, he bypassed the living room, with its green leather couch and chairs that cost more than several months of my take-home pay, and offered me a seat at the glass table in the dining nook. There was nary a speck of dust, a smudge nor a fingerprint upon it, and I imagined that he tipped his maid as well, if not better, than he tipped his limo driver. I watched him over the tiled counter as he mixed us drinks in the kitchen.

Wordlessly, he handed a glass to me, then toasted, "To absent friends." A shadow crossed his features; he drained most of his drink off in one gulp, then went back out to the kitchen and topped it off.

"What was I talking about?" he inquired, finally sitting down across from me.

Stevens was erudite, intelligent. He was good-looking and classy. If it wasn't for the fact that I didn't trust him as far as I could throw the entire building that housed his condo, I might've been inclined to change my mind about fighting him off if he suggested anything ulterior, despite the age difference. His charisma, not to mention the liquor, made me feel a little intelligent and classy myself, so I said, "Mourning the absence of Melinda, wild and free, and under the influence of the demon weed, you'd just suggested kissing David."

I expected the return of his shark-like smile, but there was just a glimmer of it, as at a fond memory sadly recalled. "Ah, yes. David closed one eye and considered, as one might ponder the suggestion of a minor crime. Shoplifting, perhaps. At last he said, 'All right.'

"We made out, and felt each other up over our clothes, but before any zippers could be unzipped or button-flies unbuttoned, like something out of *Leave It To Beaver,* my mother knocked on the door at the top of the steps and said, 'Are you boys all right down there?'

"I knew it was but a gracious prelude – Mom didn't want to catch me doing anything I shouldn't be doing, any more than I wanted her to catch me. If she knew I had a girl with me, she'd give adequate time for bra straps to be adjusted and seat backs and tray tables returned to their full upright position before she'd come downstairs.

"The empty beer bottles had already been stowed, but there was the pipe and baggy still on the coffee table, so out of instinct and past experience, David waited a heartbeat before saying, 'All's well, Mrs. Stevens,' while I hastily stuffed the contraband under the couch cushion.

"The door opened and Mom glided down the steps to check on us. A commercial was playing on the television, and to make conversation, she asked us what we'd been watching.

"I had absolutely no clue, Janet. I'd simply forgot what we'd not been watching, and I was pretty sure that David didn't know either. But he was a quick thinker, and he seized the *TV Guide* from the table and gave Mom a fairly good run-down of the episode of *Baretta* that may or may not've just concluded.

"David remained seated while I somewhat awkwardly arose, turned on the lights and shut off the TV. Mom exchanged a few more pleasantries with him, then bid us good night.

"When she was gone, David stood up, adjusted his jeans. He grinned at me and said, 'Don't do the crime if you can't do the time,' a reference you won't recognize, because you're too young. It was from *Baretta,* the show we hadn't been watching on TV.

"We stood there looking at each other in silence for what seemed like a long time. Finally David stepped over to me and kissed me quickly on the mouth. 'That was certainly something different, John,' he said.

"It was one of those rare times in my life when I had no words, so I just nodded. David picked up his keys from the table – the moment was lost. There wasn't gonna be any further exploration of this *something different* tonight. He said he'd see me tomorrow, and went home."

Stevens sighed, looked at the glass of Seagram's in his hand for a long moment. I was reminded of Adam Walker, staring into his coffee cup. That seemed like it'd been a long time ago. When I realized that it'd only been yesterday, I drained my drink.

Stevens did likewise, then rose and took our glasses out to the kitchen for a refill. There was no toast this time. His absent friend, now absent forever – Stevens needed to tell someone about that friendship. Like Adam's need to *explain* about his own relationship with David – John Stevens also had to talk to someone about him, and also like Adam, the only person he had was a stranger, a cop he barely knew.

He sat back down and rubbed his hand over his face. He took a deep breath, let it out, then continued. "I went up to my room, but couldn't fall asleep for a long time, because I was thinking about David. I couldn't get him out of my mind."

He smiled suddenly. "I wouldn't want you to think – I wasn't suddenly *in love* with David, Janet. It was just that it'd been such a surprise – I'd just discovered myself to be one of nature's most fortunate creatures. A hedonist. A bisexual. And seeing as how my first foray onto the other side had been so cruelly interrupted . . . I was frustrated. I wanted David to come back so that we could see this *something different* through to what I was sure would be an awesome conclusion.

185

"But the moment for fruition never seemed to want to present itself. Throughout the rest of high school, sometimes, if we were alone for a second, David would grab me and kiss me – 'For luck!' he'd say, and then walk away. And that was okay, although the thought crossed my mind occasionally that he was . . . *teasing* me.

"It was another conundrum. I didn't feel the need to explore this thing enough that I looked elsewhere for it. I was just a kid in high school and it wasn't a mainstream thing like it is today – I wouldn't't've even known where to look. But I remained curious about David. It wasn't like it consumed me. I dated plenty of girls, and so did he. But when he'd kiss me like that and then just walk away, it would hit me. I *wanted* David.

"I didn't know what he wanted. There was never a private moment where an opportunity to talk about it presented itself. Except once . . ."

Stevens laughed. "It wasn't hardly a private moment. We'd already been accepted to SFSU. We'd decided we were going to study law – UCLA was closer and his dad said it was better – but David didn't want to be a legacy. He didn't want go to school where Eddie had gone. He wanted to get away from Eddie, make his own way, even though Eddie was gonna be paying for it. I wanted to get away from the home fires, too, so we'd picked SFSU. It was a good school, far enough away, but not too far." Stevens waved his hand, dismissing SFSU.

"Anyway, we'd already been accepted. We were at a party on the night of high school graduation, and who should be there but Melinda, joined at the hip as she'd become with the little drummer boy. She was drunk and soppily sad that most of her friends were going away to college. She wasn't going. She and Scott were planning to go on the road with his band. That didn't happen." Stevens's grin was drunk-mean, vindictive. "Within a year, Melinda got pregnant, and Scott – *for my nineteenth birthday, I got a union card and a wedding coat* – Scott got a haircut and went to work selling Chevys at his uncle's car dealership. That's what I heard, anyway." The attorney waved his hand again. Melinda and Scott's ultimate fates were collateral to the story.

"So we're there at this party, and Melinda, commenting on our choice of schools, says something like, 'The Lord only knows what kind of trouble Davey and Johnny are gonna get into, so far from home!'

186

"David looked at me guilessly and said, ' I know exactly what kind of trouble Johnny wants us to get into,' and it was like he was telling me that as soon as we got away from our parents and everything we'd previously known, he was down to once again explore that *something different.*"

Stevens sighed. "And as things turned out, that's exactly what he was saying."

"But it wasn't with you," someone said, and I was surprised as hell that it was me.

Stevens gazed at the ice in his again empty glass. He nodded, then went on as if I hadn't spoken. "We *packed our hopes and dreams, like a refugee . . .*" He looked up at me suddenly. "Surely you recognize that one? You are *from* California, right?"

"I am," I said. Regardless, I had no idea what he was talking about.

"It's an old Eagles song," he explained, and I thought, *Like there's any* new *Eagles songs.* I tried to think of one, new or old, and failed.

"It goes, *there is no more new frontier, we have got to make it here,* but David and I didn't take it the way Henley meant it." Stevens slowly swirled his ice. "The song was a lament, about how the west had been ruined. Whatever. We were going to take over the west. Be the best damned lawyers . . ."

Stevens rose to make himself another drink. I told him mine was still good. From the kitchen, he told me, "So we came to Frisco, all anticipation, glad to be away from home for the first time, ready to take over the world. I also anticipated that I was finally going to get to . . ."

He returned and regained his chair. "David had, in so many words, promised me that. We had a great set-up, a little cozy dorm room. I pictured how it was gonna happen, eventually . . ." Stevens looked up and met my eyes. "We hadn't been there a week before Billy Munro shanghaied us and took us over to Max's house. I looked around and thought, *This is even better.* The commonplace moralities of the times weren't just relaxed at Max's; they were *nonexistent.*

"But the first weekend . . ." Stevens uttered a chuckle: drunken defeat. "The *very first* fucking weekend! David disappeared with Billy. And when they came back, it didn't take long for me to realize that I'd been pre-empted. Billy had shown David *something different* as casually as he'd showed him the Golden Gate Bridge. It was absolutely no thang to the party boy. But David was hooked. *Hooked on Billy.*

"Because I was miffed at being passed over, I went out and immediately found myself another dark-haired, blue-eyed guy, neither David *nor* Billy, and then another one. I was in San Francisco, where *something different* could be had for the asking. Neither of Billy nor David noticed that I'd been gone for a few days, but Max smiled curiously at me when I came back. 'Where ya been, Johnny?' he said. 'Looking for love in all the wrong places?'

"I hated Max at that moment because he saw through me, recognized all my provincial ideas about relationships. The girls I'd known – it'd never been just about sex to me. It was about intimacy, making those happy memories . . ." Stevens looked down at his drink with a kind of embarrassment. "I was nothing but a romantic schoolboy, and Max knew it."

Stevens abruptly gulped his drink. "There wasn't a lot of romance to be found in anonymous pick-ups in San Francisco. Max knew that, too. He said, 'There's nothing but the wrong places around here, Johnny. We're all just ships passing, transitory, temporary. Relationships that last a lifetime aren't started in college. Have fun. Take what you can get, and be happy with that.'

"My attitude changed overnight. Our house was Party Central – whatever I might be looking for – temporarily, of course, and you couldn't call it love – it showed up promptly at dusk damn near every Friday night, and I discovered that Max was right. Nobody wanted a connection. We were all there for a good time, not a long time.

"Billy was the poster child for this philosophy, and the first time David saw a partner that wasn't him come out of Billy's bedroom, he was shocked. Billy laughed at him. *'All you need is love, love,* little brother,' he said. *'Love is all you need.'*

"Billy didn't know anything about *love* – I doubt if he actually ever loved anybody or anything in his life. It was of course *sex* to which he referred. That was all he needed, all he wanted. Like I said before, he'd let you love him, but when the next person came along, you had to get back in line.

"David made himself accept it. He was proud – he wouldn't admit to being in love with Billy, any more than I'd admit to being . . ." Stevens gulped his drink. "Any more than I'd admit to the fact that I felt that David'd snubbed me *for* Billy.

"David ignored the fact that Billy was a whore by becoming a monk. He remembered that the reason he was in college was to get those credits, so he put his nose to the grindstone. David stayed shut up in his room, studying, whenever Billy was on the boulevard. But when he was home, David forgot about higher learning; his baser instincts ruled him." Stevens chuckled. "School was a breeze to me, so I remained a whore all the time, not unlike Billy himself.

"Maybe now you understand why I, unlike David and everybody else, was immune to Billy's charm. When I ran into him at that A Pi party – David was at home, waiting for him like a new bride – you might say that Billy and I teamed up. We went through that sorority house like Ted Bundy, like Richard Speck." Stevens grinned wickedly at what was undoubtedly a look of shock on my face. "Oh, I see you get that way-back allusion. Old music's lost on you, but if I mention ancient crimes . . . I guess all cops know about those."

"Those were kind of famous ones, Counsellor."

I was fine with him using my first name, but for some reason, I just couldn't bring myself to call him *John*. Maybe it was because he'd just referenced infamous mass murders to describe a collegiate sex romp. Maybe it was because some part of me, untouched by alcohol, wanted to remain professional. These details he was telling me about David and Billy – I suddenly strove to remain a cop conducting an unasked-for interview, instead of a pal listening to a drunken story.

He continued. "Like roosters loosed in the hen house, Billy and I serviced the sorority sisters. *All alone, or in twos* . . . When we weren't pleasing the ladies, Billy and I pleased each other. I was curious to know what all the fuss was about, and I must say that he lived up to his reputation."

Stevens swirled the ice in his glass. "When I'd had my fill of Billy and the ladies, I went back home. Like I said, there was David, waiting. When I saw him, I was surprised at feeling an unexpected wave of disgust – for myself, for Billy and those girls – but mostly, I discovered that I was disgusted with David. Max had undoubtedly told him where I'd been, what I'd been doing, *who* I'd been doing, but he just stubbornly ignored the pain it caused him. All he cared about was if I knew when Billy was coming home.

"The idiot way he acted wounded me, and some cruel part of me wanted to hurt him in return. Maybe that's why I'd messed around with Billy in the first place; it was definitely why I said to David –

189

just in case he *hadn't* been told – 'I understand why you're so hung up on him, *little brother.* He's a lot of fun.'

"It was a mean, whorish thing to say, but David didn't react. He knew what Billy was, what he did – he did it with everybody, regardless of how much David loved him. What difference did it make if he did it with me, too?"

Stevens rubbed his hand over his face again, to avoid having to look at me. "David's depressingly stoic acceptance of the fact that his lover was a whore, and his best friend was a whore, and that they were whores with each other, depressed *me.* 'Let's get out of here,' I suggested. 'Let's go see and be seen. Let's go over to that place on Taravel and shoot some darts.'

"And that was when we met Ginny. While Billy was away, David fell in love with someone else, someone who loved him back. When Billy returned, Max told him of this happy development, and Billy, in his magnanimous largesse, ceased making overtures to David, allowing him to be steadfast in his loyalty to Ginny." Stevens shook his head. "To use another ancient, now taboo saying: I thought it was mighty white of our Billy, to not tempt David to stray from his burgeoning monogamy.

"Billy absented himself from the house more than ever, and David was truly happy for the first time since we'd arrived at SFSU. He'd pledged himself to these new feelings he had for Ginny, because she returned them. He didn't give himself time to reflect on the fact that he still loved Billy, because Billy wasn't there.

"This delusion evaporated when Ginny came up pregnant and wanted to get married and move back to Riverside. Though he'd ceased sleeping with Billy, it was still an agony for David to leave him. Billy didn't care either way. He chastely kissed David goodbye, wished him *rotsa ruck* with marriage and fatherhood and UCLA, and promptly took off again. He didn't come to their wedding, didn't show up at the going away party. Ginny never even met him, and neither David nor I heard a word from him until he showed up on the doorstep ten years later.

"Billy was still as striking in his early thirties as he'd been at school. You saw his picture. I worried – well, I didn't actually *worry* – but I was curious to see if David's long-dormant desire for the love that dare not speak its name would flare up and singe him, now that its one and only object had returned. But Billy maintained his policy of not tempting David. Why should he bother? He was too busy –"

"Fucking David's wife." Again I was surprised that the words came from me.

Stevens smiled wryly, nodded. "David was so busy fighting down his own adulterous thoughts, that he didn't notice Ginny acting on hers. I'd observed – I'd *studied* Billy's interactions with people when we were in college, so I knew what was going on from the outset."

He grinned. "Here's a historical crime for you, Cop Lady. It was in England, in the 20s. Edith Somebody. She was married to some old guy, and then she met some young guy, decided she was in love with him, and the two of them decided to off her husband."

Once again, I had no idea what he was talking about, but I didn't want to let this drunken officer of the court know that he was more well-versed in the annals of crime – *foreign* crime, no less – than I was, so I didn't say anything.

He picked up his phone, scrolled. "Elementary, my dear Watson. Edith Thompson and Freddie Bywaters. How did we live before Wikipedia?" He read, *The twenty-six-year-old Edith was immediately attracted to the eighteen-year-old Bywaters, who was handsome and impulsive and whose stories of his travels around the world excited Edith's love of romantic adventure. To Edith, the youthful Bywaters represented her romantic ideal; by comparison, twenty-nine-year-old Percy* – that was her husband – *seemed staid and conventional. Percy welcomed the youth into their company . . . Percy invited Bywaters to lodge with them.*" Stevens grinned. "Who does that sound like? Bywaters murdered Percy, and both he and Edith were hung for it."

I must've looked shocked again, because Stevens said, "I'm not saying that Ginny and Billy contemplated murdering David because he stood in the way of their love, Janet." He shook his head, laughed. "Billy never loved anyone in his life, and Ginny was having her cake and eating it, too."

I recalled Mrs. Walker's interview. She'd told us that David had said just those words to her, when he'd found out about the affair: *No. Virginia Nicole Leeds is not gonna have her cake and eat it too, this time. I want a divorce.*

Stevens was saying, "Our own little drama of homemade sin hasn't always reminded me of the Thompson murder because of the possibility of any murderous thoughts. It was the picture."

He held up his phone. In a tree-shaded and grassy English garden, Edith Thompson sits on a high-back wicker couch. Her hands lie demurely in her lap, and she gazes pensively at something out of frame.

"You gotta wonder," Stevens said. "What's she thinking about?"

To Edith's right on the couch – not inappropriately close by any means – a handsome, dark-haired, nattily dressed young man is reading a book.

"He even looks like Billy a little bit, don't you think?" Stevens asked.

To Edith's left, her husband – he looks much older than twenty-nine – is reading a newspaper. He's sitting in a wicker chair, very close to Edith – at first I thought that they were all sitting on the same couch together. From their body language, both men appear to be ignoring the young woman seated between them; they're engrossed in their reading.

But once you realize that the man on her right killed the man on her left out of love for her . . . Stevens was right. I had to wonder: What was she thinking about?

"There used to be a big glider in David's back yard," Stevens said, "and the three of them used to sit on it together, just like in this picture."

The image of an airplane with a slender fuselage and enormous wings formed in my more-than-a-little-drunk brain. "A . . . Did you say *a glider?*"

"It's like a rocking chair, but instead of rocking . . ." He moved his hand back and forth like a metronome. "It . . . *glides.*" He didn't have a gesture for that; his usually razor-sharp mind was at a loss for a more thorough description.

"The three of them would sit on it sometimes, Ginny in the middle, just like Edith. I would sit across from them; we'd laugh and talk. Billy would say something witty and David would look at me, communicating that his ability to maintain his marriage vows was waning. Out of the corner of my eye I would see Billy and Ginny's shared smile, and it was obvious to me that she'd already compromised hers."

Stevens sighed. "It was on an afternoon not unlike tonight – Trust me when I tell you that I'm not actually an alcoholic, Janet."

That was the second time that he'd used that expression: *Trust me when I tell you that I'm not of a mind to seduce you,* and *Trust me when I tell you that I'm not actually an alcoholic.* I was drunk enough to indeed trust him on these two points, but not yet drunk enough to trust him any further than that.

"I'm almost a teetotaler," he was saying. "But at those times when my own foolishness and the foolishness of those around me gets a little too much, I'm afraid I turn to the bottle for solace. It doesn't really offer any solace, just an eventual blotting out of those things I don't want to think about.

"Tonight, it's my own stupidity and delusions I want to forget, but can't. On that long ago afternoon – summer was ending. It was Labor Day. I'd gone to the office, because I didn't have anything else to do. David showed up, too – always a hard worker, was David Walker.

"But I'd hoped to be alone, so I took off and went to a bar around the corner, just down the street from here. They tore it down a couple of years ago." Stevens waved his hand; another unimportant detail. "I wasn't looking forward to the party at David's house that night, to watching Ginny and Billy making eyes at each other right under his unsuspecting nose. I hated Billy and Ginny for being so fucking obvious about it; I hated David for being so oblivious. I hated myself most of all for the fact that I still associated with any of them.

"So I was sitting in this bar, drinking the afternoon away, hating pretty much every aspect of my life. Like I say, I'm not generally much of a drinker, because, as you're now aware, drinking makes Johnny talky. And a talky lawyer – well he's not much good to anybody, is he? But it seemed the thing to do at the time.

"David waltzed into the bar, looking for me, babbling about the party, and why was I drinking already, and didn't I want to save some sobriety for all our friends and clients that were coming to the house later? They weren't any of them really my friends, just acquaintances. He was the only friend I really had. And Billy Munro, whom he'd once upon a time *been so friendly with* was making a fool of him with his beloved bride, and I just couldn't take it anymore.

"I said, 'You know they're carrying on behind your back, David,' even though I knew he *didn't* know. David had a lot of delusions – about Billy, about Ginny, about love and loyalty – but this wasn't one of them. He hadn't seen the way they looked at each other and then lied to himself about what he'd seen. I knew what was going on, what had been going on all summer, but David sincerely had not a clue.

"I looked at my watch and said, 'It's two o'clock – you're not expected back until, what? Four? Nose to the grindstone, as always. Sarah's not in school today, but they probably sent her over to the neighbor kids'. No one's gonna see Ginny sneak into his room. They're probably going at it right now.'

"I wasn't trying hurt him, Janet. But when I drink . . ." He swirled the ice in his glass, again half empty. "Sometimes I think that I see how things *should* be. David had to know that they were making a fool of him." Stevens set his glass on the table and pushed it aside. Maybe he was done drinking for tonight.

"David blinked at me in dumb disbelief, his mouth hanging open like a little kid that'd dropped his ice cream into the dirt at the fair. He didn't ask me if I was sure: we'd been friends for half our lives, and he knew I wouldn't make this kind of unbelievable, traitorous statement if I wasn't sure, as we say in the law game, *beyond the shadow of a doubt.*

"He stared at himself in the mirror behind the bar for some time. When the bartender approached to take his drink order, I shook my head and he moved away. David didn't drink when the truth got too much for him, like I do. He made a plan and he *acted.*

"'Come on back to the office with me, John,' he said at last. 'I know how to get rid of Billy.'"

The attorney's phrasing made the cop in me sit up a little straighter, made her attempt to banish the encroaching drunkenness. I also pushed my glass aside. John Stevens was far gone; he'd been drinking all day. He'd been seized with this relentless need to talk – would it lead him to confess what he knew about Billy's disappearance?

The realistic part of me didn't think so; that kinda shit only happens in the movies, on TV, usually right before the last commercial break. But still, I leaned forward and listened a little more keenly to whatever he was going to say next.

"David had the logistics of the thing down perfectly. He called the house; Sarah answered, and he asked her to put Uncle Billy on the phone. David told him that since the job in Frisco had fallen through, we had a business proposition for him – could he come in to the office so we could lay it out? 'If you like it,' David said, 'then we might really have something to celebrate tonight.'"

Stevens unconsciously waved away the next unimportant detail even as he spoke it. "For all I know, David might've actually been considering offering Billy some kind of job. A clerk or an

194

investigator or something. He'd never discussed it with me, but the summer was drawing to a close, and Billy'd been talking about leaving." He shook his head.

"But the best laid plans of mice and men and all – David surely didn't have any kind of business proposition for our Billy now. It was just a ploy to get him downtown.

"When David hung up, he instructed me: I went up to the house and waited until I saw Billy's car pull out of the driveway. I had to hide the Jag – it's kind of distinctive." Stevens winked. "I parked down the street and stood behind the bushes. When he was gone, I drove on up to the house. As luck would have it, Sarah and Ginny were busy in the kitchen with party preparations – they didn't see me sneak into the house. I went up to Billy's room and stuffed all his belongings into the one battered suitcase he'd arrived with. I snuck back out of the house and drove back to the office.

"David and Billy were sitting in David's office, chatting, maybe talking about this business deal that was now never going to happen. I dunno. I went to my office and set the suitcase just inside, beside the door.

"My office was bigger; David never cared about such things, but I've always appreciated a little ostentation. There was my desk, of course, and a small table and chairs, a couch. All to make the clients feel more at home. The safe was also in my office.

"I appeared in the doorway to David's office, and he rose, and gestured for Billy to follow us to my office. I stood a little off to one side; David went around behind my desk. He'd already taken the money out of the safe –"

"Why did you have so much cash at the office?"

Stevens grinned wickedly again. "For emergencies, Detective." He paused and his smile fled. "I've already told you what happened next. David told Billy that he knew what'd been going on. Billy looked at me in surprise. It was plain that he'd known all along that I knew, but he'd expected me to keep his secret for him.

"David said, 'Since you're down on your luck, here's a little bit of money.' He tossed the envelope full of cash to the edge of the desk. 'Now you'll never have to come back here again.'

"Billy said he'd have to go back and pack; David pointed to the suitcase by the door. Billy counted the money, then picked up his suitcase and left.

. "We watched through the window. Billy put his suitcase into the truck of his car, opened the door and threw the money onto the seat. He looked up once, but I knew he couldn't see us. Then he drove away.

"David's composed anger broke. He sobbed, saying he couldn't believe that they'd done this to him. He collapsed onto the couch and put his face in his hands and cried. I sat beside him and put my arms around him. He hugged me tightly, and I said that everything was gonna be all right, the way you would to a heartbroken child.

"He looked up and babbled that he was so sorry, that I'd always been there for him, and he'd always just taken me for granted . . . Then he kissed me."

Stevens picked up the drink I'd thought he'd discarded, and drained it. He put one hand over his face and looked down at the table. "I knew it was wrong. David had just had the shock of his life; his vulnerability was . . . incomprehensible. He didn't really want . . . But I kissed him back, because I, ladies and gentlemen of the jury, am a son of a bitch.

"One thing led to another – I told myself I was *comforting* him. That's another one of those delusions I've harbored all these years – that I was comforting David in his moment of need. But that wasn't it at all, not in the least. When he kissed me . . . All the desire I'd stuffed down into a hole since the day he'd come back all smiles and giggles after he'd spent the weekend with Billy – all of it came roaring back, and yes, I hugged him and kissed him and wiped away his tears, finally experiencing all that intimacy that I'd always told myself was the only thing I wanted.

"But when the moment finally arrived, I enjoyed it with a brutal vindication singing in my blood. *Fuck you, Billy! And fuck you, too, Ginny, you heartless, rutting bitch! It's finally Johnny's turn!*"

Stevens ran his hand through his hair, usually so perfect, but a trifle disheveled now. "David started making promises. He'd come to stay with me, *tonight.* He'd divorce Ginny, we'd move the office to LA, get a place together. We'd leave Riverside behind, just like we had when we'd left for college. Everything would be as it *should've* been then. He started to apologize again, started to kiss me. I looked at my watch and told him that there'd be time enough for all that again later. Now . . ." Stevens grinned viciously. "Now it was time for him to go home and dump his cheating wife.

"The opportunity didn't present itself immediately, as there was the Labor Day party to be endured first. I was in a good mood – a great one, actually, so I didn't have anything else to drink. David was coming to grips with what had happened, slowly – like I said, his attitude became *easy come, easy go.* He was halfway to talking himself into our bright and shiny new future in LA *together . . ."* Stevens sighed. "But there was still the accusation, the break-up to be enacted, so he had a few drinks to steel himself for it.

"Sarah ran out from the kitchen and gave me a hug, told me goodnight. I looked around for David and when I didn't see him, I figured that he'd gone into the kitchen to drop the bomb. He was always thinking, was David – he didn't wait until the guests departed, because if Ginny didn't take the news well, and felt the need to cause a scene – she wasn't likely to do that if she still had a house full of people. It would be handled calmly, with David in control.

"I went out onto the back patio for some air, considering that it might just be the last time I'd be at the Walker estate. There were party-goers standing around in twos and threes, but I wasn't in the mood for small talk with the sycophants and general hangers-on that Ginny called friends.

"My mood was too exceptionally light for all that – the afternoon I'd spent with David had become an idyll in my mind. The idea that I'd taken advantage of him in his vulnerability – that thought had been buried. No. This shock had simply made David come to his senses. His future – *our future* – was so bright, I had to wear shades.

"So I slipped past the guests, thinking I'd wander out to the glider, sit and enjoy the evening air by my lonesome until David was done telling Ginny he wanted a divorce. My eyes adjusted to the darkness; there was half a moon, so I had no trouble seeing the glider there ahead of me. I'd just about reached it, and had begun to tote up how much said divorce was going to cost David, when I saw a cigarette glowing a few more feet ahead, just there, in the trees.

"These were not the type of party-people who were likely to be sneaking off to the woods for illicit activities – if the idea struck anyone to do so, there were plenty of spare bedrooms in the house for such things. So I immediately thought the smoker under the trees had to be some kind of intruder – someone casing the house, waiting for the party to wind down and the lights to go out.

"I said, 'Hey. This is private property. If you don't leave, I'm gonna go back inside and call the cops.'

"He stepped out where I could see him and said, 'You're gonna have me arrested now? I thought we were friends, John.' It was Billy.

197

"'We were never friends,' I told him.

"'You wound me,' he said. 'After all we once meant to each other.'

Stevens grinned at me. "I said, 'It was only once, Billy, and it meant nothing.' I asked him what he was doing there. "You think you're gonna extort more money out of David? That twenty large not enough for ya?'

"He said the money was fine, and he'd go, just like David wanted him to. Then he said, 'I just thought maybe . . . Maybe I should . . . Say goodbye better. If you'd just go in and get him, tell him I'm out here . . .'

"'He's *saying goodbye* to Ginny right now.'

"Billy was astonished. 'Over *this?* Aw, that's not right, John. What about Sarah?'

"I told him that Sarah would be all right. Ginny would be all right. Even David would be *all right,* if he'd just take his money and go. But Billy wanted to argue with me. He demanded that I go back to the house and fetch David for him, so he could explain. There was no need for him to divorce Ginny. Billy said he just wanted to tell David that, then he'd leave; he just wanted to *say goodbye.*

"I saw it all clearly then, Janet, as if in a vision. The three of them, sitting at the dining room table, after the guests had departed. There would be tears – not from Ginny or Billy, but from David. Billy would apologize: 'I'm sorry, David, I just tripped and fell into your wife.' And David would forgive him. If I gave Billy the chance to plead his case, *David would forgive him.*

"I could see how it would shake out. Billy would leave – *for a while.* David would divorce Ginny – he'd never forgive *her.* But Billy . . . Hell, it was just how he was. David would ask himself how he'd ever thought it could've ended up any other way. *Everybody* loved Billy.

"Billy would leave, but he'd come back. David had given him twenty grand – there was more where that came from. Once Ginny was no longer in the picture, Billy would come back, take David up on that job offer. He'd let David pay him – *keep him.* And eventually, he'd do what he always did. He'd go visit Ginny again, or it'd be someone else. If I let Billy talk to David, David would let him hurt him again.

"I wasn't going to let that happen. I took him by the elbow, and said, 'Step into my office, Billy.' I led him back under the trees – I

198

couldn't have David, looking for me, randomly glance out the window and see me out there talking to him."

Stevens took a deep breath and slowly let it out again. "It took some oration – but I've always thought I had a little Clarence Darrow in me. I explained that nothing could be gained by his talking to David. It would just make him feel angry and betrayed and heartbroken all over again. I told him I'd tell David that he'd stopped by –"

"Did you?" The cop in me was suddenly fully awake, on the alert.

"Of course I didn't, Janet." A flash of annoyance. "I persuaded Billy that it would be in the best interests of all parties involved if he just took his money and went back to San Francisco, as had been the original deal."

But he didn't go back to San Francisco . . .

"He agreed, and left. If I would've told David that he'd been out in the woods, all apologetic, David would've told himself all the lies again – Billy really did care about him – and he would've changed his mind. Billy wouldn't've had to've actually spoken to David – if I told David that he'd come back to apologize, that would've been enough. David would've forgiven him. Somehow, Billy would've weaseled his way back into David's life again. So, no, I didn't tell him. Billy was finally gone, and that was the way it needed to be.

"I was again totally disgusted with the whole situation, so I didn't even go back into the house. I just went home. David was already there when I arrived – his showdown with Ginny had been brief.

"The rest, as the saying goes, is history." Stevens looked at his glass, found that it contained nothing but melted ice, and staggered out to the kitchen to make himself another drink. From there he said to me, "Now that I've told you the true tale of Davey and Johnny, I imagine that you can understand my melancholy tonight?"

"Give me a moment before I reply," I said. "I *have* been drinking, you know."

But I didn't need a moment to gather my thoughts because I was toasted. There were the slow motor responses and the beginnings of a headache, a dim ringing in my ears – physical things, without remedy until my system processed the alcohol. But my mind was as coldly, as relentlessly sober as if I'd never had a drink in my life.

John Stevens, wallowing in drunken, grieving vulnerability, had just confessed to murder. It was textbook:

Opportunity: The dark woods; as far as David Walker knew, Billy was already gone. He'd told Virginia the same. No one would miss Billy except for Max, and that wouldn't be for a while.

Means: A stray branch or a rock, applied bluntly and forcefully to the back of Billy's unsuspecting skull. Or maybe slick Johnny had simply strangled him with his bare hands.

And of course, motive: Stevens had just experienced the culmination of a decade and a half's lust for David Walker. David was making promises. If David heard Billy's apology – he would've forgiven him; *Billy would've weaseled his way back into David's life again.* And Stevens couldn't be having that.

Parker was wrong. David hadn't murdered Billy in a jealous rage, and Stevens hadn't helped him hide the body. *Stevens* had murdered Billy in a different kind of jealous rage, and David hadn't known anything about it. I was as sure of it as I was sitting there, slow and sloppy of movement, but crystal clear in thought. Because surely, John Stevens hadn't simply *talked* Billy into leaving.

And he wanted me to tell him why I thought he was sad? I needed a minute.

He returned and handed me an icy bottled water. The drinking was indeed concluded.

He eyed me carefully and said, "Perhaps you require a denouement; an epilogue, a what-happened-next? Because I'm going to be damned pissed if I've wasted my time, your time, and way too much good liquor, and you fail to grasp why, at this moment, *I have lost all my mirth*, Janet." He smiled.

"Proceed, Counsellor." It was all I could think of to say.

"Post Ginny and Billy, David and I did live happily ever after for a very short time. We never did get a place together – our tastes in accommodations were too dissimilar. We wound up living across town from each other, with the office in the middle.

"Once we were all settled in the big city, the practice flourished. David told himself that he loved me. And he did, really, in all the ways I'd always told myself that I'd wanted him to love me: the cuddling and the intimacy, the laughing memories made in bed. But relationships started on the rebound seldom last, and after about six months, David's desire for intimacy waned. In half a year, we went from lovers to bedfellows to platonic old friends again.

"There wasn't someone else. The truth that David had never actually been attracted to me in that way simply reasserted itself.

200

David had never really been attracted to *anyone* in that way, at least not enough to act on it. Except, of course, for charming Billy.

"I'd catch David sometimes, staring absently into space, and from the look on his face I could tell what he was thinking about. He didn't want me, but our Billy still cavorted through his imagination. We went back to being friends and business partners. We'd always made a killer team as lawyers."

But you're the only one that's actually a killer.

"David dated women. He was attractive and single and there are legions of ladies in LA that would've liked to've snagged a wealthy attorney. But none of them meant anything to him. He was never gonna let another woman hurt him like Ginny had done.

"I also dated my share of women, and they never failed to take the edge of the unrequited desire I still had – would apparently always have – for David. There've been offers from men . . ." Stevens raised his hand and let it drop to the table. "But no one that was appealing enough to inspire me to waste my time. David would still sometimes surprise me with a quick, unexpected kiss – *For luck!* And I had all my lady friends. I was content.

"Yet now, as creeping old age sets in, I wonder if I'll ever be content again." Stevens's gray eyes were emotionless. "You still don't get it, do you?"

"You're sad because someone you loved is gone," I said lamely.

"Someone I loved is gone." Stevens laughed. "Twice. I grieved for David seven years ago, and now I'm grieving for him all over again. Is that what you think?"

I nodded.

"There's more to it than that. When Sarah showed us Adam's photograph, it was like looking through a portal into the past. He looked so much like Billy that I knew that it'd only be a matter of time before David got in touch with him."

"So you knew that David was –"

"Attracted to him? How could he not be? But David played it off. He'd say, 'Yeah, Adam looks a lot like Billy,' but then he'd bookend it right away by reminding me that Adam was only seventeen. He'd chuckle and say, 'Besides, *the heyday in the blood is tame, it's humble, and waits upon the judgment.*' And I had to admit that this was accurate. It wasn't like David had ever been on the boulevard, trolling for a date, and certainly not now that he was pushing fifty."

"Did you think that Adam thought . . ." In my mind, this sentimental journey was now definitely an interview again, *an interrogation* – and my question was cumbersome, so I rephrased it. "Did David tell you that he'd told Adam that he wasn't his father?"

Stevens nodded. "He told him right away. 'Look kid, we can hang out and watch the game, but I'm just an old guy that was once married to your mom. I'm not your long-lost daddy. Sarah's mine, but you're not.' He said Adam didn't care; he just liked palling around with David."

"You didn't know that Adam was –"

"Gay? Bisexual?" Stevens shrugged. "It gets harder to tell just by looking at them every year, and the idea that Adam might be – it wasn't the first thing that came to my mind, believe it or not. Just like Billy, or David, or Max, or myself, for that matter – Adam's not exactly effeminate, so I didn't have that stereotype to guide me. I thought he was just a regular seventeen-year-old kid, happy to be in Los Angeles with the grown-ups. I didn't see him too many times. I didn't get to watch him and David interact."

I pressed. "So you never suspected that they were –"

"And the circle comes back around and is completed," Stevens said with another hard sparkle of annoyance. He didn't like being pressed. "That's what I told you earlier, Janet. I *did* suspect, with a kind of awful certainty, when no bodies turned up. But it was only for a second. I told myself that while it was certainly true that David and I hadn't been intimate for decades, I believed he still loved me. He'd never abandon me, he'd never abandon his daughter. . . He'd never be so cruel as to allow us to believe he was dead, just so he could take off with some teenaged kid that looked like Billy Munro. The whole idea was insane.

"And the kid – I didn't want to think that he'd do such a heartless thing to his mother. I didn't know Adam at all, but I knew Ginny. David never forgave her and I never really did either, but after her son died, she needed somebody. I had nobody – in one fell swoop, Ginny lost her beloved son and I lost David. We sort of just fell in together.

"She never saw the depth of my grief, because she had none whatsoever of her own for David. He didn't know anything about boats – his ineptitude had proved to be deadly. He'd taken her precious boy from her. She blamed David, hated him.

"She might've considered for a hot second that I mourned for my best friend, but she quickly dismissed that. She's the embodiment of selfishness – I was there to comfort *her*." Stevens chuckled darkly. "But she's also smart and witty and not averse to sleeping with her dead ex-husband's old partner when the nights are particularly cold and dark and lonely. Ginny comforted me without realizing that she did so."

Stevens sighed. "But all that is neither here nor there anymore. Ginny's son is back, and she'll no longer want to engage in the kind of clandestine liaison that would've made her friends at the country club cluck and shake their heads in pity if they knew about it. It was okay when she was lonely – Sarah's finally got her own life. But now that Adam's back, Ginny no longer needs me."

"Is that why you're sad?" I asked softly.

Stevens grinned at me as if I was a small child raving about the Easter bunny. "Now, Janet – even after our brief acquaintance – I think you know me better than that." His smile fled. "No. Like I told you before, it's contemplation that's driven me to drink."

And to confess.

"When David came back and Ginny killed him all over again, I still didn't want to believe what we've found out to be true: he and Adam faked their own deaths in order that they could live together in connubial Greek bliss, *erastes* and *eromenos,* removed from the disgust and outrage that their relationship would engender in Adam's mother and David's daughter, in the conservative California Bar Association, in society in general." Stevens frowned, not sorrowful now, but indeed, disgusted.

"And I still might've been able to continue in ignorance . . . Perhaps fate has given me *the right* to subject you to this boozy confession. Maybe the gods, in their mercy, have permitted me to bend your ear, because my inability to delude myself any longer . . . It's your fault, Janet."

A small cold fear whipped through me, like an iced wire. On television, seemingly stable persons often suddenly display a homicidal madness: you never would've guessed that the mousy accountant was in fact deranged. It made for must-see TV. I believed John Stevens was a murderer, but he knew that he could never get away with killing me – this wasn't a dark woods, and I wasn't a nobody that wouldn't be missed. But maybe that didn't matter to him. Having to face the truths he didn't want face – I still wasn't quite sure what those were yet – somehow, *I'd* made him face them. Maybe he'd confessed to murdering Billy because he didn't intend on letting me leave here.

Or maybe it was all bullshit. Regardless, I had a gun and he was a drunk old man. I said with a somewhat disrespectful grin, "How's that, Counsellor? You're all in a tizzy because I found Adam and brought him home to his mother?"

"Not because you found him, Detective. After Ginny shot David – I *wanted* you to find him. I wanted to know *why*. I wanted to hear that Adam had wanted to escape from a drug-possession beef, or a pregnant girlfriend, or something –"

A little hometown jam –

"– and David, bored with his life, had agreed to help him out. To go with him. For kicks. I wanted to believe some innocuous, plausible lie like that. And so I would've been allowed to believe – Adam doesn't want anyone to know, does he? Why hurt his mother and sister with a bizarre truth that doesn't matter in the slightest anymore?

"So Ginny and Sarah received their convenient lie. But not me. You and Sergeant Lover-Boy had to bring Adam *to me*. To help him concoct his fiction."

"It was *Adam's* idea to come to you."

"But you could have refused. You could've dissuaded him, told him . . . told him it's perjury."

"No one's gonna be testifying to it in court . . . John."

He went on as if I hadn't spoken. "So there I am. Adam is sobbing, telling me how much he loved David. I'm appalled at his tears, at his *unmanly grief*, appalled at what it was telling me: everything I'd suspected for that brief moment was true. David had abandoned me, Sarah, everything he'd known, for a pretty boy that reminded him of Billy Munro, so he could live the life of which he'd always dreamed, just him and Billy; a little house, a little store." Again Stevens sighed. "And this realization led me to contemplate the immutability of fate. And that would make anyone depressed."

When I looked at him blankly, he rolled his eyes. "It's another concept from our old friends, the Greeks. That whatever we do, no matter how we attempt to dodge them, to equivocate with them, our fates are set. In my case, it didn't matter what I'd done for David –"

"You got rid of Billy for David . . ."

A look of utter astonishment animated Stevens's features. "You're a cop through and through, aren't you, Janet? You're still on the clock. You're still *investigating*. You're still trying to find out what happened to Billy." His sly, shark's grin returned. He wasn't surprised at all. "The rest of my sad story means nothing to you."

"That's not true, John," I said genuinely. "You're grieving. You hurt. You needed to talk to somebody and I'm . . . I'm honored that you chose me."

He laughed. "And you think that in the unguarded process of pouring out my soul – I didn't say *I got rid of Billy,* Detective. I simply appealed to his logic: nothing could be served, nothing good could come from him talking to David."

"No one's ever talked to Billy again, John."

He shrugged elaborately. "That's what we call circumstantial, my dear Watson. Or more accurately, *absence of evidence is not evidence of absence.* Nobody ever talked to Billy again – nobody *you* talked to. Yet there's a world of people *you didn't talk to.* Maybe he's shacked up with one of them, right now."

"It seems unlikely," I said. I didn't feel like bringing up all the other things that pointed to Billy being dead. He'd just shoot them down, each and severally: pew, pew, pew.

"Nothing regarding Billy's absence is prosecutable at this late date, Janet. Nobody misses him, except for Max Haycroft and you. And all the missing in the world doesn't matter – not a DA in this country would touch it. You have no *evidence,* Detective, that I or David or anyone else *got rid of Billy.* Without evidence, there's no case."

Even sad and drunk, John Stevens *was* as smart as he thought he was. Smarter than me. He hadn't confessed to anything. I felt foolish, like a crusading newbie, like Parker. Again I thought that unsubstantiated accusations of murder in the first degree were something for angry, vengeful tough guys on the street corner, not law enforcement.

"When I said it didn't matter what I'd done for David, I wasn't talking *about getting rid of Billy,* specifically." Stevens shook his head. "I was talking about all of it, everything I did to try to show him what a truly worthless individual Billy was. Not to mention all the emotion I wasted on caring about him.

"I was trying to tell you about the immutability of fate. None of it mattered. If I hadn't talked Billy into leaving, David would've forgiven him, because *David loved Billy.* This is the fact that I'd always made myself ignore. It didn't matter that worthless Billy didn't love him back.

"Since Billy *did* leave . . . It didn't matter how many years passed. David would never forget him." Stevens said acidly, "As we discovered, he still carried his picture in his wallet.

"When he saw Adam, and Adam turned out to be bisexual, David left me and everything else behind because *Adam looks just like Billy, and David loved Billy.* Even if I'd known what he was going to do, there's nothing I could've done or said to change his mind. I couldn't have changed *anything* – not when I was twenty, not when I was fifty. David wanted Billy, and not me. I knew it all along, but deluded myself into believing otherwise.

"When Adam was crying in my office – I couldn't delude myself any longer. What we'd had for the briefest of moments – it hadn't made any impression on David at all. He'd forgotten about it, hadn't even mentioned it to Adam, with whom he *shared everything,* or at least that's what the blubbering kid told me.

"But David hadn't told him about us because it hadn't meant enough to him to even bear mentioning. He'd never told Adam that if there was any kind of emergency, he could turn to me because he loved me and I loved him. Coming to me – Adam decided that all on his own. I'd been David's business partner – *maybe* I could be talked into conspiring in this new scam. As far as he knew, that's all I'd ever been. David's law partner. The kid was very cautious at first; he didn't know me, because David had never talked about me.

"Our friendship had meant nothing to David. The thought had never even crossed his mind how devastated I would be at his death. That was all just collateral damage to his living his dream." Stevens paused. *"I am Jack's wasted life.* So, yeah. I thought I'd have a drink or two."

I had nothing to say. He was still deluding himself. He was drowning his sorrows, not because fate was immutable, but because he'd murdered a man in his quest to alter that fate. The murder was what had possessed Stevens with the need to drink. He'd killed Billy because he thought it would mean happily ever after with David. He'd only had that for six months, and then after twenty years of missing Billy, David had just run off with Billy's son.

But still I wondered – why had Stevens felt the need to tell it all to me? *To pay it forward,* the cynical cop said. *You can't change the unchangeable. Stevens couldn't do anything about David loving Billy, and you can't do anything about him killing Billy. Welcome to despair and self-loathing and hatred. Welcome to John Stevens's world.*

I smiled to myself, and almost felt a touch of pity for him. I wasn't going to be miserable and bitter and resentful like he was – I wasn't going to despair over things I couldn't change concerning people I didn't know. It wasn't right that he's murdered Billy, true, but I wasn't a crusader for justice, like Parker. You can't win 'em all. Slick Johnny wasn't the first guy to've gotten away with murder, and he wouldn't be the last.

"I dunno, Counsellor," I told him. "I think you'll get over it."

****

I'm a lot of things, but impolite isn't one of them. Despite what Stevens said, I hadn't still been *on the clock* when I'd run into him. In deference to his company and conversation, I'd turned off my cellphone. That's what adults do, and besides, it would save the battery in case I needed it later.

Standing in the lobby of Stevens's condo, waiting for the cab he'd called for me – I'd foregone the limo – I turned my peasant Android back on again. Parker had called, left no voicemail. Then he'd texted: *Where r u? I thought we were gonna finish the report. I'm sorry I'm late. I got hung up at the Walker's.*

Then about ten minutes later: *Seriously, where r u? Your car's in the lot, but ur not here.*

I looked at the time of his message and at the current time, and was amazed that only two hours had elapsed since Parker'd texted me, since John Stevens had begun his never-gonna-be-prosecutable confession.

My phone lit up in my hand. Parker was calling again.

"What the actual fuck, Jan?" He was adorable when he was annoyed. "I thought we were going to finish –"

"It's all handled, Parker."

"I saw that. Where are you? Why is your car still at the station?"

"I ran into John Stevens at The House of Ale –"

"Really? Did you go there to see the band?" He giggled, his annoyance forgotten at the image of me rocking out at the bar.

"When you didn't show up, I finished the report and took a walk around the block."

"I called . . ."

"Yeah, you called after a minute. By then, I was already deep in conversation with Mr. Stevens. He had some interesting things to say."

I could hear the frown in Parker's voice. "I'll bet."

Oh, Parker, my perfect partner, you have absolutely no idea. What was that tagline Stevens had told me? From the old cop show

207

he hadn't been watching the night he fell in love with David Walker? *Don't do the crime if you can't do the time.*

He did the crime, Parker, and since he's never gonna do the time, he took the time *to tell me all about it. You pegged the caper, but you got the perps wrong. But it doesn't really matter that it was Johnny and not David what killed Billy, because I can't prove it.*

I didn't tell Parker about Stevens's confession. That was just one I'd keep to myself. It would just piss him off, make him even more frustrated about the injustice of a world where police work seldom plays out like it does on television.

"Where are you now?" he repeated. I told him that I was still at Stevens's condo, waiting for a cab.

"Cancel it," he commanded. "I'll come get you. Sheesh, Jan. You can't be standing around in the dark all by yourself."

I laughed in surprise. Wasn't he cute? "I've got a gun, Parker."

"Whatever. I can't believe you just left me at the memorial service."

"Really?" I said before I could stop myself. It was my turn to be surprised. "You seemed right at home with the caviar and the high society." *And Sarah Walker.*

"Oh, it was all right, I guess. They're all right. It was a family thing, though, and I felt like an outsider. The cop at the funeral." He laughed. "Besides, it's Friday night. I've been wondering where you were all this time. Let's get a drink."

The one thing I didn't need was another drink. My hangover tomorrow was going to be one for the record books. *Call Guinness.* I grinned to myself, wondering if John T. Stevens, Attorney at Law, had ever seen *Super Troopers.* I knew Parker had seen it.

I told him where I was, *standing around in the dark all by myself,* and he said he was on his way.

While I waited, I did a little contemplation of my own on the immutability of fate. Maybe slick Johnny would've been able to control his destiny a little better if he'd just spoken up. If he'd just once told David that he loved him, before college, before he even met Billy Munro, maybe David would've reciprocated. Or maybe not. If John had spoken up and David had turned him down, then John could've manned up and accepted it, way back then. Maybe he could've gotten on with his life, found another David.

But he decided that it was better to wish than to know – and when the time came to admit that he'd really known all along, it wasn't very pretty.

208

I decided that I wasn't going to be like that. I wasn't gonna wind up old and bitter, lamenting *what might have been,* because I hadn't had the guts to risk rejection, speak up and say my piece. I wasn't going to pine in silence for my young partner anymore.

I'd tell that I wanted him. I'd do it tonight!

But probably not.

****

Also by LM Foster

A Passing Resemblance
Contrariwise – A Tale of Twins
Corvino
Crypsis
Duck Feet
Our Endless Needs
Peter's Sisters

Two Green Keys
Two Green Keys
Adapted for the Screen

One Wilde Ride Trilogy:
Part One: It Might Have Been
Part Two: An Exceptional Boy
Part Three: What Should Never Be

Stars and Guitars:
Talk To a Movie Star
Where The Guitars Play

Tom and Wiley:
This Carnival of Strange
Wiley Royce
Generally Recognized as Safe
Wiley Royce Versus The Martians

www.ingramcontent.com/pod-product-compliance
Lightning Source LLC
Chambersburg PA
CBHW051504170626
46811CB00002B/637